GUESSING GAME

The man, his face a mass of blood, opened his eyes, groaned, sat up, and did a double take when he saw the handguns pointed at him.

Camellion pushed his right foot against one of Doherty's legs.

"Sit up or I'll put a slug in your gut. It's question-and-answer time."

With another moan, Doherty managed to twist around and sit up, bracing himself by putting his hands flat on the floor.

"Who are you p-people?" he croaked. "You're not police. Are you Officials?"

The Death Merchant moved closer to the man, his "elderly" face a mask—which, in a sense, it was.

"Tell me, snake-belly: What has four wheels and flies?"

Doherty's words stumbled all over themselves. "I—I don't know. What has—"

"Shut up!" shouted Camellion. "The penalty for not knowing the answer is death!"

Camellion raised the CZ and pulled the trigger. There was a splat, and Doherty fell back dead, a blue-black ringed hole in the middle of his forehead.

THE DEATH MERCHANT SERIES:

#38 in the incredible adventures of the

DEATH MERCHANT

THE BURNING BLUE DEATH

by Joseph Rosenberger

PINNACLE BOOKS   LOS ANGELES

This is a work of fiction. All the characters and events portrayed in this book are fictional, and any resemblance to real people or incidents is purely coincidental.

DEATH MERCHANT #38:
THE BURNING BLUE DEATH

Copyright © 1980 by Joseph Rosenberger

An original Pinnacle Books edition, published for the first time anywhere.

First printing, April 1980

ISBN: 0-523-40702-5

Cover illustration by Dean Cate

Printed in the United States of America

PINNACLE BOOKS, INC.
2029 Century Park East
Los Angeles, California 90067

The average man believes that "reality" is that which can be seen and touched. If it is not tangible, then it is illusion and hallucination.

Apart from religious beliefs, generated from myths, half-truths and superstition, the fact remains that while everyone wants to "go to heaven," no one wants to die.

The basis for this deep dread of death is that man is terrified of the unknown, and, in spite of his religious "beliefs," simply cannot realize that he is able to live and function without a physical body.

Death is nothing more than the *permanent* separation of the astral self from the physical body, the *permanent* separation of you from the body you are presently inhabiting.

Modern science, especially nuclear physics, has proved that the *invisible is the real*, that our five senses perceive only *phenomena*, and that all realities of the universe are invisible to us while we are in this time continuum.

True reality, true consciousness, has never been perceived by any of the ordinary senses.

The modern man thinks that he is a "body" possessing a temporary mind. The truth is that it's the other way around. *Man is a spirit, possessing a temporary body*. Man goes on forever. . . .

Impossible? Not anymore impossible than the fact that two thirds of the human body is composed of water.

Think about it. . . .

Richard Camellion
Votaw, Texas

THE BURNING
BLUE DEATH

Chapter One

Richard Camellion, with a mug of black coffee in one hand and a small glass of *bessenjenever* in the other, stalked from the kitchen into the living room, a feeling of failure nagging at him. He put the mug of coffee and the glass of red-currant gin on the end table, dropped into an easy chair and glanced in disgust at the stacks of letters piled high on the kneehole desk across the room. He had expected maybe fifty letters. He had received hundreds.

The letters had come from every part of the world, many handwritten on cheap paper, others typed on personal or business stationery. Most of the letters had been written in the language of the senders. Quite a few, though, were in English. Stacks of letters from London, Paris, Rome, West Berlin, Tokyo, Johannesburg, Rio de Janeiro, Buenos Aires and other cities the newspapers of which had carried Camellion's advertisement: "Scientist doing special research seeks information as to how spontaneous human combustion can reduce a man or woman to a handful of ashes within minutes. This terrifying phenomenon is on the increase throughout the world. Send any information you may have to Justin O. Bystrom, Ph.D., Box 3742-EC, Amsterdam, Netherlands. Europe."

At least the interview the previous evening on the television talk show had gone well—on prime time, too. Everyone in Holland watched Govert van den Wenckebach, the "Johnny Carson" of the Netherlands. Naturally the interview would generate a lot of momentary interest. But would it cause the people he was after to come looking for him? He hadn't mentioned Johan Heijermans, the Dutch military attaché in Belgrade, Yugoslavia, who had been found dead in the bathroom. All that had been left of the man was half a charred foot and three fingers of his left hand. The rest of him had been gray ashes—and a bathrobe singed only slightly on the inside! However, Heijermans had not died in Yugoslavia. He had been on leave, and had perished in Amsterdam.

During the TV interview, the amiable Van den Wenckebach, who spoke excellent English, had not mentioned Heijermans, because he didn't know how Heijermans had died. The Dutch authorities, like other governments whose citizens had been mysteriously incinerated, had not given the true facts to the public. The press had been told that Heijermans had died of a massive coronary. The casket had not been opened because "the fall down the stairs" had smashed in Heijerman's face.

But Dutch Intelligence knew the truth. So did the CIA, which had contacts in the Ministry of Justice. The murderers knew the truth!

They have to be wondering who I really am, Camellion mused, *who I am working for and how much I—we—might know!*

Camellion adjusted the earphone in his left ear, took a sip of gin and used a swallow of coffee as a chaser. The clock on the wall over the desk read 2:48 AM, but the early morning hour didn't bother the Death Merchant, who was a night person, a creature who loved the deep shadows and the quiet blackness of long nights.

Deep in thought, he sank lower in the high-backed chair, certain that if last night's interview with Van den Wenckebach didn't bring the bedbugs out of their murderous woodwork, nothing would.

The "box" advertisement in *Het Vrije Volk*, Amsterdam's leading newspaper, had brought only a response of ten letters. Eight letters had been from curiosity seekers. Another had been from a self-styled parapsychologist who offered the theory that SHC—spontaneous human combustion—was caused by a combination of "certain kinds of cosmic rays and moonlight"!

The last letter had been from a religious fanatic. This woman was *positive* as to the cause. "Akriel" had told her in a "vision" that "evil spirits" were responsible, that it was

2

"Satan burning his own." Oh yes, she had explained that "Akriel" was the "chief assistant to the angel Gabriel."

Thinking about the letter, Camellion couldn't help but smile. *If sin could cause SHC, the whole human race would have been reduced to ashes 10,000 years ago!*

The slightly twisted smile lengthened. Camellion decided the CIA must really be grinding its teeth over "cost factors." Not only had the Agency shelled out thousands of American bucks for the advertisements—not to mention the time and caution of the case officers whose agents had placed the ads in various countries—but it was costing American taxpayers a small fortune for the rental of the five-room house in the country section of Aalsmeer, the wholesale marketplace for Holland's flower-growing industry, located just outside Amsterdam.

A house in a secluded locale had been necessary, an absolute must. Living in a hotel or an apartment would have made a kidnaping too difficult for whoever was responsible for the worldwide SHC assassinations. Amsterdam, famed for its narrow houses, was one of the most overcrowded cities in Europe. The Death Merchant had needed a secluded house with a large yard. A country house. The CIA had found one, but at a rental cost that was, in Dutch guilders, the equivalent of $3,285 a month. The spooks in the Company's financial office had to be grinding their teeth.

The house the CIA rented for the Death Merchant wasn't all that great, not $3,285-a-month great. It was a clapboard house painted white, with a stone foundation, a large front porch and a small back porch. A fairly large yard was enclosed by an iron fence painted blue. The house had a two-car garage behind it, and a tool shed attached to the garage. Old elm and linden trees, now frosted with snow, were everywhere. A dirt road led from the cobbled main road to the garage.

The furniture was old and massive but well-kept, much of it antique, other pieces at least of period value. Yet, as the Dutch would say, there wasn't anything *capsone*—pretentious—about the place. The house did have a lot of rooftop flourishes on and around its spout gable, but this was customary in the Netherlands. The Dutch, who call themselves *Nederlanders*, believed that crowning the

3

houses with ornamental gables provided an irresistible opportunity for artistic and architectural expression.

But what mattered to Camellion was the locale, which was perfect for his scheme. The house could be approached without too much risk, without neighbors seeing anything suspicious. This was especially true after sunset. The closest house was "down the road a ways" as they say in Texas, and it did not have any occupants. According to Kroon, an Amsterdam banker owned the property, but used the house only during the summer months. It wasn't very likely that the owner would put in an appearance with six inches of snow on the ground and the temperature hovering at 15 degrees F—unusually cold for January in Holland.

The house occupied by the Death Merchant did offer numerous places, both inside and outside, where he could conceal his motion detectors. If anyone got within six feet of any detector, the intruder would trigger a warning. An inflated flea couldn't flutter without Camellion's being warned. Around fence, yard, house and garage, there were twenty-six sensors.

There were two special detectors in the '78 Targa, the car that the stoic Kroon had brought to the garage. Their range limited to twenty inches, these stations—one in the trunk and one under the front seat—provided extra protection. Another sensor was in the Audi that Camellion had rented in Amsterdam.

Such sensors had saved the Death Merchant's life in the past. Without them, he wouldn't have dared to risk his life in the present. The enemy might think he was a sitting duck, but he wasn't. All the sensors had bass compensation boosting circuits and double-frequency oscillators, this refinement enabling Camellion to pick up a warning signal either on the earphone receiver or on the base receiver inside the house. It was the earphone receiver that was important. Without it, he wouldn't be able to detect intruders while approaching the house, in which case the enemy could ambush him inside the garage or the house. Impossible with the earplug. The stations constantly emitted a "quiet" (all-OK) signal. Should the enemy invade while he was away and find the central receiver, it still wouldn't matter. If the enemy smashed the station, they would eliminate the "quiet" signal; if they turned off the power, there would be a steady heterodyne whistle in the earphone.

4

There would be because there was a carefully hidden inferential switch in the base station that had to be shut off when the power pack was not functioning. The inferential circuit had its own mercury batteries. Malfunctions? Only one chance in a thousand.

Camellion finished the glass of *bessenjenever,* chased it with the remainder of the coffee, got up and went over to the single lamp burning in the room. He switched off the lamp, walked over to the front window of the living room, carefully moved one of the heavy drapes several inches to one side and looked outside. It was as quiet and tranquil as the inside of a cathedral. Soft moonlight sparkled on snow diamonds. Icicles hung from the mailbox attached to the fence post left of the front gate.

He put the drape into place and started for the first bedroom to turn on the light. It would make them think he was going to bed, assuming someone was watching. *They could come in the daytime,* Camellion thought. *Not too likely. Might not be home. Or they might not come at all.* Camellion was gambling that the enemy would come before dawn. They had better! If they came later, they'd walk into a trap that wouldn't be of his making. It was a sure bet that the Dutch Bureau of Security would be watching him closely, and probably come to question him within a day or so. The TV interview would cinch that.

Camellion was in the tiny hallway between the living room and the bedroom when the "quiet" hum in the earplug changed to a steady *berp-berp-berp-berp!* It was all he could do to keep from jumping up and down and giving a rebel yell.

Cast your bread upon the waters and your hook into the pond and you're sure to get a nibble, he thought excitedly. *Now to reel them in!*

He hurried into the first bedroom and switched on the typical cheap Dutch table lamp. He took off his suit coat, draped it over the back of a chair, opened the closet door and took out a cream-colored club tote and what looked like an oversized attaché case. He unzipped the club bag, unlatched the attaché case, tossed the top half back to the bed and glanced quickly at the rows of lights on the panel of the sensor-receiving station in the other half of the case. Three of the tiny bulbs were flashing red. Pulling the shoulder holster out of the bag, Camellion leaned down to read

5

the labels over the flashing lights. Invaders were at the rear of the back fence—or had just crossed over it—and within six feet on either side of the east and west fences.

Camellion quickly slipped into the shoulder holster, fastened the straps, pulled out the 9mm Parabellum Star autopistol and checked it. Fully loaded, one cartridge in the firing chamber. He pulled the other two weapons from the bag. *Damn Kroon and Spare!* Especially that bald-headed Spare, who was Kroon's control officer. Both weapons were .45 Colt 1911A1 autoloaders, but modified in a way that was ridiculous. Each Colt had been fitted with a long barrel, a pistol grip in front of the trigger guard and a banana-style extension magazine that held 55 cartridges. Both .45s had been altered to fire full automatic.

Camellion pulled from the bag several spare magazines for the Star and a pair of goggles. Called a holographic one-tube goggle, the device employed thin-film diffraction optics and advanced electronics. Harvey Spare had explained to Camellion that human-engineering specialists had designed the device so that it amplified dim visual light and near-infrared electronics. The goggles had also been designed so that the image-intensifier tube, which extended from above the bridge of the nose, did not block any portion of the wearer's view.

Camellion put on the goggles and centered them in such a way that the five-inch-tall intensifier tube was resting against his forehead. He switched off the lamp and turned on the tube of the goggles. *Well now, how about that!* The pitch dark room was bathed in deep reddish twilight.

He returned to the sensor-receiving station. The first three lights were no longer blinking, but others had taken their places. He leaned down to read the labels illuminated by tiny penlight bulbs beneath the plastic. Four of the sensors on the back porch were blinking. So were two on the front porch, as well as one to the west by the window of the first bedroom, and one to the east by the window of the dining room.

Close. The enemy was very close, and what they would do next was predictable. They weren't going to rush the house or they would have already done so. They had been waiting and watching. Now that the bedroom light was out, they would wait until they thought he was asleep. Then they would enter.

6

Camellion took two silencers from the club tote and began to attach them to the barrels of the .45s, thinking that in this kind of snatch-and-grab setup, the enemy would have walkie-talkies and one, maybe two, cars parked down the road.

Once the silencers were in place, Camellion closed the sensor station and shoved the case under the bed. From now on he would depend on the earphone receiver. Having used the sensors numerous times, he had a lot of practice and could tell from the sound just about where the enemy was. The louder the *berps* and the faster they ran together, the closer the enemy would be.

A silenced .45 "machine pistol" in each hand, he left the bedroom and moved to the front of the hall. He would have preferred to capture all the invaders, a task which could have been accomplished very easily with ultrasonic sound. The CIA would not approve the use of the device. The Company feared that, once it left the American Embassy in Amsterdam, it might fall into the wrong hands. *So I have to do the job the hard way*, thought Camellion.

It was unlikely that the goofs on the east and west sides of the house would smash the windows to get in. They were stationed there to make sure he didn't escape. How to get at them was a problem. The others would creep in through the front or back doors. An ordinary skeleton key would open the old-fashioned locks.

The Death Merchant waited, knowing he was in the best defensive position possible. The hall, no longer than eight feet, was in the center of the house and contained four doors. Directly in front of him was the door to the living room. In back of him, to the east, was the door to the dining room. To the west, the door to the first bedroom. To the north was the hall door to the bathroom.

He partially pushed open the door to the living room, thinking that he wasn't all that safe. It was the bathroom with its three doors that bothered him. Other than the door at the north end of the hall, there were two more entrances to the bathroom, one from each bedroom. The first bedroom had one window. The second bedroom had two, one on the west side of the house and one in the rear. *No point in worrying about those windows now!* Camellion thought.

The *beeps* and *berps* in the earphone suddenly became louder and closer together. The invaders were making their

7

move. They had unlocked the doors and were coming in.

The Death Merchant thumbed off the safety catches of the .45 Colt machine pistols and looked around the edge of the doorway. In the reddish glow of the holographic goggles, he saw the three men who had just sneaked into the living room through the front door, which was standing wide open. Two of the men wore overcoats, and felt hats with narrow brims. The third joker had on a Cavalry Twill stormcoat with a fur collar, and had a round lambskin hat perched on his head. Each man had a pistol in his gloved hand. The one wearing the lambskin hat advanced with a hand-held night-sight device before his eyes, the other two behind and on either side of him.

The man with the night scope spotted the Death Merchant and yelled in surprise and fear. "Justin O. Bystrom" was supposed to be in bed, but there he was in a doorway, some kind of weird-looking weapon in his hand.

The man with the night scope didn't have time to raise the 9mm FN Hi-Power automatic in his hand, much less lower the night-vision device from his eyes. Jan Herwijnen didn't have time to do anything but die. No sooner had he yelled than several .45 Silvertip hollowpoint slugs stabbed him in the chest, the grand-slam impact knocking him off balance.

With the sound of the noise suppressor no louder than a light cough, the Death Merchant raked the two other men, who were blind in the darkness. Although moonlight gleamed through the open front door, Pieter Gracht and Bemhard Brug were facing the darkness, their backs to the opening and the front porch.

It wouldn't have made any difference if the living room had been illuminated by a searchlight. In a panic, the two were still at the peak of shock from hearing Herwijnen cry out, still emotionally petrified as Camellion's 185-grain slugs poked through their overcoats and punched into their bodies.

Gracht fell to the floor with flattened-out hollowpoints in his stomach and chest. Brug, his lungs and heart punctured by Silvertip lead, fell almost on top of Herwijnen, over whom the wind, blowing through the open door, had blown flakes of snow. Now snow flurried over and around the dead bodies of Brug and Gracht.

During those few brief moments, Camellion made his decision. He spun around and put .45 projectiles through the three other doors, exhausting the magazine in the Colt. He placed the empty weapon on the floor and, hearing windows being smashed on both sides of the house, picked up the second Colt that had been altered to make a submachine gun. *Survival time!* The pussyfooting around had ended!

He turned and darted through the door into the living room.

Just as much of a realist as the Death Merchant, Hendrik de Jeer, the leader of the group, also sensed that the time for stealth had come to an end. De Jeer, and the three men who had come through the back door with him, had heard Herwijnen yell and the slight coughing sound of the silencer on the Colt .45. De Jeer, scanning the area through an infrared night scope, had seen not only Herwijnen but Gracht and Brug get clobbered with slugs he presumed to have been fired from a silenced submachine gun.

Without taking the monocular night scope from his right eye, De Jeer nudged Klaus Eickner, who held the walkie-talkie, and whispered frantically, "Tell Rodley and Kemgelt to get in here—fast. Bystrom's using a machine gun."

Wishing he were back in West Germany, Eickner was whispering into the walkie-talkie when slugs chopped through the door between the dining room and the hall. None of the bullets even came close to De Jeer and his companions, since Camellion's line of fire was at such a slanting angle that most of them struck only one end of a china cabinet against the west wall. A few went through the doorway between the dining room and the kitchen.

"Let's kill him," hissed Michael Régene. "Everything has gone wrong. He was waiting for us."

He jerked his head to the left as glass from the lower part of the dining-room window crashed inward.

"We can't kill him," muttered De Jeer. "Our orders are to take him alive." He said in a louder voice, "Turn on the lights."

William Kemgelt, standing by the wall to the left of the doorway between the dining room and the kitchen, flipped the light switch on the wall. At once the dining room was bathed in light from the hurricane light fixture hanging above the dining-room table. At the same instant, De Jeer,

Eickner and the other men spotted Camellion. He was in the living room, standing to one side of the archway, only ten feet away, some kind of machine pistol in his hand.

"Take him alive!" shouted De Jeer in Flemish. He tossed the heavy infrared scope at Camellion and darted to the right. The other men, their eyes on the man they presumed to be Justin O. Bystrom, rushed forward, reasoning that they could always kill him if they were forced to.

Camellion had time to get off two lines of fire before the night-vision device struck him in the chest. A stream of slugs poured from the black mouth of the silencer, the first half-dozen blowing away Charles Rokin, who was frantically trying to crawl through the broken portion of the bottom window in the dining room. The left side of Rokin's head, neck and shoulder exploded in ripped cloth, flesh, bone and blood. Half inside the window, the corpse sagged, so butchered as to be unrecognizable.

The rest of the big .45 projectiles slashed into William Kemgelt, who had been moving quickly—but not quickly enough—from the light switch. He had time to see only a goggled man swinging some kind of machine pistol and wonder about the silvery tube lying vertically against the man's forehead. A blink later, Kemgelt was a candidate for a mortuary, Silvertip hollowpoints tearing into his body and pitching him against the wall.

Angry at himself because he hadn't been able to dodge the night-vision device, the Death Merchant fought the stabbing pain in his breast bone and tried to swing the .45 Colt toward the other men in the room.

As incredibly fast as Camellion was, the sharp, stabbing pain in his chest had slowed his reflexes. Even so, he might have succeeded if the Colt hadn't had a long noise suppressor and if Hendrik de Jeer hadn't been so nimble-footed.

De Jeer grabbed the hot, rounded silencer with his gloved left hand, pushed the cylinder and the .45 to one side and swung the Heckler & Koch P-9 pistol, in his right hand, at the left side of Camellion's head.

The Death Merchant ducked the P-9 and let go of the modified Colt. He had no choice. His right hand had been around the butt of the Colt, the fingers of his left gripping the forward pistol grip mounted to the frame. He didn't have time to fight De Jeer for possession of the Colt. The two other men were rushing at him and he needed both hands for what he had to do.

De Jeer, surprised and tossed off balance by Camellion's sudden release of the Colt, didn't have time to take a second swing. Camellion let De Jeer have a left-legged powerhouse kick, the sole and heel of his jodhpur a battering ram that crashed into the lower part of the Dutchman's car coat and smashed into his groin. A choked cry of agony jumped from De Jeer's mouth and it seemed as if his hooded eyes might pop out of their sockets. Overcome with shock from one of the most painful blows a man can receive, he started to sag while Michael Régene did his best to dent Camellion's skull with a viciously swung Czech CZ-75 autopistol. Klaus Eickner, cursing under his breath in German, swung at the other side of Camellion's head with the Luger and tried to kick him squarely between the legs.

The Death Merchant had other plans. Ducking the autopistols, he pulled in his stomach, arched himself in the middle, grabbed Eickner's right foot with both hands and twisted savagely to the left, jerking the man off his feet and throwing him toward Régene, who managed to jump to one side. Eickner fell flat, the unscheduled fall knocking the wind out of him and smashing his face against the rug.

Genuinely afraid, Régene tried to raise the Czech pistol and put a bullet in Camellion's chest. The Death Merchant grabbed his left wrist, pulled outward, and Régene's finger contracted on the trigger. The handgun roared, the 9mm slug missing Camellion's hip by a foot. Before the Belgian could even try to free his wrist and again use the autopistol, Camellion right-handed him above the bridge of the nose with a *Tae-Kwon-Do Sangdan-Chirugi* high punch, then grabbed him with both hands by the front of his rust-colored jacket and flung him to the left, straight into another man who had just rushed into the room from the door between the dining room and the hall. Camellion assumed that the newcomer had been stationed on the west side and had entered the house through the window of the first bedroom.

Out cold from the high punch, Régene crashed into Lawrence Rodley, who had a nickel-plated .38 Taurus revolver in his right hand. Both men went down, the unconscious Régene falling on top of Rodley, who desperately

11

tried to free his right arm and fire at the tall man in the weird-looking goggles. Pushing against Régene, Rodley could see Eickner, blood streaming from his nose, trying to reach the Luger he had dropped. Rodley hoped he would succeed. Eickner didn't. Camellion pulled the Star from the shoulder holster, switched off the safety and fired. The 9mm Parabellum struck the kraut in the side of his neck, went all the way through his throat and came to rest in one of the table legs. Blood spurting six inches from his neck, Eickner flopped back down again, jerking slightly, dying quickly.

A frantic Rodley had almost freed his gun arm from Régene's body when Camellion's Star roared again. Rodley heard the 9mm projectile pop into Régene's skull, yelled in terror and let the Taurus revolver slip from his fingers. He found himself looking into the smoking muzzle of a Star and heard a voice saying calmly, "I'll never dance at your wedding, friend. Neither will you, if you don't behave yourself."

Rodley held his breath and waited, expecting a bullet to hit him any moment. The slug didn't come. Unconsciousness did. Camellion slammed the side of the Star against his head, and Rodley's universe dissolved in darkness.

The Death Merchant looked around the dining room, then turned his attention to the living room. Holy hell! Eight bodies were in the two rooms. Eight and a half, counting the dead dummy who hung in the dining-room window, his head and arms dangling almost to the floor. One of the bodies was groaning and starting to move—the turkey he had kicked in the groin.

Casually, Camellion walked across the room and picked up the P-08 Luger that had belonged to Klaus Eickner, and, for a moment, he looked at the wrecked chunk of humanity. Hendrik de Jeer, his back to Camellion, was trying to get to his feet, his groin white-hot agony, bile and slime dribbling from his mouth.

"Tsk, tsk. You have ring around the collar, fella," murmured Camellion and pulled the trigger of the Luger. The 9mm slug struck de Jeer in the base of the skull and made his head snap forward. Dead, he half twisted and fell sideways to the rug.

12

The Death Merchant carefully placed the Luger on the floor and thought of how confused the Dutch police would be. He wasn't concerned about his finger- or palm-prints being found on the butt of the Luger, or, for that matter, in any part of the house. He always coated his hands and the soles of his feet with Kessalene, a special liquid that looked like ordinary water, but when dry could not be detected and would make it impossible for prints to appear for several months, yet enabled the "wearer" to wash his hands as often as he wished.

Camellion went to work. He moved across the dining room, switched off the light, went into the kitchen and closed the back door. The housing of the old-fashioned lock, mounted on the outside of the door, was undamaged. The invaders had used a skeleton key.

He retraced his steps, went into the living room, glanced at the three bodies frosted with snow and looked out the front door. Damn it. More snow was falling, not heavily but steadily.

He hurried to the first bedroom, turned on the lamp, went to the closet, pulled aside a loose piece of fiberboard and picked up the medical kit resting between the two studs. He unzipped the kit and took out a hypodermic syringe and an ampule filled with 300 milligrams of Thorazine. He filled the hypodermic with the powerful tranquilizer and returned to the living room. He removed Rodley's leather bomber jacket, rolled up the unconscious man's left shirt sleeve and shot the Thorazine into his arm.

Camellion hurried to the bedroom, any number of thoughts crisscrossing his mind. It was not very likely that anyone had heard the shots. The wind was wailing too loudly and the nearest houses were too far away. Besides, at this hour all the good Dutch people were sound asleep. The snow was another matter. The country road had already been treacherous before this new snow had started falling. Now, with fresh snow, even an A.J. Foyt would have to be doubly careful driving into Amsterdam. The drive would be one long risk; yet there wasn't any other way. *I can't fly*, Camellion chuckled, *and I don't have a pogo stick!*

If he slid off the road and became stuck? Worry about it when and if it happened.

* * *

13

4:45 AM. The Death Merchant was almost ready to leave the house. He had packed three suitcases and put them into the trunk of the Targa. In the third suitcase rested the sensor-receiving station and the medical kit. He had picked up all the handguns, and they—including the two modified Colt .45s—were in the club tote, also locked in the trunk of the Targa. Into a large paper bag he had dumped the various personal items taken from the pockets of the corpses. The bag was between the legs of Rodley, whom Camellion had dumped in back of the car, on the floor between the seats, and had covered with a blanket. Now all he had to do was make the phone call and get to Amsterdam in one piece.

He thought of the owner of the house. A banker in Amsterdam. What a shock the poor man would get. His name and the house would be on the lips of every *Nederlander* for weeks to come. The publicity would extend to the dead men in the two rooms, provided the Dutch police, or INTERPOL, had their prints on file. But there wasn't any way the rental of the house could be traced to the Agency, and "Justin O. Bystrom" was about to vanish quicker than Carter's campaign promises.

The Death Merchant picked up the telephone and dialed a number in Amsterdam. The phone on the other end rang seven times before a sleepy voice said, "Yes?"

Camellion recognized Harvey Spare's voice.

"Yes, what?"

A short pause. "The ragged rascal ran around the rugged rock—and do you know it's ten to five?"

Camellion laughed. "I didn't get any sleep at all. Visitors came calling. I've got one fish and leaving now."

"You're going to Drumhead's?"

"No. I'll be at C-Sixteen-F."

"All right. I'll see you about noon. Anything else?"

"No."

"Good luck, and watch yourself."

Camellion hung up the phone, took a final look around through the holographic one-tube goggles and reached into his pocket. He pulled out a folded square of paper, opened it and dropped it over the dead man, who had been wearing the round lambskin hat. The paper was supposedly from the *Front de Liberation de la Bretagne*—the Liberation Front of Britany—a French nationalist group that

14

bohemians, along with a smattering of bourgeois. These floating houses range from sleek, expensive craft to ramshackle hulks that flout conventional notions of comfort and sanitation.

Now, these snow-covered houseboats looked forlorn and abandoned, while their occupants shivered and condemned the unusually severe winter.

Richard Camellion drove cautiously through the gloom of the dawn. Several times he skidded on the country road but each time managed to straighten the Targa and prevent sliding into the deep snow on the side of the road. Reaching Rijksweg 4, one of the highways leading into Amsterdam, he breathed a lot easier. He couldn't increase speed, but at least he had more room in which to maneuver and there was less chance of skidding into drifts.

There were few cars on Rijksweg 4; however, traffic increased when he turned onto Vijzelstraat. By American standards traffic was thin. Even so, something was still conspicuously absent: There weren't any bicycles!

Most cities are prisoners of the internal-combustion engine. Amsterdam is devoted to pedal power, the main reason being that the bicycle is ideally suited to Amsterdam's gentle gradients and narrow streets. This explains why Amsterdam is one of the least polluted cities in Europe. Bicycles—equipped with baskets and panniers to carry everything from sandwiches to small children and animals—are the personal transportation for two out of every three Amsterdammers.

But not this January morning.

Full daylight. Camellion was crossing Dam Square, the favorite meeting place for young people, which originally gained prominence because it fronts the Royal Palace. For a moment he caught sight of the Virgin of Peace gazing down from her vantage point on the roof of the palace, flakes of snow fluttering around the Rod of Mercury in her left hand and the olive branch in her right. The words of the Roman poet Horace jumped into his consciousness: *"Coelum non animum mutant qui trans mare currunt."* The old boy was right. Traveling does change your sky, but not your mind. You take yourself wherever you go, be it down the road a piece or the middle of Asia. . . .

Having crossed Dam Square, Camellion turned right and

17

rechecked his bearings. Damn it. Now wasn't the time to become lost. He was right on course. He was on Raadhuisstraat. Ahead was the bridge that crossed the Singel Canal, and beyond it the bridge that crossed the larger Herengracht.

Fifteen minutes more and he passed the Anne Frank House and turned left on Rozenstraat. He was only a fifth of a mile from "home." He speeded up slightly. Only a mile away, on the Herengracht Canal, was the Drumhead Station—Jacob Kroon's houseboat. But how do you carry an unconscious man from the back seat of a car to a houseboat without being seen and reported to the police? The odds are that you don't.

Finally, there it was: Number 487, a three-story house with a bell gable and a massive lions-head doorknocker. Station C-Sixteen-F, the safe house.

Camellion turned into the narrow drive. His wheels started spinning. Grateful that the Targa had an automatic transmission, he quickly rocked the car, alternating from low to reverse . . . forward then back, forward then back . . . and treading lightly on the throttle for two reasons: Spinning wheels have no traction; and he didn't want to give convulsions to the transmission and rear end by switching directions every few seconds at full throttle.

The wheels grabbed hold and the vehicle moved ahead, skidding slightly on the driveway. Camellion straightened out, fed more gas to the engine and rounded the curve. He stopped in front of the long garage and waited while the electric eye raised the doors. More relaxed, he drove inside. The doors silently started to lower.

There were two other automobiles in the garage, a Renault sedan and a Toyota Mark II. Two men, wearing leather coats and caps with earflaps, got out of the back seat of the Renault.

It was two-thirty in the afternoon before Harvey Spare arrived at the house, explaining that he hadn't been able to leave the American Embassy because of an important meeting with the CIA's chief of station in Amsterdam.

Spare and Camellion immediately started for the third floor, accompanied by a woman who had introduced herself to the Death Merchant as Joanna Luprich. "I'm a physician," she had said.

18

He hadn't asked her what an MD—and a woman doctor at that—was doing at a Company safe house in Amsterdam. In the first place, it wasn't any of his business. In the second, nothing about the CIA surprised him. He did know that the house was, ostensibly, owned by an elderly Dutch couple named Huysman. Spare had given him that tidbit of information seven weeks ago.

"He's only been awake for the past half-hour," Dr. Luprich told Spare as the three of them trudged up the stairs. "Our friend here gave him a massive dose of Thorazine— three hundred milligrams—and it's taken us all this time to get him awake. He's having a bad time of it, but it's nothing serious."

Spare broke step. "What do you mean, a bad time of it?"

"Side effects of the Thorazine," the woman explained. "He has slight jaundice and dyspnea and dyskinesia."

"I know what jaundice is, but break down the rest of it into English." He added crossly, "Keep it simple."

"He's having trouble breathing, shortness of breath, and he can't coordinate his arms and legs." Her tone became accusatory. "Don't worry. He'll be in good health when you or whatever his name is"—she glanced at Camellion— "kill him."

"Bystrom," Camellion said with a straight face. "Justin O. Bystrom."

"Uh-huh. And I'm Dr. Mayo!"

Reaching the third floor, they went into a room in the middle of the hallway, a windowless room that contained several short-wave transmitters and receivers, four filing cabinets and an assortment of massive baroque furniture. It took only a glance to see that the various pieces had been chosen only because of pragmatic need. Nothing matched.

The man, sitting in a wooden swivel chair by the radios, looked as grim as the furniture. He sat as rigid as a poker, and had a bony chin and suspicious gray eyes.

"I'll check on our visitor," Dr. Luprich said and started across the room.

"Fine. Get him in shape for questioning," Spare called after her. "Don't come back here unless I send for you."

The woman tapped lightly on a metal door on the west side of the room. A man in the next room opened the door and let her in. The door closed.

"She's strictly NTK,"[1] Spare said to Camellion, who walked over to a table on which lay numerous personal items a man would carry in his pocket. There was also a small open box on the table.

"I found this stuff on the bodies," Camellion said. He pulled out a chair and sat down. "The junk in the cardboard box is from the guy I brought back with me. His name's Lawrence Rodley. He's British."

Spare sat down at the table across from the Death Merchant, a concerned expression on his lined face. Spare's expression in normal times was usually melancholy. He was of medium height, in his forties and the skin was puckered beneath his neck, suggesting that he had once been much heavier.

Spare sat down across from Camellion at the table. "I couldn't ask in front of her, but how many men did you have to terminate?"

"Seven," Camellion answered. He then proceeded to give a report of what had taken place at the country house outside of Aalsmeer, finishing with, "It wasn't until toward the last that some of them tried to kill me. They realized I was winning. I'm positive the prime directive of the group was to kidnap me. We can assume we know *why*. It's the *when* and the *where* we have to find out. I'm hoping the man I brought back can give us a lead."

"I'm inclined to believe he's only 'hired help' and doesn't know much," Spare said. He shook his head from side to side. "Seven bodies! What a stink they'll make—and that's not a pun. I'm talking about the press when the bodies are discovered."

Camellion had picked up a passport taken from one of the dead men and was looking through it. "Discovery will take time. Weeks, perhaps. By then, 'Bystrom' and this face will have disappeared."

Spare did a double take. "You mean . . . ?" He stared at the Death Merchant, whose appearance was that of a man in his sixties, a comfortable, pleasant appearance. He was half-bald, with a small, neatly clipped beard, long, curved sideburns almost to his chin, a large nose and a mole in the center of his left cheek.

"No, this isn't my real face," Camellion said. "I'd have

---

[1] "Need-to-know."

to be a first-class idiot to appear on Dutch television and let our 'friends' know what I really look like!"

Spare, noting the expressionless face of Camellion, believed he saw a gleam of satisfaction in his eyes, which were an odd color of blue. He thought of asking the man across from him his real name, but dismissed the impulse as being unreasonable.

"It was a good job you did on Wenckebach's program last night," Spare said. "Damned good. They did a good job at the Center when they briefed you about SHC in Washington. I'm glad you didn't mention Senators Wilder or Lake on the program. Their names would have been a giveaway to the enemy about who you're really working for."

The Death Merchant smiled inwardly. The experts at the Center in Virginia hadn't told him a single thing he didn't already know about spontaneous human combustion, the mysterious burning death that consumed human beings in a manner totally incomprehensible to medical science. SHC was a conflagration of flesh that occurred instantly, often generating such a fantastic degree of heat that the body of the victim was reduced to a few pounds of ashes in a matter of minutes. No one knew why or how it occurred. Yet, in 135 established cases throughout history, the bursting blue flames continued to mystify and astound medical men and police investigators.[2]

"I'm rather curious," Spare went on. "Was it true what you said about Dickens, or just part of the act?"

"I didn't even exaggerate on Wenckebach's program," Camellion said. "Charles Dickens was familiar with the burning blue death, and he did use it to knock off one of his characters in *Bleak House*. Ambrose Bierce used the mysterious phenomena in some of his writings. Bierce himself turned out to be a mystery. He was one of the leading American writers of his day. He simply vanished. As I explained on the interview, both writers were criticized because people tend to disbelieve anything they consider 'impossible,' anything that 'just can't be.'"

[2] SHC is not listed in the *Standard Nomenclature of Disease* of the World Health Organization's classification of death causes; yet there are doctors, firemen, and special investigators—including agents of the FBI—as well as relatives of the victims, who have had contact with the horrible results.

"Well, you have to admit that SHC is hard to believe," Spare said in a low voice.

"Sure it is, but so was going to the moon at one time. Yet the evidence is irrefutable. All through history, the burning blue death has claimed victims all over the world. Since colonial days, SHC has been noted throughout the U.S. But the first real case to come to the attention of the public was that of the Rooneys in Ottawa, Illinois. On December 27, 1885, SHC killed Mrs. Rooney in the kitchen. Her husband suffocated to death from the fumes."

"I know, I know," Spare said, making a motion with his hand. "What gets me is the terrific heat involved. It takes as long as eight hours to cremate a body by conventional means, at a temperature of two thousand degrees Fahrenheit. To reduce most of the body to ash, and to do it within minutes, would require temperatures between five and six thousand degrees. It seems to me that science should be able to find the answer."

The Death Merchant put down the passport and gave Spare a long look. "It could be that science can't see the obvious. Or the real answer might be too fantastic for the human mind to conceive, much less accept."

"The human body is ninety percent water," Spare said thoughtfully. "I'd like to know how a body can become so critically combustible that it bursts into spontaneous flame." His gaze became fierce, almost savage. "How can a fire start *inside* the body and be so selective that it burns only human tissue and only slightly harms nonliving matter? I'm wondering how many 'accidental deaths due to smoking' are really cases of SHC? Did you know that SHC is not even recognized by the American Medical Association? That's ridiculous!"

"It's not mentioned in any AMA publications," added Camellion, "nor in its bible, the *Index Medicus*. This doesn't mean that medical people have totally ignored the burning blue death phenomenon. Many AMA members have studied SHC from every angle. They haven't gotten anywhere, except to prove that alcohol doesn't cause SHC. Years ago it was thought that only heavy drinkers were prone to be struck. The thought now is that anyone can go up in flames."

"Yes, I read the photostat of the report from the Center." Spare frowned and moved closer to the table, the legs of his chair scraping on the bare floor. "What makes SHC such a threat, according to the report, is that absolutely nothing is known about its cause or prevention. It's anyone's guess as to who might be susceptible. The conclusion of the Company's medical people is that there will be more victims."

"Our only course is to proceed on the basis of theory," Camellion declared. "Spontaneous human combustion is a fact. The only reason it's mysterious is that we don't know the physical laws in operation that trigger the process. What really matters is that some group, somewhere in the world, has not only discovered those laws but has figured out how to induce SHC, how to direct it, apparently, at any human being. From the selective number of assassinations, we can deduce what this group is after—world power."

Harvey Spare's eyes narrowed. "I hope to Jesus Christ it's not the Soviets," he said bleakly. "The way our gutless Congress is doing nothing about commie encirclement, all we need is for the ivans to have developed artificial SHC."

"It's up to us to find out," Camellion said drily. "This stuff on the table might give us a lead. I doubt it. I'm putting my rubles on the Englishman in the other room. He doesn't know the top people, but one clue is all we need for a start."

Spare looked at the items on the table—billfolds, packs of cigarettes, some cigars, lighters, keys, a few penknives and other personal material.

"This guy, Klaus Eickner, was a kraut," Spare said, looking at the identification card in one billfold.

"They were all Dutch, except two: Eickner and Michael Régene. Régene was Belgian, according to his passport. I'm glad he and Eickner were there. I dropped a 'Liberation Front of Brittany' warning. Too bad they both weren't French."

Spare counted the passports. "*Hmmm*. Three of them." He picked up the thin booklets and looked at the names and photographs. "Eickner, Régene and a Hollander named De Jeer."

"All three also had international driver's licenses," said the Death Merchant. "And a fourth guy—Jan Herwijnen."

"It all adds up to a large, well-organized international organization," said Spare crisply. "The dead men weren't

23

carrying cover documents. But you're the one who'd know that. I assume the photographs on the IDs and in the passports match the crumbs you terminated?"

"They match. They didn't use false ID because they expected the job to be easy. They thought I was asleep. Any word from your sources in Dutch Intelligence?"

"They were armed, of course?" Spare picked up a small shoe box. The box was orange bordered in black. The printing was blue and in Old English.

"Handguns, the best. They're downstairs." The Death Merchant's voice suddenly had a sharp edge. "Give me the latest on Dutch Intelligence."

Spare opened the cardboard shoe box and looked at the various colored cigarettes inside.

"We won't have word for a day or so. But you know as well as I do that after last night's broadcast, the Dutch Intelligence Bureau will check you out even more than after your ad appeared in the *Het Vrije Volk*. Until last night's telecast, they figured you were an eccentric." Spare gave a light laugh. "Amsterdam's noted for its cuckoos. Fruitcakes gravitate to Amsterdam the way oddballs migrate to California."

"That's the danger point: Dutch Intelligence," Camellion offered. "If Dutch agents go out to the house, they'll find the eight bodies. I don't suppose it matters."

"You're safe here." Spare watched Camellion pick up the open shoe box and dump its contents next to the other items. There were a billfold, keys, several letters, and a box of cigarettes similar to the one in Spare's hand.

Camellion looked at Spare. "Anything strike you as being peculiar?"

"I'd quit and become a street sweeper if I didn't notice," the CIA case officer grunted. He picked up the box of cigarettes Camellion had dumped out of the shoe box and held it in his right hand. "These two boxes of Marmis Premium cigarettes—gold filter-tipped cigarettes. These are an exclusive brand and expensive. You wouldn't expect ordinary gunmen to have them." He turned one of the boxes over and read from the back. " 'Kemper Marmis's guarantee: Never, never, do we use any flavorings. We do not use saltpeter or any additives in our custom-made cigarettes. We screen our tobaccos for our particular blends and select only the top ten percent of the tobacco presented to us.

24

Our cigarettes are absolutely pure—selected from the best, and custom-made for those who know that nothing can hold a match to the taste and mildness of our pure tobacco.' Note the address: 4164 Bond Street, London, England. That's in the West End, the very heart of London."

"The cigarettes I dumped from the shoe box belong to the Englishman I brought here," Camellion said. "The second box of smokes I took from Régene, the Belgian."

"To me, it adds up to zero." Spare sounded gloomy. "Two boxes of expensive cigarettes don't necessarily mean anything. A lot of people have expensive tastes. I have a brother-in-law who would live on skid row—if he had to—just so he could ride around in a car he can't really afford and put on a big front." .

"The cigarettes are all we have," Camellion retorted, leaning back in the chair. "I found a ticket stub in Rodley's pocket. According to the date, he came from London to Holland on one of the English ferries. Either he gave the cigarettes to Régene, or Régene bought them in London or from someone in Europe. Or someone could have given both boxes to Rodley. I've a hunch though that Rodley and Régene were together when they bought the cigarettes at Marmis."

"What's the difference?" Spare spoke rhetorically. "No matter how they got the cigarettes, I don't see how that can help us find out who gave them their orders, and we both doubt that Rodley knows anything of value." His shoulders sagged and his expression became philosophical. "In the long-range scheme of things, I don't suppose it matters. The way American society is falling apart, I seriously doubt whether we'll have a working nation twenty years from now. And the damned liberals are constantly making conditions worse."

A smile twisted the corners of the Death Merchant's mouth. "I'm a card-carrying skeptic myself. I don't believe we're captains of our ships. Come to think of it, I don't even believe we're deck hands on a rudderless dinghy!" The smile faded and his tone became serious. "We do have a nation of paradoxes. The know-it-alls condemn smoking on the basis of sheer statistics and preach the value of running; yet almost nothing is done about fifty thousand automobile deaths a year, a third of which are caused by drunk drivers."

25

"Or the twenty-five thousand deaths a year caused by firearms each year," rejoined Spare. "For the life of me, I can't understand why Congress won't listen to Senator Kennedy and others who want to ban all firearms!"

Camellion said in a lazy way, "Yeah, Senator Kennedy would like to have strict gun control in the States and put in the clink any person who owned a weapon. I just wonder what kind of penalty he'd prescribe for a man who drives his car into a creek, accidentally kills one of the passengers, and then uses his power to keep authorities from performing an autopsy on the corpse?" He looked straight at Spare, whose face was beginning to redden. "It seems to me that the antigunners have a double set of legal standards: one for themselves and one for us poor folk. I know six Senators who would like to ban all firearms; yet they have permits to carry weapons. To their way of thinking, they'd give gun permits to 'special citizens,' but deny them to ordinary citizens. Or don't you agree with me?"

Spare glared at Camellion, who knew damn good and well that he didn't.

"Are you saying that antigunners are hypocrites?" demanded Spare, his eyes and voice filled with bitter resentment.

"Hypocrites and misinformed, misguided, unrealistic fools!" snapped the Death Merchant. "If you want to stop crime—and that's the idea behind gun control—you don't take guns away from honest citizens. You punish criminals who use firearms. You execute the sons of bitches! We can't do that because it's 'cruel and inhuman punishment'! Damn the victim and his family. Society is only supposed to be concerned about the rights of the criminal. There's always any number of half-brained psychiatrists and silly sociologists ready to offer an excuse why this or that piece of trash raped half a dozen women or murdered three or four people. You see, the 'poor fellow' was 'deprived' as a child, or he was born in the ghetto, or his mother didn't breast-feed him. The dear liberals—a lot of them tinged with a commie pink—never run out of excuses why a criminal isn't responsible for his own actions." Camellion suddenly grinned, pushed back his chair and stood up. "But shucks! Let's not argue over gun control, Spare. We're all God's children. It's just that some of us are more childish and unrealistic than others. Let's go question Rodley."

26

Camellion turned to walk into the next room, feeling greater satisfaction when he noticed that the man by the radios, across the room, was smiling. Then the man winked at Camellion, proving he was in agreement with what the Death Merchant had said.

"Hold on!" A sullen Spare cleared his throat, got to his feet and put his hands flat on the table. He would have liked nothing better than to smash Camellion in the face. At the same time, all his protective senses warned him that he had better not try. There was an aura of death about the man who used the name "Bystrom," giving the impression that here was an individual used to every form of violence, a man more at home in a graveyard than in a sunny field filled with flowers and singing birds.

Spare said firmly, "Before we go in there, we've got to decide what kind of interrogative technique we're going to use on Rodley. There are any number of techniques which—"

"Which aren't applicable here," Camellion snapped, cutting him off. "We don't have the time to use sophisticated techniques. I'm going in there and—"

Spare's eyes flashed angrily. "What the hell do you mean, we don't have the time?" he demanded sharply. "He's our prisoner. He's not going anywhere."

"He's not, but I am. Don't forget the enemy higher-ups. They know the kidnap attempt was a failure. The men who tried didn't come back. To the other side that means they're either dead or captives. Should the whole organization go underground, that leaves us making a long dash on a short pier. And don't give me an argument. You read your orders from the Center. I'm in command, and I don't intend to pussyfoot around."

Spare cleared his throat again. "Very well," he said stiffly. "How are you going to question the man?" His manner became more conciliatory. "We do have the elements of fear and confusion on our side. Rodley can't be very happy! You knock him out in the country house and he wakes up here, only he doesn't know where 'here' is—plus the fact he's weak and sick."

"You'll see how I'm going to do it," Camellion shot back and started for the door. "Just make sure you're fast on the uptake when I start with the 'incrimination' method. And

27

get Doctor Luprich out of there. Humanitarians make me want to vomit."

"I understand she's a very good doctor," Spare offered. "Internal medicine is her field."

"She doesn't belong in the Company. She's not a realist."

Camellion knocked on the steel door. One of the CIA men on the other side swung open the door and Camellion and Spare walked into the room. Like the other rooms on the third floor, this room was also small and windowless. Not that the third story didn't have windows. A fiberboard wall, painted light gray, had been built six feet from the windows. To assist in hiding the wall from anyone in the house next door, large window boxes rested on the windowsills; however, the plants were three feet tall. The real secret of disguise lay in the special optics of the windowpanes in the old-fashioned cross-squared windows. To anyone looking directly through the glass, the wall would appear to be on the other side of the room. Since chairs and couches had been placed at various points along the wall, everything would appear normal to the outside viewer.

There was a daybed in the room. On the bed sat Lawrence Rodley, dressed only in his shorts. In front of him, in a semicircle, sat three CIA men, one on a box, the other two on turned-around chairs, their elbows on top of the short backs.

Doctor Joanna Luprich stood by a hot-plate on a table, sipping coffee. Wearing gray slacks and a cable-stitch pullover, she was about thirty-five, had a hardy face, luxuriant black hair and a so-so figure.

Spare looked at her. "How is he?"

"He's recovering nicely," she answered. "He'll be back to normal in a few days."

"You can leave, Doctor," Spare said, thinking that the prisoner would be dead within hours and suspecting that Camellion could be totally ruthless when he had to be. "Take your coffee with you, if you want."

The woman put down her cup, glanced at Spare, gave Camellion a go-to-the-devil look and left the room.

The Death Merchant walked over to Rodley and looked down at him the way a housewife would look at a dead cockroach. The Englishman stared back, his cowlike eyes mirroring anger and fear.

A 200-pounder, his black bushy eyebrows gave him an

air of fierce expectancy, while the broad bulkiness of his body made even casual movements seem aggressive.

"Recognize me, Rodley?" Camellion reached into his coat pocket and took out a .22 Minx Beretta automatic. From another pocket he pulled a noise suppressor.

Several of the CIA men glanced at each other and tried to catch Harvey Spare's eye. Spare stared straight ahead at Camellion and Rodley.

"You're the bloke who gave me the bashin'," Rodley said thickly. He watched Camellion screw the silencer onto the extra-long barrel of the Beretta.

"Where were you born, Rodley?"

The man rubbed a hand across his forehead. "In London, guv'nor, within sound of Bow bells."[3]

Very quickly, Camellion pulled back the slide of the Beretta and placed a cartridge in the firing chamber. He grinned sinisterly at Rodley, then turned and looked at Spare. "We catch the weasel in the hen house, dead to rights, and he doesn't even know he's trapped. He's a bloody bloomin' liar, he is! By the way, did you get the report yet about the tobacconist in London?"

"The report should be here in a few hours," Spare said seriously, proving that he was lightning fast on the uptake. He added the windowdressing. "Scotland Yard phoned just before you arrived. They've arrested the other three. Inspector Kellon said they had talked and implicated Rodley!"

"In wot?" burst out Rodley, gaping at Spare. The CIA man only smiled at him. Rodley turned to Camellion, a frantic look on his ashen face. "Listen, guv'nor. I've told the truth. It wasn't my idea to go muckin' about that house. The whole bloody business gave me the shivers, it did."

"Oh, shut up, stupid," Camellion said pleasantly. "You're no more a Cockney than I am. 'Within the sound of Bow bells, huh?' No Cockney could ever manage that *th* in *within*. A real Cockney would say *wivin*. Besides, there

---

[3] St. Mary-le-Bow in the City section of London. The "bow" refers to the arches on which the church was built. The true Londoner, the Cockney, is the one who has been born within sound of the huge bells of St. Mary-le-Bow. They can be heard for miles.

should be at least two diphthongs in Bow. You, Mr. Rodley, are a lying son of a bitch."

"I'll be damned!" exclaimed one of the CIA men.

Camellion turned to the man. "They should have you blokes study speech behavior. It's very simple. You see, the vocal apparatus of a human being is capable of making many thousands of sounds. Speaking a language is different. You must utter certain programmed sounds."

The Death Merchant returned his attention to Lawrence Rodley, who was becoming increasingly nervous and couldn't take his eyes off the silenced Beretta dangling in Camellion's left hand.

"I'll ask you again, stupid," Camellion said in a soft voice. "Where were you born?"

"In London, in the East End." This time there was no fake Cockney accent; this time Rodley spoke in the accent of the lower-middle-class situation comedies that are the staple of British television.

"Keep talking, ole darlin'," Camellion said, grinning.

"I know you fellas ain't the Dutch police," Rodley said, a quiver to his voice. "I want to know what I've been implicated in. I demand my rights. I demand to see a barrister."

Surprised at the man's brazen audacity, Camellion stared at Rodley for a moment, the smile fading, his mouth changing into a hard, grim line. Without warning, his hand flashed up, the silencer on the Beretta whispered and a glass, resting on a card table, exploded into dozens of pieces.

Rodley jerked and threw up his arms, fell back on the bed and let out a screech of fear. Spare and the three other Company men in the room also jumped, startled at the Death Merchant's unexpected action.

Camellion moved closer to the daybed and pointed the Beretta straight at the head of Rodley, who thought his time to die had come.

"Here are your rights!" Camellion snarled. "Unless you tell us what we want to know, the only attorney you'll ever see will be in hell." Then he took the long shot, at the same time prepared to cover it over with Rodley should he be wrong. "We know that you and Régene obtained those cigarettes from the Marmis shop. Tell us the rest—and sit up, damn it!"

Rodley sat up and blinked, his face frozen in confusion.

"We brought the cigarettes before the meeting," he choked out. "Paid for 'em one an' four a box. But what have cigarettes to do with this?"

The Death Merchant lowered the Beretta and pointed it at Rodley's right foot. A look of panic skidded over Rodley's flushed face. His mouth opened. His eyes went round.

"Ever seen a man shot in the foot?" Camellion snapped. "Tell me that first lie and you'll have a bad limp for the rest of your life—*which should be about two hours!* Now *talk,* damn you!"

"All we were told—me and Régene—was that we were to come to Amsterdam and meet this Dutch chap. Hendrik de Jeer was his name. It was De Jeer who—"

"We know where the meeting was held," Spare spoke for the first time, jabbing a finger at Rodley. "But we want to hear you tell us."

"In the back of the tobacco shop, the back room," Rodley admitted, looking somewhat surprised.

Camellion turned to Spare. "You know, it's possible I won't have to shoot him in the foot, after all. I think he might be telling the truth."

"I have my doubts," Spare said. "He still hasn't told us the name of the man who told him and Régene where to meet De Jeer in Amsterdam."

Camellion turned and stared at Rodley. "And you haven't told us who else was at the meeting in the back room."

"There was only me and Régene and another man," Rodley said quickly. "The third man didn't give his name. We didn't ask."

"Three of you were in the back room, at the meeting?" Camellion said.

"Three of us, yes."

"At Marmis's tobacco shop?"

"That's right, but I didn't kill anyone. I'm not a tocker."[4] Rodley's voice became a whine, the plea of a man who knows he's balanced on a tightrope between heaven and hell. "After we met De Jeer, he told us about you living at the house at Aalsmeer. He said it was a snatch job, but that there wouldn't be any trouble. He gave us five hundred pounds each. But I didn't kill anybody."

---

[4] British underworld slang for "murderer."

Camellion believed that Rodley was telling the truth, but he had to be positive; he had to be absolutely certain.

His hand flashed. The silencer went pop. Rodley yelled and jumped a foot off the bed. Camellion had shot him in the arch of the right foot.

Rodley fell back on the bed and moaned, blood dripping from his foot onto the floor, spittle dribbling from the corners of his mouth.

"Sit up, you damned liar!" roared Camellion. "Or I'll start shooting off your toes, one by one. I want information—*now!*

Still moaning and making *ou-ou-ou* sounds, Rodley managed to sit erect, his body shaking with pain and terror. He looked down at his bloody foot, his face turning the color of chalk.

"I need a d-doctor," he wailed. "I'll bleed t-to death."

"You'll need an undertaker if you don't answer me!" warned Camellion. He swung the Beretta toward Rodley's other foot. The man screeched like a woman about to be raped, jerked up his leg and held up his hands in front of him.

"Wait! *Wait!*" he almost shouted. "It was Mr. Marmis. He told us to come to his shop. Me and Régene met him in a pub in Soho. He bought us a pint and said he knew we was petermen,[5] and asked us if we'd like to make five hundred pounds a piece for a job in Holland. He said the job would be easy and that we wouldn't have any trouble with the bobbies. Me and Régene, we said sure. Our only concern was not being caught and sent across. Oh God! My foot hurts. I need a doctor."

"This third man at the meeting wasn't Kemper Marmis?"

"I swear he wasn't. Marmis and his clerks were in the front of the shop," moaned Rodley. "We waited in the back room. This third man, he came from another room in the back. He must have been back there when we arrived. I know he didn't come in from the front, at least while me and Régene was there."

"*Wot* did 'e look like?" asked Camellion in a mock-Cockney accent. "Tell the truth. I don't want ta shoot yer

[5] A safecracker who uses explosives.

other foot. Lookin' at the one that's already bloody gives me the shivers, it does."

Rodley, pain etched in his pale face, thought for a moment.

"He was a heavy sort of man. Tall, a good meter. Weighed maybe fourteen stone. What I noticed the most about him was his hair. Brown hair, it was. He wore it long, almost as long as a teddy boy's. He didn't offer his name. Mike and I didn't ask."

"By *Mike*, you're referring to Michael Régene?"

"Yes, Michael Régene."

"The guns you men used in the house?" Camellion said in a harsh tone. "Who gave them to you?"

"Hendrik de Jeer," Rodley spoke promptly. "Me and Régene met De Jeer at the dock. We came over on one of the ferries. He took us to his house in the afternoon. That same night, we drove to Aalsmeer. Me and Régene rode in the car that De Jeer drove." He looked up at Camellion in awe and dread, rivulets of perspiration coursing down his cheeks and forehead. "God! You did it all. You killed everyone, all by yourself, everyone but me!"

"I didn't come here to swim in the Zuiderzee," the Death Merchant said, a glimmer of a smile on his lean, ruggedly handsome face. "You're right, I killed them all with my nice little Colts. You I saved for information."

"Please get me a doctor," moaned Rodley, who had raised his right foot off the floor and was holding his leg, his hands around his knee. "Get me something for this pain."

One of the CIA men, feeling sorry for Rodley, shifted uncomfortably on his feet.

"Are there any questions you want to ask him?" Camellion looked at Spare, who had taken out a handkerchief and was mopping his brow.

"You've covered the full field," he said.

Camellion focused on Rodley. "OK, jazzbo. We'll get a doctor to look after your bloody foot." Once again he caught Spare's eyes and motioned with his head toward the door.

"Frank, give the subject a hypo to kill the pain," Spare said to the CIA man wearing a gray lambswool sweater, gray whipcord pants and black town and country oxfords. "In his right arm, Frank."

33

"Right," Frank said.

Twenty seconds later, Spare and Camellion were in the next room, walking toward the table.

"Do you believe he was telling the truth?" Spare asked.

The Death Merchant pulled out a chair. "I think he was. We're going to proceed on the basis that he was. We have to. How are you going to terminate him? I trust you're not going to have the lady sawbones do the job with drugs?"

Spare said soberly. "Rodley's already dead, or in the process of dying. The hypo I told Frank to give him was filled with poison from the sea wasp. It's a deadly little bastard in Australian waters. Rodley will be dead before Frank will have time to pull out the needle. Ever hear of the sea wasp?"

Camellion didn't look up from his task of unscrewing the silencer from the Beretta. "For its size, the sea wasp is no doubt the deadliest creature alive. Its poison is even more potent than a tiger snake's."

"You're a marked man," Spare said ominously. "The other side is out to kidnap you, find out who you are, what you know, and then terminate you. The interview with Van den Wenckebach didn't have anything to do with their coming after you, unless of course Rodley lied. Like you, I don't think he did."

The Death Merchant put the silencer in one pocket, the Beretta in another. "Yeah, Rodley and Régene came to Holland before the program was even on the air. It was the advertising that brought the worms to the surface."

"You could end up a bucketful of ashes," Spare said.

Camellion grinned. "First they have to know who to look for and where to look; and believe me, I've been hunted by the best."

Spare didn't comment. He would be glad when Camellion left the safe house and was out of the country. Just having him around made one think of a cold drizzle falling in some dark and forgotten cemetery. . . .

Chapter Three

To ask a Londoner about London as a whole is to open the door to dozens of vague generalities. The trouble is that London is so big, so sprawled out. If you wanted to put the entire city under your shoes, you would start at Charing Cross Station, London's geographic center, walk 18 miles north, 18 miles south and the same distance east and west. Even so, you would still have missed many places of significance to the Londoner. You would have missed 20 square miles of territory and most of the city's 7,397,014 inhabitants.

The vastness of London did not concern Richard Camellion, who had been in London for thirteen days. He had flown to London from Amsterdam, disguised as a senior citizen—gray-white hair, small, fuzzy beard, wrinkled skin and a cane. His expertly forged French passport identified him as "Henri Chaunalt" of Paris, France, the stamps in the passport indicating that Monsieur Chaunalt had been visiting in Rome, and from Rome had gone to Amsterdam.

British customs officials at London's Heathrow Airport had accepted without question the passport and his explanation that he would be in London for only two weeks.

Four hours after "Monsieur Chaunalt" had left Heathrow Airport, the Death Merchant was in a well-kept two-story brownstone house on Bayswater Road, just north of Hyde Park, consulting with Raymond A. Hohfeler, the chief of station of the CIA unit at the American Embassy in London.

"Henri Chaunalt" no longer existed. The Death Merchant's new identity was now Casimer Anthony Mohilowski, an American of Polish ancestry, from Cleveland, Ohio, USA. The small photo in his American passport was that of Camellion's actual face, but with some difference. The face in the photograph sported very long sideburns, a shaggy mustache and a short but full beard, neatly trimmed.

The well-oiled network of the CIA swung into action. Contacts within Scotland Yard's Special Branch revealed that Kemper Marmis was a third-generation Turk whose parents had immigrated to Great Britain in 1896. Marmis had served in the British Army during World War II, had been wounded in France, and had been honorably discharged. He did not have a criminal record. Since 1958 he had owned and operated Marmis's Fine Tobaccos of Distinction on New Bond Street, which was an extension of Old Bond Street. Very discreet inquiries of other shop owners on New Bond Street resulted in the report that Marmis was well-liked and held in high regard. The same fine reports were received from Marmis's neighbors in the district of Knightsbridge where he lived with his much younger wife and two children. His first wife had been killed in World War II during a German bombing raid over London.

On the surface, Kemper Marmis was not a likely candidate for membership in the organization that held the secret of the burning blue death.

On the tenth day of his stay in London—he was residing at the brownstone house which was owned by a retired American business executive—Camellion had a long conference with Raymond Hohfeler and Norwood Clark, Hohfeler's chief aide. Both men were dubious about Camellion's belief that Kemper Marmis was an important lead. They didn't, however, argue with him when he outlined his scheme, explaining that he would need the services of two experts from Q-Department.[1] The London CIA section, too, had received an ultrasecret directive from the Center in Langley, Virginia to give Edward Walker, Camellion's cover name, "your full and complete cooperation."

[1] Officially there isn't a Q-Department. Unofficially, this is the assassination and "gunmen" department.

"It's a crazy damned scheme," Hohfeler said. He was a dark-haired man with confident and reassuring gray eyes. In his thirties, he seemed young to be the chief of station in London. "So ridiculous it might even work."

"Why couldn't we kidnap Marmis?" Norwood Clark offered, looking at Camellion. "Going in the shop and using gangster tactics does not seem the right approach to me." He didn't give Camellion time to answer. "Sure, I know. You want to snoop in those back rooms."

"I'd like to know what you expect to find?" Hohfeler frowned for a second. "Granted. There is a complex of rooms behind the establishment, but Marmis uses them in connection with his business. You know, storage, etcetera. I see nothing unusual about that."

"We can't be positive that—what was his name again?"

"Rodley," supplied Camellion.

"We don't know that he didn't lie," finished Clark.

"His kinesic behavior indicated that he told the truth," Camellion said earnestly. "We don't have any other leads. "We might as well pursue the one we do have. Can either of you offer a better suggestion?"

Neither Hohfeler nor Clark spoke.

Camellion leaned back and let his eyes wander around the sparsely furnished room. There was a walnut desk in the rear. Books on every subject lined two walls. A leather sofa and four leather tilt-back chairs. Numerous knick-knacks. The one that caught Camellion's eye was a fifteen-inch-high bronze statue of the Hindu goddess Umā, the husband of Siva.

"I did suggest putting the grab on Marmis," Clark said, breaking the brief silence. We could black bag him on his way home." He motioned with one hand. "It would be a cinch. But what you want to do! Hell, it's like trying to get sunlight to the bottom of a mine shaft."

Hohfeler took a cigarette from a pack of Kent Golden Lights.

"He has a point, Walker. If you don't mind my saying so, it seems you're determined to thumb down the highway when you could be riding first-class."

Camellion locked his fingers on top of his head and tilted back the leather chair. "Gentlemen, I'd like nothing better than to go first class. But have you asked yourselves what the other side will do if Kemper Marmis turns up missing?"

"In my opinion, they're already underground," announced Hohfeler. "The dead men you left back in Holland made sure of that." He glanced at Camellion and lit his cigarette.

Clark interposed, "Fortunately for our side, the Dutch Police will find all the bodies. It was a good idea taking Rodley back to the house in Aalsmeer."

"That part of the plan was Spare's idea," Camellion said, taking a flat box of dried apricots from one of his suit-coat pockets. "I only hope that the Dutch police don't do an autopsy on the bodies. If and when they find the bodies, if an autopsy's performed, they'll discover that Rodley died of a strange poison."

"It all depends what the Dutch police tell the press," Clark said. "We know for fact they don't always give all information to the media."

"There's also a day-and-a-half difference between Rodley's demise and the deaths of the other men," said Camellion, opening the box.

Hohfeler joined in. "Personally, I don't see the connection between the bodies in Aalsmeer and Marmis, in the sense that a snatch job wouldn't help us achieve our goal. Or should I have said *your* goal?"

A slight dig on Hohfeler's part? If so, Camellion didn't give a damn. His past successes had been due in part to intuition, and he was trusting the same subconscious perception now.

"I have a hunch we might find something of importance in the rear of Marmis's shop," he said and took an apricot from the box. "Marmis isn't working alone. Kidnap him, and whoever is working with him will close up shop—and that's not a pun. The entire organization might go deeper underground than a salt mine. Then where will we be?"

He put the apricot into his mouth and began to chew.

Raymond Hohfeler said straight out, "Constructing an operation on a 'hunch' is not what I consider to be intelligence work. Suppose something goes wrong and the bobbies grab you or one of the Qs? What then?"

"Hell no, it's not intelligence work by textbook standards," said Camellion. "But there are times when you've got to go on a gut feeling, especially when time is working against you."

Clark looked carefully at Camellion. "It's a gamble

you'll be taking, an enormous gamble. Thank God for silencers . . ."

Camellion smiled slightly. "The way I've planned the invasion, the chances for success are on our side. I'm not a novice at this sort of thing. Believe me, I have had more than enough experience.

Clark cleared his throat—tipping off Camellion that he was worried. His "eyebrow flash" proved it.

Hohfeler exhaled smoke through his mouth and nose, his eyes moving upward. He wished he had never laid eyes on the man who called himself "Walker." Under ordinary circumstances, there was never any difficulty in operating the London station. The CIA watched the KGB and other known agents of Communist nations and tried to find out who the "unknowns" were. Everything proceeded smoothly. One even had a drink now and then with one of the KGBs at a diplomatic reception. The only trouble was when those gun-happy, violence-prone coverts showed up. God in His sweet heaven! The whole business could turn into a shootout. Right in the heart of London! And suppose Ambassador Cherlin found out? Hohfeler's official post in the American Embassy was that of cultural attaché, but Cherlin knew he was the station chief. On the other hand, he had definite orders from the Deputy Director of Operations to cooperate in every way with Edward Walker. More thoughts blossomed in Hohfeler's mind, involving vague rumors about an incredible individual who at times took special assignments for the Company—the infamous Death Merchant.

Could Edward Walker be the Death Merchant? Hohfeler wasn't about to ask him. He wasn't even going to mention what he suspected to Clark. . . .

Norwood Clark said reflectively, "You know, Walker, depending on what happens in the tobacco shop, the Yard might get into the act. That's another howdy-doody we'll have to contend with."

Camellion cocked an eyebrow toward Clark. *This joker is incredibly average*, he thought. "I won't ask how many 'moles' you have in the Yard. It's none of my business and you couldn't tell me."

Clark looked startled for a moment, then clamped his mouth shut and looked at Hohfeler.

"We do," Hohfeler said, a trace of pride in his voice.

"Even in the Special Branch. This gives us channels to MI5."[2]

Camellion smiled at Norwood Clark. "Our problem is solved. We'll always know what the Yard is thinking and doing, should it become interested in Marmis. How soon can you bring the Qs here?"

Hohfeler crushed his cigarette in an ashtray next to his chair.

"I can have them here by tomorrow afternoon." He looked gravely at the Death Merchant. "Understand that I have to radio the Center about your proposed operation. The D/DO has to give his OK when Qs attached to the London Station are used."

"When you radio, put in a request for me," Camellion said. "Ask the Center that I—use the cipher W-Two-B—want all the available data on Dr. Morris K. Jessup, the astrophysicist."

"Is that all you have on him, his name?" Surprise shone on Hohfeler's face.

"What does he have to do with the burning deaths?" inquired Norwood Clark, taking a pack of British Player cigarettes from his shirt pocket.

"Back in 1955, Dr. Jessup published a book called, *The Case for the UFOs*," Camellion said. "He was found dead in his station wagon in Dade County Park in Florida, in April of 1959. Police listed his death as a suicide. They found that a hose had been attached to the exhaust pipe of his station wagon and looped into the closed interior."

Clark gave a low laugh. "Don't tell me that you think UFOs are responsible for SHC?" He laughed again and licked his lips.

The Death Merchant yawned. *Clark, old bloke, yer a blinkin' 'oly'ock. And a damned dumb hollyhock at that!*

Camellion answered pleasantly enough. "I'm interested in Dr. Jessup because of a series of strange letters he re-

[2] MI5 is Britain's second intelligence branch. Equivalent to the FBI, MI5 is responsible for counterespionage in England itself. However, it has no powers of arrest. When it is ready to move in on a spy ring, it does so through Scotland Yard's Special Branch. It's the Yard that makes the actual arrests.

MI6 is military intelligence, England's spy and espionage arm, or "Her Majesty's Secret Service." The telephone number is WHItehall 2730.

ceived from a man who signed himself 'Carlos Miquel Allende,' but that's another story." His piercing blue eyes darted to Hohfeler, who seemed to be studying him. "Make sure you put in my request, and have the Qs here tomorrow."

London's West End is not an "end" at all. It's the center of the city. All the famous places are in the West End. In the West End is Piccadilly Circus, the hub of the universe for the British, the "Times Square" of London. Nelson's Column, Trafalgar Square and two other famous squares, Berkeley Square and Grosvenor Square, are all located there. Berkeley Square, once a distinguished residential center—Clive of India lived there—has been taken over by business firms. St. James Street is a very special world of splendid men's shops and clubs. Crescent-shaped St. Regent Street is one of London's better shopping streets. There are many other streets, among which are Bond Street and Oxford Street. But the heart of the fashionable West End is Mayfair, the district bounded by Park Lane on the west, Bond Street on the east, Piccadilly on the south, and Oxford Street on the north.

In spite of all this so-called elegance, the West End is drab by day and very ugly, so ugly that various members of Parliament have proposed tearing it down. Always the members of Parliament change their minds when they learn that the new buildings would be even uglier.

At night, the West End undergoes a miraculous change. Then it becomes the center of the most exciting city in Europe, perhaps in all the world, offering something for all tastes, from the most elementary to the most intellectual—from whores to concerts, from peep-shows (heterosexual or homosexual) to discussions on God, the space-time continuum and the universe. Another paradox is that one's person will be fairly safe in the West End—day or night—unlike, say, Times Square in New York City.

Neil Reeder, who knew London the way Camellion knew the Big Thicket region of southeastern Texas, was behind the wheel of the Aston-Martin convertible. The Death Merchant, wearing an expensive tweed all-weather coat, his left arm in a sling, sat beside him.

Reeder was a thin, young man, not yet thirty-four. Al-

41

ways immaculately dressed, he had a large round face, a high forehead, and a backbone filled with steel. The fact that he could end up dead or spend years in a British jail—if Camellion's plan failed—didn't bother him. If it did, he was sure doing a fine job of not showing it. When Camellion had explained to him and Plymale, the other Q-man, what was expected of them, Reeder's only comment had been, "When?—and give us the details."

"That's another thing about London," Reeder said. "Ever since Parliament passed the streetwalking act, you don't find the girls walking in the vicinity of Mayfair and Leicester Square." He giggled almost like a woman. "That act sure gave a shot in the arm to the call-girl system. Just as expensive are the hothouse sluts that bloom on bar stools. Those mattress testers are watered with weak whisky just as they are in the States."

So far the Death Merchant was pleased. He looked at the watch on his right wrist: 2:09. The schedule was perfect. The weather was on his side. Like the rest of Europe, Great Britain was in the icy grip of one of the worst winters in years. Earlier in the day there had been snow flurries and the sky had taken on a blue-purple appearance. The snow had stopped right after lunch. Now, almost at the middle of the afternoon, the ceiling of heaven had softened, with the sun trying to poke aside the clouds and blow its hot breath on chilly London.

The roads were crowded, traffic slow because of patches of snow and ice. Reeder, however, had assured Camellion that the streets around Bond would be free of ice and snow.

"That's one thing I like about the British," Reeder said. "They don't let the snow pile up." Like a tourist guide with a motorboat mouth, he rattled on, "I'll tell you another thing about the West End. It contains three of the hotels favored by most Americans—the Hilton, the Dorchester and Grosvenor House. All three are not far from the big Marble Arch on Park Lane."

"Yes, I know."

"You can head south on Park Lane and hit Piccadilly. Make a left and there's Green Park. Right across from Green Park is Buckingham Palace. Westminster Abbey, the Houses of Parliament and the British Museum are all in the West End."

As if I didn't know, but why tell him? the Death Merchant thought, glancing at the wide-angle rear-view mirror. Klyment "Clem" Plymale and the Morris Minor were nowhere in sight. The flow of traffic had forced him to drop back.

"We seem to have lost Plymale," Camellion said, again glancing in the rear-view mirror. "He has time to catch up, though. We'll have to wait after we're parked. What are our chances of parking on New Bond Street at this time of day?"

Reeder did not answer immediately. He slowed the Aston-Martin, shifted gears, turned carefully onto Baker Street and increased speed slightly.

"Oh, we'll find space to park in," he said confidently. "The rush won't start until four-thirty, after the business offices close. By then, we'll be long gone. You still figuring on blowing up the joint?"

"It all depends on what we find in the back," Camellion said. "Our first concern must be our own safety. If the Yard gets in on this, MI5 and MI6 will not be far behind!"

"Hell, good men like us don't have to worry," laughed Reeder. "We've always obeyed the commandments Moses brought down from Mt. Cyanide."

Amused at Reeder's malapropism, the Death Merchant glanced at the map in his lap. Another two blocks and Baker Street would run into Orchard Street. One long block on Orchard, a left onto Oxford, then two blocks on Oxford would take them to the end of New Bond.

On Orchard they passed long-established shops, which conveyed the feeling of an era when London, the real London, was confined to a small central area, including a small perfume shop, a meat market, an apothecary shop and other small businesses.

They turned onto Oxford and quickly covered the short distance to New Bond Street. With other vehicles, Reeder made the turn when the bobby, from his island station in the center of Oxford, waved them on.

Every single parking space on the left side of the road was filled—in Merry Ole England, one sits behind the steering wheel on the right side of the automobile and drives on the left side of the road.

"Go on down to Old Bond," Camellion ordered. He took a small walkie-talkie from the compartment in the dash and pressed the signal button four times. It was almost a minute before Klyment Plymale answered.

"I'm on Oxford," Plymale said. "A moving truck got in front of me. I'll contact you when I'm parked on Conduit Street. If I can't park on Conduit Street, I'll try for a spot on Regent Street. Acknowledge."

"Acknowledged—and out," Camellion said.

Reeder drove slowly, although on New Bond Street traffic was thin. Camellion watched the numbers. At length, on the right side of the street he saw the number 4164, and the sign, printed in Old English: MARMIS. FINE TOBACCOS OF DISTINCTION.

Kemper Marmis and two clerks! Camellion thought. *How many in the rear? Or could I be totally wrong. We'll see. . . .*

They were almost to the end of New Bond when Reeder spotted a parking place and expertly turned into the tiny area.

They waited, neither speaking. Ten minutes later, the walkie-talkie started to buzz. The Death Merchant switched on the device. "Yes?"

"Couldn't find a spot on Conduit," Plymale said. "I'm on Regent. Any special stamps you want me to buy?"

"Sit tight. I'll tell you when. If you don't hear from us within forty-five minutes, take off. Acknowledge."

"Understood. Over."

"Out." Camellion turned off the walkie-talkie and slipped it into the left-side pocket of his overcoat. Slipping one arm through the open coat, he adjusted the woolen Prince Edward cap and slipped a fur-lined deerskin glove over the white Bakelite hand of the artificial arm, which filled the left sleeve of the specially tailored overcoat. He buttoned the single-breasted overcoat with his right hand, slipped his right hand into a glove and, still using his right hand, adjusted the blue cloth sling in which rested the artificial arm.

To Camellion's right, Reeder put on a red, green, and white Scottish wool tam-o'-shanter over his gray hairpiece, and slipped his hands into a pair of gray gloves.

"The last operation like this I took part in was in West Berlin," Reeder said. "We almost got our butts shot off, but we kidnapped the traitor."

"What was he?" asked Camellion, picking up the walking stick from the floor.

"A 'she.' A double-agent that got one of ours terminated." Again Reeder giggled like a woman. "She had an accident. She walked in front of a car on the Kurfürstendamm and was killed."

Neither man was worried that, later, anyone would recognize them. Kemper Marmis and his two clerks could look through the Yard's mug albums until icebergs floated down Piccadilly! They still would not find photos of Neil Reeder and "Edward Walker." Camellion's uncanny talent with a makeup kit had changed their features. The Death Merchant was a man in his sixties, the contours of his face very different from the originals. Reeder looked fifty, his naturally clear skin pockmarked and ruddy, a purplish birthmark on his right cheek.

They got out of the automobile. Reeder buttoned his Melton British warmer while Camellion patiently waited. The two men started walking south to the corner, the coldness tingling their faces, gusts of wind blowing up little clouds of powdery snow from the front of shops and from mounds piled toward the edge of the sidewalk.

They came to the corner, crossed the pavement to the other side of the street and began walking in the opposite direction. They did not hurry; they could not. To any person who might have bothered to notice, Camellion had been in some sort of accident. His left arm was in a sling and his right leg had a severe limp. For this latter reason, he used the walking stick.

Finally, number 4164: MARMIS. FINE TOBACCOS OF DISTINCTION.

The front of the shop was quaint and old-fashioned—two rounded sections of windows, each section composed of twenty-five separate panes of glass, each held in place by twenty-five individual frames painted white. Now, much of the glass was frosted over. Two wide stone steps led to the door between the window sections.

"You first," Camellion said, a lilt to his voice. "I'm all crippled up. Remember?"

They walked up to the shop and Reeder opened the door.

A bell tinkled.

Chapter Four

Camellion and Reeder saw at once that the shop was well-stocked. Shelves lined the three walls, behind the glass display cases on two sides of the room and the counter toward the rear.

Cigarettes of every nation, brand and description were in the cases and on the shelves, plus Kemper Marmis's own special blends, including the familiar Marmis Premium cigarettes in the orange boxes bordered in black. The cartons were also orange and edged in black. There were Marmis's queen-sized cigarettellos, London Ovals in various colors, English Naturals with gold-banded cork filtertip, Turkish Rounds, Havana Rounds, and Black Beauties with silver-banded cork filtertip.

Cigars of every length and blend. These were Marmis's Custom-Made Havanas that are extra-mild. With various names: the Matzos, the Twist, the Pencil-Slim, the Half-Corona, the Churchill, the Knicks and others.

A giant photograph on the rear wall showed three different-colored cigars. Below was the wording "Colors from left to right are Double Claro, Natural English Market, Maduro."

Boxes of gift assortments. The most expensive was the "Fine Life" selection, which contained 150 "carefully selected cigars (five cigars to a container, thirty containers in all) in this luxurious humidor, hand-tooled in 14K gold and lined with velvet. The lock is solid brass."

The cost in English pounds was the equivalent of 175 American dollars.

Various kinds of cigarette and pipe lighters, all the way ⟍⟍ the cheap kind that anyone could afford to a few that were solid gold and retailed as high as $2,145.

Cigarette cases (*I wonder who uses them?* Camellion thought) and pipes. Hundreds and hundreds of pipes made of Mediterranean briar, or root briar, or Greek or Corsican briar. Pipes with various names—the Bent Scoop, the Canadian, the Pot, the Apple, the Half-Scoop, the Tall Bowl. And of different finishes: virgin finish, or tan sandblast, or walnut goldband or black sandblast. Some presmoked. But all would "insure a cool smooth smoke from the first puff."

All kinds of humidors, some covered in leather. Ashtrays of a hundred different shapes. Over 50 different kinds of tobacco pouches. Sixty blends of pipe tobacco. Anything a smoker might want, he would find at Marmis's tobacco shop.

A nonsmoker, Camellion only wanted Kemper Marmis—and a complete inspection of the rooms behind the shop.

Several male customers were being waited on by the two clerks behind the counter. The young employees were impeccably dressed, as was Marmis, who was behind one of the display cases to the right of Camellion.

Neil Reeder walked to the counter, took a position to the left of the elderly man, who was buying a box of cigars, and pretended to be interested in Marmis's "portable humidors"—roll-up tobacco pouches in bright plaids.

Leaning heavily on his walking stick, Camellion limped over to where Kemper Marmis had bent down to arrange small brown boxes of cedarwood on the top shelf of a case. Each little box contained twenty Tiny Specials—"The Kind of Cigars Lord Byron would have Smoked."

As Marmis stood up and smiled at Camellion, one of the customers left the shop.

"Good afternoon, sir. May I help you?" Of medium height and slightly on the pudgy side, Marmis had a pleasing baritone voice. He didn't look like a Turk. In his early fifties, his hair was dark, streaked with gray at the temples. His eyes were dark but skin was as fair as a Norwegian's. He wore gold-framed eye glasses.

The Death Merchant, his right hand holding the walking stick, his left hand around a Czech CZ autoloader, stalled, waiting for the other customer to leave and almost praying that no one else would come in from the outside.

"Cigars," said Camellion, faking the age-worn voice of an elderly man. "Trouble is, there are so many different kinds. The various selections simply amaze me."

Marmis nodded understandingly. "Were you buying for yourself or for a friend?"

"For a dear friend," replied Camellion. "He likes a mild Maduro."

From the corner of his eye, he noticed that the last customer had turned from the counter and was walking toward the door.

"May I suggest the Statesman?" Marmis said suavely. "The Statesman is my own special blend. It's a mild cigar, made from the finest of tobaccos, naturally dried, without any flue curing."

The instant the front door closed, Camellion and Reeder swung into action. The two clerks drew back, and their eyes widened in fear and astonishment when Reeder calmly reached inside his British warmer, pulled out a Walther P-38 autopistol, to which was attached a silencer, and said in a chillingly calm but low voice, "Move one single muscle and I'll blow your faces off."

Kemper Marmis thought he was having an hallucination when he saw a hand and a silenced pistol poke through the Death Merchant's overcoat. He changed his mind when he heard Camellion speak. "Go to the front door and lock it. If another customer walks in before you have a chance to lock it, tell him you're closed for the day. Make any wrong moves or attempt to warn anyone and I'll kill you—customers, too, if I have to."

Marmis, tight-lipped and frozen-faced, glanced in the direction of the two clerks and saw that they were covered. Then he moved from behind the display case and walked to the front door. The fact that he retained his composure was proof enough to Camellion that he was on the right track.

"Careful how you take the keys out of your pocket," warned Camellion. "I'd just as soon put a bullet in your belly as bounce a bedbug off a baseball."

Marmis took a ring of keys from his pocket and used one to lock the vertical deadbolt lock.

"Now, reverse the sign," ordered Camellion.

Without a word, Marmis turned the sign on the door so that CLOSED faced the outside.

"What is it you men want?" Marmis asked, his voice tight and controlled. "You're welcome to what money we have."

"Hurry up and get to the back room," snapped Camellion, noticing that Reeder was already marching the two clerks into the first room in the rear. "We're going to see what you have back there."

Watching Kemper Marmis closely, Camellion saw the barest hint of alarm and fear flash over the man's face—more evidence that he had something to hide!

"There isn't anything of value to you back there," Marmis said and started for the first room in the rear.

"Hold it and don't move," Camellion said. They had reached the counter. Reeder, moving behind the two clerk was in front of Marmis, and Camellion did not want to risk the Turk giving the Q-man a violent shove.

"Now move," Camellion said.

Once Camellion and Reeder and their three prisoners were in the rear room, Camellion closed the door to the front of the shop, ordering Marmis and the two clerks to face the wall and put their hands on top of their heads.

On one side of the room were filing cabinets, an old-fashioned roll-top desk and a table, on which were ledgers and an adding machine. On another table were cups, saucers, a box of tea and a double-burner hot-plate. A small refrigerator was along one wall. There were several chairs and an expandable metal garment rack. Against the rear wall were tobacco drums, each containing a special blend, and huge cartons of various kinds of cigars, cigarettes, and other smokers' supplies. In the center of the cartons was the door to the next room.

"You chaps made a mistake," one of the clerks said nervously.

"Be still, Norman," Marmis said. "They aren't robbers."

Neither Marmis nor the two clerks had time to say anything else. Reeder slammed the barrel of his P-38 against the back of one clerk's head while Camellion put the second clerk to sleep with a right-handed sword-ridge chop, and tapped the side of Kemper Marmis's head with the rounded side of the silencer attached to the Czech CZ auto-pistol.

Without even a moan, Marmis and the two clerks dropped to the floor and lay still.

"Get on with it," Camellion said, unbuttoning his overcoat with the fingers of his right hand. "I'll cover you, just in case."

Reeder reached into one of the pockets of his British warmer, took out a two-inch-long metal tube and got down on one knee. He placed the P-38 on the floor, unscrewed the tube in the middle, tilted one section and let three blue tablets fall into his hand. He opened the mouth of the first clerk by squeezing the man's cheeks between his thumb and forefinger. He dropped a pill into the man's mouth.

The pills, a combination of flurazepam and diphenhydramine, were powerful sleep inducers, and would render a man unconscious for a minimum of six hours.

"When are you going to drop the IRA leaflets?" asked Reeder, opening the mouth of the second clerk.

"When we leave," Camellion replied. He frowned. Could he have heard a slight noise in the next room?

Neil Reeder had just dropped a F-D pill into Kemper Marmis's slack mouth, and was starting to stand up when the door to the second room opened and a heavy-set man began to step through the opening. Wearing corduroy pants of a faded brown color and a dark blue Shetland sweater, the man froze, shocked incomprehension on his face—but only for a second.

"It's a raid!" he yelled hoarsely, his accent unmistakably Irish. In one quick motion, he tried to step back into the room and at the same time pull the British Webley .455 Mark VI revolver from his belt.

"Hell!" Reeder spun, dove to one side and swung up the P-38.

The Death Merchant's reflexes were much faster. His left hand was a blur as he mentally positioned the target and pulled the trigger of the Czech CZ twice. The noise suppressor popped with less noise than a toy cap pistol, the two 9mm jacketed hollowpoint bullets striking the man in the chest and knocking him back into the store room.

Hampered slightly by the artificial arm in the left sleeve of the overcoat and by the sling around his neck, Camellion darted to the door, his right hand reaching for the second Czech CZ fastened in a spring-clip under his left armpit. Reeder charged right behind him.

Camellion had pulled the second gun and thumbed off the safety by the time he streaked through the door and sprinted to the left. In that instant, he saw that the two windows in the back wall had been bricked over and that the door to the alley was of metal and secured by an iron bar. More boxes and cartons stacked against the walls and in the center of the room. And two men! A skinny gaunt-faced piece of trash in gray pants and a red-striped shirt. He was between the door and some boxes in the center of the room, looking as though he had just dropped dead and was staring at the Gates of Hell. Confused by the ale he had been drinking below, Albert Collins was slow to react. And thinking that he and O'Conner were facing an "old duffer" only added to his confusion.

The head, shoulders and chest of Arnold O'Conner protruded through a square opening toward the center of the floor. A large wooden carton had been bolted to the trapdoor, and now both trapdoor and crate were tilted so that the edge of the crate rested on the floor.

With a cry of alarm, Collins reached for the British .38 Enfield "pistol" in a shoulder holster as O'Conner tried to pull a 9mm Beretta from his right hip pocket.

A snarl of a grin on his face, the Death Merchant fired both Czech autoloaders simultaneously. The bullet from the left CZ-75 smacked Collins high in the chest and pitched him back against a stack of cartons marked "Samplers for the Armchair Adventurer." The slug from the right CZ cut into O'Conner's throat, just below the chin, and bored through the back of his neck. The Irishman dropped the Beretta and, with a river of red rushing from his throat, sagged and rolled down the wide wooden steps.

Neil Reeder didn't have an opportunity to inquire of the Death Merchant what their next move might be. Much to his astonishment, Camellion raced straight to the open trapdoor.

The Q-man's eyes widened as he stared after the deadly individual who called himself "Edward Walker." The man had to be some kind of a crazy-brave nut! How did he know what lay in the secret room below? He might be going to his own execution!

By no means was the Death Merchant the risk-taking oddball that Reeder suspected he might be. Camellion had charged the trapdoor opening for two very good reasons. Earlier in the afternoon, psychic conditions had been just right and he had caught sight of Reeder's aura.[1] The bio-electric emanations had been a pale blue, tinged with deep green and some yellow, this type of radiation indicating that Reeder would not die in the near future. Since Camellion would be with Reeder, he reasoned that he, too, would be safe. The second reason was equally as logical: to hesitate would give whoever was below a chance to think, a chance to organize. The key to success was attack. Attack while the enemy was rattled and still befuddled by the suddenness of the assault.

Careful not to slip on the wooden steps slick with O'Conner's blood, the Death Merchant stormed down the stairs, his eyes raking in the panorama before him. The rear wall of the basement room was filled with shelves of canned goods. The room contained a large electric hotplate on a wooden box, and a table and six chairs. To the left, metal bunks, one on top of the other. Half a dozen army-type cots to the right. And nine pairs of eyes staring up at him, some of their owners holding handguns.

As the men in the room below ducked, the Death Merchant dodged to the right and, almost throwing himself down the steps, began firing the two CZ-75s. Now all that counted was speed, more speed, and accuracy, both of which were composed half of talent and half of experience.

He particularly wanted to kill the man in the northeast corner of the room, the leathery bloke who was frantically trying to swing shut the square door of a large safe built into the stone wall. Camellion could see only the man's legs below the knees and his head and shoulders, the large door hiding the rest of the man's body. That most of the man was hidden by the safe's door made little difference to Ca-

---

[1] Invisible electrobiochemical radiation, sometimes called the Od, Odyle or Odic Force. Although the human aura can be detected by sensitives and some clairvoyants, it was not until 1911 that W. R. Kilner devised ways of showing it experimentally: First by looking at the human body through a dilute solution of a dye called *dicyanin;* second, by looking at a very bright light through a strong alcoholic solution.

The aura must not be confused with the etheric double, which is a part of the physical body, or with the astral body—the inner you.

mellion, whose first 9mm slug went slightly off mark. He had aimed at the man's right shoulder, but the hollowpoint bullet hit Tyrone Holmes just below the right ear, bored through his throat and instantly made him forget about closing and locking the door of the safe. The slug even erased all his thoughts about living.

Desmond O'Day and James John Flynn, two experienced IRA gunmen in their thirties, were the first to recover their surprise at seeing the weird "three-armed" figure racing down the steps. O'Day snapped off a shot with a Heckler and Koch autopistol; Flynn fired a French F-1 autoloader.

As four other men, who had been drinking gin with ale chasers at the table, dove to the floor, Wayne Colburn and Bowles Devlin, between the table and the bunks stacked by the west wall, jerked out their weapons. Like O'Conner, Lynch, and Collins, the two men had been about to go upstairs to the toilet and relieve themselves of all the gin and ale they had drunk. The "three-armed" intruder had been their first shock. The sudden appearance of Neil Reeder—at the top of the steps as the Death Merchant reached the bottom of the stairs—was their second.

O'Day's 9mm slug streaked by Camellion's left side. Flynn's projectile came much closer, ripping across the right side of Camellion's overcoat, in the vicinity of the waist. The two IRA men didn't know it, didn't have time to think about it, but they had pulled triggers and held iron for the last time.

Just as Bowles Devlin's soft-nosed .32 bullet, fired from an Italian Bernardelli autoloader, struck the artificial arm in the left sleeve of Camellion's overcoat, the Death Merchant's missiles caught Flynn and O'Day.

Jimmie Flynn screamed as a 9mm slug smacked him in the stomach and the impact slammed him against the shelves on the north wall. Half-unconscious and full of burning impossible agony, he went down, cans of Spam, Pork 'n' Beans and peas tumbling down around him.

O'Day was luckier: He died almost instantly, sounding like a bull frog giving its final croak when Camellion's bullet hit him in the upper lip, gave him four free tooth extractions, stabbed through his throat and left a hole the size of a thumb in the back of his head. The French F-1 pistol slipped from his hand, he folded like a soggy strand of macaroni, fell and lay still.

Muttering curses, Bowles Devlin leveled down on the Death Merchant with a .45 Argentine HAFDASA pistol at the same instant that Camellion, now off the steps and on the floor, ducked to the right and cut loose with the Czech CZ in his right hand.

Devlin's big .45 flat-nosed slug came within several inches of Camellion's left side; yet he had blown his one and only chance. The Death Merchant's first slug smacked him low in the chest and started to send him spinning in a whirlpool of blackness. He never felt the second bullet that cut into his gut and performed a crude, bloody colostomy—without charge.

Next to Devlin, Wayne Colburn uttered a loud *"Oooooohhhhh!"* and spun from the impact of Neil Reeder's slug that hit him in the right side of the abdomen. Reeder's second projectile zipped in at an angle between Colburn's shoulder blades, bored a tunnel through his left lung and stopped when it hit the inner side of a front rib. Colburn collapsed, a look of disbelief and terror forever fixed on his face.

The four men who had been at the table felt as if they were caught between being struck by lightning or blown away by a tornado. In less than a minute, the two invaders—they couldn't be the police!—had killed five men. What made the situation so terrible was that none of the four had a weapon with him, and they knew that they didn't have time to reach the pistols and the two British submachine guns on a shelf above the army cots on the east side of the room.

The four did the only thing possible under the circumstances: They rushed the Death Merchant and Neil Reeder!

Brian Roach and George Meehan, underneath the wooden table, reared up and, with all their might, sent the table flying toward the Death Merchant, who attempted to dodge but only half succeeded. All he had time to do was throw up his left arm in an effort to prevent the tabletop from smashing into his face and chest. Camellion sidestepped, but one end of the table crashed against him and he felt himself going down, falling backward. Worse, the re-

54

flexes involved in protecting himself against the table, had caused his hands to open and the Czech autoloaders fell to the floor. Part of the table fell on top of him.

Damn! the Death Merchant thought. *I'm a thousand miles from heaven and only a few inches from hell!* Angry at himself, he struggled to free himself from the table. It wasn't heavy, only cumbersome.

Thomas Doherty and Sean MacFainolin, the two other men who had been drinking at the table, had not forgotten Neil Reeder. The Q-man drew a second autoloader, a Smith & Wesson .38 autopistol, intending to cut loose with both the S & W and the Walther P-38. He wasn't slow. In fact, he was extremely fast. It was just that he had been caught off guard by Doherty and MacFainolin's throwing several chairs at him. Reeder ducked the first chair, but the end of one leg of the second chair caught him in the left shoulder. He felt a stabbing pain, automatically stepped back, tripped over the bloody corpse of Arnold O'Conner at the bottom of the steps and almost fell sideways to the concrete floor. By the time he had halfway straightened up, Doherty and MacFainolin had jumped over the bodies of Devlin and Colburn and were on him.

The Death Merchant, now enraged, pushed the end of the table from his body, a strange phosphorescence in his blue eyes. Incredibly fast, but at a disadvantage because of the artificial arm supported by the sling around his neck, he was almost to his feet by the time Brian Roach and George Meehan reached him and attacked.

"Goddamned peeler!"[2] yelled Roach and aimed a right-legged kick at Camellion's stomach, a power-smash that would have shocked him into the world of nightmares had it landed. It didn't.

Camellion's hands shot out. He caught Roach's right foot and twisted to his right. Roach howled in pain, the powerful twist sending red-hot stabs of agony all the way to his hip and beyond. His body half turned in the air and, arms flying, he fell heavily to the floor.

Meanwhile, George Meehan had jumped with both feet on the overturned table, but only because he hadn't been able to stop his own rush. Believing that the table would

[2] British and Irish slang for a policeman.

pin Camellion to the floor, Meehan had started to jump as Camellion was freeing himself from the end of the table. He didn't crush Camellion. He did jar his own feet so much that the soles tingled. Quickly, he straightened and turned toward the Death Merchant.

Now fully on his feet, Camellion spun to meet Meehan's attack. He also saw that Reeder was in one hell of a mess. Big Tom Doherty had clamped his left hand around Reeder's right wrist, his right hand around Reeder's left wrist, and was effectively knee-blocking the Q-man's efforts to knee him in the gut. While the two men struggled, Sean MacFainolin was bending to pick up the Walther P-38 that Doherty had twisted from Reeder's right hand.

Meehan, a rough-and-tumble barroom fighter, swung and anvillike right fist at Camellion's jaw. The Death Merchant ducked and, while his right hand streaked to the back of his neck, he chopped Meehan across the bridge of the nose with a left half-vertical knife-hand blow.

All in the same moment, thumb and forefinger of his right hand found the black Lexan handle of the Jakal. With a lightning-quick motion, he pulled the commando knife from the holster on his neck and expertly threw it at MacFainolin, whom he had recognized as being one of the most-wanted leaders of the IRA.

Years of practice paid off: The five-inch stainless steel double-edged blade cut into the left side of MacFainolin's neck and buried itself all the way to the end of the handle. It was the day of the Jakal and the beginning of the eternal night for MacFainolin.

The IRA leader's fingers slipped from the butt of the Walther P-38, and he jumped as if stung in the butt by an atomic hornet. Blood gushed from his mouth in torrents, accompanied by loud gurgling. He danced a fast momentary two-step; then his legs became hot wax and he went down in a spray of blood—dead by the time he hit the floor, his death automatically giving Reeder the edge against Doherty.

Horrified at the way MacFainolin had died, Tom Doherty hesitated for only a fraction of a second. He still held Reeder's wrists in both hands, but for a moment he forgot all about the Q-man's knees. That wink in time was all Reeder needed. He kneed Doherty in the groin—once, twice! Shock flowed over the Irishman's face. No longer was it ruddy; now it was the color of slate. With the supreme agony in the lower part of Doherty's body, his hands might as well have been putty. Reeder jerked both wrists free and counterattacked. A right-handed sword-ridge chop to the left side of Doherty's neck! A left fist-hammer to the Irishman's face, just above the bridge of his nose. A final right uppercut to Doherty's chin. Out cold, the IRA terrorist dropped.

The Death Merchant's knife-hand blow to the bridge of George Meehan's nose made the IRA gunmen feel as though a grenade had exploded against his face. Blood poured out of his nostrils and he couldn't see. He was finished and knew it.

And the Death Merchant knew it. A back-knuckle fist-head to Meehan's jaw finished him off. His knees folded and he sank unconscious to the floor.

Camellion and Reeder looked around them, at the bodies sprawled on the floor. The smell of blood filled the air with the odor of death, with the dank, rank smell of the grave.

"I wonder if this qualifies us to work in a funeral parlor," quipped Reeder, breathing heavily. Sweat poured down his face and his British warmer was smudged.

"It will qualify us to be customers in an embalming room if we don't work fast." Camellion slipped the sling from around his neck and began to pull the artificial arm from the left sleeve of his overcoat. "Go upstairs and take a look around. I don't think the shots were heard down here, but who knows? Be careful how you look into the front of the shop."

"It's not likely the shots were heard," said Reeder. He picked up the P-38 and the S. & W. .38 from the floor. "I noticed that the door to the alley is metal and that the windows have been bricked over."

Pulling the deerskin glove from the hand of the artificial arm, Camellion regarded Reeder with impatient eyes. "After you take a look, use your walkie-talkie and contact Plymale. If everything seems to be all right, tell Plymale to be in the alley out back in fifteen minutes."

"Fifteen minutes!" exclaimed Reeder. "Why so long?" He shoved a fresh magazine into the butt of the P-38 and pulled back the cocking slide.

"Do as I tell you—move!" Camellion's voice was scathing, although his lips barely moved.

Making a face of annoyance, Reeder stepped over the body of Arnold O'Conner and started up the steps, careful not to walk in the blood that already bore imprints of his own and Camellion's feet.

The Death Merchant placed the artificial arm on the concrete floor, slipped his own left arm into the left sleeve of the overcoat, and took a long look at George Meehan and Thomas Doherty as he picked up the two Czech CZ autoloaders from beside the overturned table. The two slobs would dream on for a while. He shoved fresh clips into the CZs, cocked both weapons, shoved on the safeties and took a long look at the safe built into the east wall. The man he had whacked out had been in a frantic hurry to slam the large door shut. What had he been trying to conceal?

Camellion shoved one of the CZs into its clip holster. With the other Czech pistol dangling loosely in his other hand, he went up to the open safe, stepping over the body of Tyrone Holmes, and looked at the interior of the vault. There were nine two-pound packages of gelignite[3] and a brown leather portfolio in the vault. Otherwise, the vault was empty.

Aha! Pay dirt—maybe! Camellion removed the portfolio from the vertical compartment, again stepped over the dead Holmes and walked back to the front of the basement room. Once more he glanced at the two unconscious men, then up at Neil Reeder, who was coming down the steps.

"How does it look up there?" asked Camellion and placed the portfolio on the underneath side of the tabletop.

"All's quiet on the London front!" reported the Q-man. "There wasn't anyone outside the shop on the sidewalk. I contacted Clem. He said he'd be in the alley in fifteen minutes." He reached the bottom of the steps and glanced at the portfolio. "What's in the case? Or haven't you opened it yet?"

"Keep an eye on our two sleeping beauties. I'll wake them up in a minute." Camellion holstered the CZ pistol, hurried over to Sean MacFainolin, deftly pulled the Jakal from the throat of the corpse, turned and, stepping over bodies, went to the small sink toward the rear of the room.

"The man you killed with the knife," Reeder called after

---

[3] The British name for dynamite.

him. "I recognize him. He's Sean MacFainolin. The Yard's been after him ever since Lord Mountbatten was blown sky-high last year. The Yard suspects he had a hand in it."

"Yeah, I recognized him," Camellion replied, "from his picture in the London papers. The *Times* had one of him the other day."

He turned on the hot water tap, carefully washed the congealing blood from the stainless steel blade and thought of how Reeder had pronounced Sean as "*See-an*" instead of using the correct pronunciation, which was "*Shawn.*"

He dried the knife on a dirty towel and shoved the Jackal into the holster fastened between his shoulder blades. He then picked up a bucket from the floor and filled it with cold water from the second tap. He walked back to the front of the room and threw half the water into the face of George Meehan, the other half into the face of Thomas Doherty.

Soon the two IRA terrorists were moaning and beginning to stir. Several minutes more and Doherty, the first to open his eyes, sat up and found himself staring into the dark muzzle of the silencers attached to Camellion's DZ and Reeder's P-38. With another low groan of pain, Doherty fell to his back.

A few more minutes passed and George Meehan, his face a mass of blood, opened his eyes, groaned, sat up and did a double take when he saw the handguns pointed at him.

Camellion pushed his right foot against one of Doherty's legs.

"Sit up or I'll put a slug in your gut. It's question-and-answer time."

With another moan, Doherty managed to twist around and sit up, bracing himself by putting his hands flat on the floor.

"Who are you p-people?" he croaked. "You're not police. Are you Officials?"[4]

---

[4] During the IRA convention in Dublin in 1969, two thirds of the delegates voted for a peaceful political course, one that was practically Marxist. The other one third felt that Ireland could only be united through terror. It was this one third that decided to use terrorism. And so the IRA split into two factions: the *Officials,* who wanted no part of violence, and the *Provisionals,* or *Provos,* whose creed was violence and death.

The Death Merchant moved closer to the man, his "elderly" face a mask—which, in a sense, it was.

"Tell me, snake-belly: What has four wheels and flies?"

Even Reeder gave a start and looked at Camellion in surprise.

Doherty's words stumbled all over themselves. "I—I don't know. What has—"

"Shut up!" shouted Camellion. "The penalty for not knowing the answer is death!"

Camellion raised the CZ and pulled the trigger. There was a splat, and Doherty fell back dead, a blue-black ringed hole in the middle of his forehead.

"Bless my butt!" Reeder's mouth formed an open O.

George Meehan, sheer terror jumping in his eyes, put his hands in front of his face as Camellion moved the muzzle in his direction.

"No! D-don't! *Please!* I—"

"Patience, old chap," Camellion said jovially. "Boogie to a different drummer and you might get out of this alive. Mouth the first lie and you'll join the rest of your IRA idiots. Lower your hands, stupid!"

"What—what do you want to know?" Slowly, hesitantly, he lowered his hands, his eyes clouded with uncertainty.

"You're all IRA—correct?" Camellion moved the muzzle of the noise suppressor closer to the tip of Meehan's long nose.

"All but him by the safe. His first name was Tyrone. We never learned his last name. He didn't tell us. We didn't ask."

Reeder joined in. "I think he's giving us a lot of big wind."

"No, I'm not!" Meehan said quickly. "He was one of Marmis's people. Hell, you know how it is. You don't ask last names. It just ain't done."

Hot damn! the Death Merchant thought. *We're on to something, but what?* "Then Marmis isn't part of the IRA?"

"Not that I know of. He was only hiding us down here. Honest, mister. That's all any of us knew about him. I figured him out to be a Provo sympathizer."

"How did you men know about him?"

"Our cell chief told us. He knew about Marmis." Meehan pointed at the corpse of Sean MacFainolin. "That's him. He was our cell chief. He never told any of us how he knew about Marmis."

Reeder asked, "How long have you been down here?"

"Two months. Marmis was going to smuggle us into Londonderry. On some ship. He didn't tell us which one!"

The Death Merchant's voice was sharp. "What kind of organization does Marmis have? Did he ever mention its name?"

Bewilderment clouded Meehan's face. "I don't know if he belonged to any organization. He never mentioned the name of one around us. We seldom saw Marmis. That son of a bitch acted as though we was fifty miles below him."

"What about the vault in the wall?"

"All I know is that it was there when we came down here. It didn't have a thing to do with us. It was always locked. Tyrone opened it and was looking at some papers—they were in that brown case you put on the floor— when you blokes started all the trouble."

The Death Merchant put the question to him without any preamble, all the while watching Meehan's eyes. "How do you Provos cause spontaneous human combustion?"

Astonishment flamed in Meehan's brown eyes. Confusion skidded over his face. "What do you mean? If a man is in a bomb explosion he might catch fire. But—do you mean all at once, or what?"

"I mean instantly," Camellion said fiercely. "I mean a blue fire that can reduce a man to ashes within five minutes. What do you know about it?"

"I don't even know what you're talking about!" protested Meehan. "You've got us mixed up with something or somebody else. If God were here, He'd tell you I'm telling the truth."

Camellion sighed deeply. "God often comes calling, but most of the time we're not at home."

There was a slight *pop* from the noise suppressor attached to the barrel of of the Czech pistol. A soft thud and Meehan fell sideways, his eyes, unblinking, wide-open. He hadn't even felt a half-second of pain. The 9mm bullet had come to rest inside his head faster than the brain could interpret what was happening to the body it inhabited.

"What does have four wheels and flies?" Reeder asked, buttoning his British warmer.

Camellion picked up the artificial arm and the portfolio.

61

"A jet pilot on a skateboard. Let's get upstairs and meet Plymale.

"What about the explosive device?" Reeder started up the steps, Camellion following him. "Down here or upstairs."

"Upstairs in the back room, on one of the cartons. I'll set it for half an hour after we know that Plymale's on time."

Plymale arrived on time. Camellion and Reeder, watching through the tiny square window in the door, went out into the alley, pushed the door shut and got into the Morris Minor. The only person who had seen them was an old man pushing a two-wheeled car at the end of the alley opposite to the direction in which the car was moving.

"Drive around to Bond," Camellion said to Plymale. "The Aston-Martin is parked a block from the tobacco shop."

"How did you two do?" inquired Plymale, who was a hard-faced, pipe-smoking individual whose hands, long and slender, resembled a woman's.

"We made like Tarzan," Reeder said. "We terminated all of them."

"But we scored like Jane," added the Death Merchant from the rear seat. "All we got was this briefcase. I'll open it once we're in the other car and safely out of the area."

"How about the IRA leaflets and the bomb?" Plymale slowed the car, then carefully made a right turn, the tires on the right side skidding slightly in the snow piled by the curb at the mouth of the alley.

The Death Merchant threw back his head and laughed, harshly and without humor. "The irony of it is that the men we scratched were all Provos, with one exception," he said grimly. "Marmis and his group were hiding them out in a hidden basement. All we have to do now is find out who Marmis was working for, what organization he's connected with—and don't ask me why we didn't bring Marmis along!"

"There would have been room in the other car," offered Plymale.

Reeder, lighting a cigarette, almost snarled, "The goddamned idiot in charge of drugs at the Embassy station gave us the wrong pills. We were going to haul Kemper's tail back to 'The House,' but he's dead."

"He must have had a heart condition," Plymale said. "F-D tablets have been known to induce a fatal heart attack in subjects suffering from a heart condition, diabetes, or nephritis."

"Buffalo bull!" exclaimed Camellion laconically. "There were two clerks with Marmis, young dudes in their twenties. They were also dead. It's unlikely that they had heart trouble or diabetes or nephritis. It's like Neil said. Some dimwit at the Embassy station goofed and gave us the wrong pills.

"Over there!" Reeder said. "There's the Aston-Martin."

"The chief will have a stroke when he hears about it," Plymale said. "Someone's head will roll."

Neil Reeder drove the Aston-Martin at 30 mph on Piccadilly. Just in case anyone might be trying to follow, he and Camellion were taking a roundabout route back to "The House" on Bayswater Road; and just in case some enemy had the idea of using a "bumper beeper," Camellion had checked the automobile with a De-Bug Impedance Analyzer the instant he had settled down in the car. The Aston-Martin was "clean."

The sun was gone. Once again the sky had clouded over and was its normal winter self: a solid ceiling of low gray clouds.

"Walker, you set the device to go off in half an hour, didn't you?" Reeder said. He gave a quick glance to Camellion who was opening the portfolio, then glanced at his wristwatch.

"Exactly one half-hour." Camellion opened the case and pulled out a large 8½- by 13½-inch brown envelope.

"It should go off in another eight minutes, give or take a minute."

Camellion opened the brown envelope, pulled out six sheets of white paper stapled together in the left top corner, and got his first real shock of the day.

Tiny black swastikas formed a square border on each sheet, the crooked crosses placed an inch from the edges of each sheet of paper!

All six sheets were filled with vertical lines. On the lines and to each side of the them were markings: tiny squares, solid black rectangles, squares that were half-shaded with horizontal lines, squares with dots in their centers, squares with other markings, such as *X*s. There were shaded and half-shaded squares and triangles; squares in which were placed inverted *T*s, *X*s and other marks. There were *X*s off to themselves, not within any squares; half-squares with the bottom sections missing and dots between the side lines of the squares. Mixed in with all the squares and triangles and rectangles were symbols indicating musical notes: sharps, flats, naturals.

Reeder stopped the Aston-Martin for a red light. Waiting for the light to change, he glanced at the sheets in the Death Merchant's hands, his brow furrowing, his eyes growing chilly.

"It's not a musical score," he said in a curious voice. "It's some kind of code using musical notes and something else. I don't know what."

The light turned green. Reeder shifted gears, fed gas to the engine and turned the car onto St. James Street.

"Whoever we're dealing with is extremely clever," Camellion explained, admiration in his tone. "These sheets contain a sequence of dance steps recorded in what is known as the Labanotation method.[5] This method uses symbols to record the dancer's movements, including the direction and timing. It takes a choreographer to read them. Somewhere in the symbols is a complex code, but it will take expert cryptographers, working with computers, to decipher the true contents."

Reeder laughed lightly. "There's St. James Palace up ahead," he said with a trace of sarcasm. "I doubt if Her Most Royal Highness is receiving today, but should we stop in for a spot of tea, old chap?"

The Death Merchant, who disliked pompous titles, sneered. "Yeah, if she's not in we can have a drink with Lord High Everything Else."

Reeder became serious. "What's our next move?"

"It's time that 'Casimer Anthony Mohilowski' flies to the United States," Camellion answered. "I've got to get to the Center with these papers."

[5] Devised by a Hungarian-born teacher, Rudolf von Laban, in 1928.

Chapter Five

The four Allison turboprops were sweet music to his ears, as Camellion folded the copy of the *Times* and leaned back in the seat, streams of thought racing through his mind.

It had been an easy matter for Raymond Hohfeler, working through Ambassador Cherlin, to arrange to have him fly to the United States in a U.S. Air Force Lockheed C-130 Hercules, a multiroled transport stationed at an airfield a few miles west of Chelmsford, 12 miles northeast of London. A joint British-American effort, the main purpose of the airbase was to serve as a listening post to Communist radio transmissions. Its other function was to track Soviet satellites and "spy" on their code signals.

A bitter smile crossed Camellion's lips, the look in his eyes similar to the gaze of a rich man envying the poor for their virtues. The explosion in the second back room of Marmis's tobacco shop had made the front page of the *Times*. Much of the back room and half the wall facing the alley had been blown to smithereens. According to the *Times*, Scotland Yard was blaming the thirteen murders on the branch of the IRA known as the Officials.

Thirteen murders? Police had found the body of an old man in the second room, his corpse riddled with bits of cardboard, tobacco and wooden splinters. A two-wheeled pushcart had been found in the alley, not far from the rear door. Apparently the lock on the door had not snapped shut, and the old fart-blossom had entered to see what he could steal. Tough! But who knows how the big cookie of Fate will crumble?

The use of the word "murder" irked Camellion. Killing another human being in the pursuit of preserving freedom for one's nation was not murder. Somebody had to protect American freedom and the nation's position in the world community. The jelly-backboned liars in Washington weren't doing the job. With rare exceptions, they were all modern day Chamberlains. Washington was an expert at saddling people with more and more taxes and more and more invasion of privacy, not to mention giving the rich all sorts of tax breaks.

There was a lot wrong in the United States, much of it due to stupidity, the power of payoffs, and hypocrisy. But how does one talk to people with closed minds, with millions who insist on treating certain subject as sacred cows? All too often, honest criticism of the legitimate religions met with screaming accusations of religious "bigotry." To ask what church-owned motels, hotels and other numerous businesses had to do with religion, and why these businesses should not pay taxes was to invite fanatics to scream *"Atheist!"*

Camellion knew the real truth: The concept of religious tolerance had been stretched to the outer limits of stupidity, implying freedom from any criticism and from the payment of honest taxes. *The right to worship can never be a justification for the suspension of all reason,* he thought. *The American people must stop equating religion with nonpayment of taxes, normalcy with numbers, sanity with conformity and individual eccentricity with craziness. Yet none of this is going to help me solve the riddle of the burning blue death.*

There was one concrete fact: SHC was one of the weirdest of all supernatural phenomena, one with a recorded history that stretched back through the dark centuries and continued to baffle the entire scientific community, but the existence of which was grudgingly admitted by even the most skeptical.

The bizarre and deadly manifestation went under various names, the most common of which was spontaneous human combustion. The burning blue death was also called Autooxidation, preternatural combustion and the fire from hell.

The results, though, were always the same. The victim would suddenly catch fire for no apparent reason, blaze briefly and uncontrollably with terrifying intensity and finally incinerate, leaving behind little more than a pile of ashes.

The Death Merchant's face became intense with thought. The most extraordinary feature of all was that the victims' clothes frequently remained unscorched, objects in the room survived without even charring and articles only a foot away from the incandescent victim failed to ignite.

SHC is not an ordinary fire, Camellion reasoned. *It might not even be "burning" in the sense that we know combustion!* SHC attacked capriciously and without warning. Few of the recorded cases mentioned any sound or smell.

Another frightening aspect was the incredible swiftness of the fire. It killed 22-year-old Phyllis Newcombe in a matter of minutes, in full view of dozens of people, at midnight on August 27, 1938. The young woman was just about to leave the dance floor at the Shire Hall in Romford, England, when the horrified dancers suddenly saw her enveloped in a bluish flame. Within *five minutes,* she was a blackened mass of ash!

Complicating the problem of SHC was the fact that most coroners refused to admit the impossible! Camellion recalled one typical case he had read about in the *British Medico-Legal Journal.* Dr. Gavin Thurston, who had then been the London coroner, had commented: "Instances are extremely rare and have been described over the centuries, but authenticity has often been doubted and often the condition lies near the borderline of myth and fact. Nevertheless, there are undisputed instances, and this seems to be one, where the body has burned in its own substance, without external fuel, and in which there has been a remarkable absence of damage to surrounding inflammable objects."

Another peculiar feature about "the fire from hell" is that it appeared to *anesthesize* as it burned. Very rarely did any of the victims cry out, and then only when they saw the flames, clear-cut evidence that the screams were more of fear than of pain. Equally as perplexing, the flames usually originated in the trunk of the body, with the back being a favorite region, so that usually the victim wasn't even aware that he was burning. In seconds, he would become unconscious and drop to the floor. Another favorite region was the chest.

In other cases it seemed that the blue death originated *within* the body of the victim. People had been found with their entire interiors burned away—heart, lungs, stomach—while the outer flesh had hardly been damaged.

In 1951 the first step toward a complete study of SHC was begun, bringing in not only local authorities but the FBI as well. The case that attracted the attention was known as "The Case of the Cinder Woman" and threw the city of St. Petersburg, Florida, into an uproar.

Mrs. P.N. Carpenter owned a four-story apartment building at 1200 Cherry Street, Northeast. At about eight o'clock on the morning of July 2, 1951, a Western Union boy knocked on Mrs. Carpenter's door.

"I have a telegram for Mrs. Mary Reeser," he told Mrs. Carpenter when she answered the door. "Will you take it to her?"

Mrs. Carpenter signed for the wire and went directly to her favorite tenant's door. Mrs. Carpenter knocked on the door. No answer. Mrs. Carpenter knocked again. Worried, because it wasn't like Mrs. Reeser, a light sleeper, to miss the sound of a knock, Mrs. Carpenter pounded on the door. Still no answer. Alarmed now, Mrs. Carpenter reached to open the door. She jerked her hand back in pain. The brass doorknob was so hot it had burned her.

The woman screamed, and two men working nearby rushed to aid her. Forcing the door, they found a scene straight out of hell. Both windows were open, but the room was as hot as the inside of a blast furnace. In front of one window was a pile of ashes—the remains of the big armchair, an end table and . . . Mrs. Reeser.

Firemen hurried to the scene, followed by the police. At once it became obvious that here was no ordinary accident. The heat-eroded coil springs were all that was left of the armchair. Not a trace remained of the end table. And damned little of Mrs. Reeser: a few pieces of backbone, *a skull that had shrunk to the size of an orange* . . . and her wholly untouched foot still encased in its slipper.

Experienced firemen stared, knowing that the heat necessary for such hideous damage had to be measured in thousands of degrees. Yet the ceiling, draperies and walls had not even been scorched, although they were coated with thick soot. The pink wall paper adjacent to the chair was browned slightly, but the carpet where the chair had rested was not even singed. A wall mirror, 10 feet away, had been cracked, probably due to the terrific heat. Plastic wall outlets had fused and melted, but the fuses had not blown and the current was on.

Faced with a mystery that defied all reason, Police Chief J.R. Reichert asked for FBI aid. Scrapings from the carpet, metal from the chair, and the ashes and other remains of Mrs. Reeser were sent to the FBI laboratory for microanalysis. The report that came back only added confusion to the mess. Mrs. Reeser had weighed 175 pounds; yet *all that remained of her after the fire weighed less than 10 pounds—including the shriveled orange-sized head.*

By now, more than a week had passed and the St. Pete cops began referring to the "cinder woman" case as "impossible, weird, and unbelievable." The conservative FBI ventured to say that the case was "unusual."

The newspapers and radio began screaming for Chief Reichert to do something, not realizing that the poor man was already doing all he could and seeking what competent help he could get. He called in Edward Davis, an arson specialist of the National Board of Underwriters. Davis, a trained expert, was stumped. Admitting defeat, he said, "I can only say that the woman died from fire. I don't know the nature of the fire. Frankly, I haven't the slightest idea."

Thinking about the case, which he had read about in CIA files, the Death Merchant knew there was only one answer: *spontaneous human combustion.*

The Central Intelligence Agency, which constantly watches the world scene with a suspicious eye, did not become interested until about a year later. It was then that reports began coming in about mysterious deaths in various parts of the world. First, a nuclear scientist in France was reduced to six pounds of ashes. His death had been announced as a plane crash in which he had burned to death. It was six weeks before the CIA learned the real cause—SHC.

There were other victims of the fire from hell: a high government official in Argentina, an Israeli general. Within the space of nine months, six men and three women had died of the burning blue death. Every single victim had been either a scientist or in some way connected with the government of his or her nation.

During the three months that followed, six more persons—five men and one woman—succumbed to SHC. The first of the twelve had been a British official who held a high post in NATO. Colonel Johan Heijermans, the Dutch military attaché in Belgrade, had been another victim. Richard J. Kessel, an American expert on weather modification, had been in West Germany when he became a human torch. Lieutenant General Boris Eugeniy Vaygauskas, a high KGB official in the Soviet Union, had also gone up in smoke. He had been in East Germany at the time of his fiery death.

Another victim was Senator James Franklin Wilder. His wife had found him dead in his study, in their home in Washington, D.C. All that had been left of the Senator was a bucketful of ashes and part of his left thighbone. The leather swivel chair in which he had been sitting had not even been scorched. The press reported he had died of a heart attack. He had had a closed funeral; the casket, containing an unidentified corpse from the D.C. morgue, had not been opened.

The Scientific Research Division of the CIA had scored a big fat zero with its investigation. Nonetheless, something had to be done.

Whoever was causing the deaths had to be found.

The secret of SHC had to be found.

The CIA had asked the Death Merchant to use his unique talents in solving the deadly riddle.

Camellion stared out the small window of the high-flying Lockheed Hercules. *What have I accomplished so far?* he asked himself.

He had proved that there was a conspiracy behind the burning blue deaths. The men who had come after him in Aalsmeer were proof. Kemper Marmis? The fact that the man had hidden IRA terrorists in the basement of his tobacco shop was not any kind of evidence. That Marmis had recruited Lawrence Rodley and Michael Régene was proof enough to Camellion the man was in the conspiracy up to his eyeballs—had been, rather, now that he was dead.

Balls of blazing bumbrush! Camellion thought, suddenly

angry. *What we might have learned from Kemper Marmis if that idiot at the Embassy station had not given us L-pills[1] instead of F-D tablets.* The "idiot" was now on his way back to the States with several reductions in grade. Raymond Hohfeler had seen to that.

Camellion looked up and to his left at the sight of an airman approaching with a tray. The crewman smiled. "I thought you might be hungry, Mr. Mohilowski. This is the best we could do. Sorry that you'll have to hold the tray on your lap."

"Thank you. I appreciate your thoughtfulness," Camellion said and accepted the tray. The airman grinned and walked back toward the front of the plane. Camellion opened the sandwiches wrapped in aluminum foil—one peanut-butter sandwich and two made of salami. A pint of milk in a carton and a mug of black coffee. No cream. No sugar. *So what?* he thought. *I always drink it black.*

As he ate, Camellion speculated on the strange papers he had found in the basement vault. *Swastikas! A bunch of neo-Nazis. Or—old followers of Hitler? Or maybe a combination of both? So damned many questions. But few positive answers.*

Be that as it may, there was still no indication that any neo-Nazi group was responsible for spontaneous human combustion—unless the code within the Labanotation diagrams tied them in.

A gloomy thought born of logic crossed the Death Merchant's wind: *Suppose there wasn't any code? On the other hand, if there wasn't, why had Tyrone been in such a hurry to lock the vault? Surely not because of the gelignite!*

There was another matter Camellion had to take up with the covert spooks at the Center. A coded short-wave message had come back to London in response to his inquiry concerning Dr. Morris K. Jessup, the astrophysicist.

The reply from the Center had been short and blunt: *"Classified!"*

Camellion thought of what he had not told Hohfeler and Clark about Dr. Jessup: The letter that Carlos Allende had (allegedly) written to Jessup had revealed information about a highly secret and fantastic experiment conducted

---

[1] Suicide tablets composed of pure cyanide of potassium.

by the United States Navy during October of 1943. By using special force fields, scientists had (again allegedly) caused a United States battleship, the U.S.S. *Eldridge,* to slowly disappear into a green mist and, within seconds, reappear hundreds of miles away at a pier near Norfolk, Virginia. The *Eldridge* then winked out from Norfolk and, again within seconds, reappeared back in the Philadelphia Navy Yard.

Supposedly, this miraculous teleportation—according to Allende's letters to Dr. Jessup—was accomplished by successfully applying Einstein's Unified Field Theory.

The crew of the Eldridge also became invisible, disappearing and reappearing along with the vessel, with results that were something right out of a horror movie. Many of the officers and crew were stark raving mad. Others would lapse into invisibility, then reappear.

Others burst into flames in spontaneous human combustion—days, weeks, months later.

The computer of Camellion's mind clicked out a question: *Was it possible that SHC was tied in with the natural force fields that radiate from every single human being—with the human aura?*

The name Michael Harrison popped into Camellion's mind. One of the few writers to ever write an entire book about SHC, Harrison's theory was that when something went wrong with the aura, SHC was the result.

The Death Merchant had the same theory. *Fantastic!* Yet it seemed to be the only answer—*but let's keep in mind* Factor-X. Without the X-factor, was it possible that the aura, the bioelectrical energy of the "counterpart body" could overheat and somehow "backfire" so that its incandescent power consumed its human double?

The Death Merchant was convinced that this is what took place during SHC. Something would go wrong with the processes involved with producing the aura or its "frequency." That "something" involved natural laws of atomic physics, laws as yet undiscovered.

The aura would then consume its host.

How could this energy field create such fantastic heat?

The Death Merchant took a large swallow of milk. *How does the sun "burn"? It doesn't, not in the conventional sense.*

The heat of the sun was produced by the fusion of hydrogen to form helium, a common process in any star. In short, the sun was a giant nuclear reactor.

I think that's what happens in a victim of spontaneous human combustion—fusion of the atoms of the body, but a controlled fusion, of a type unknown to science and of a very low temperature; otherwise the heat from the victim would be in the millions of degrees. Entire blocks, if not cities, would be destroyed.

Camellion unwrapped another sandwich and took a bite.

The human body is mostly water, that is hydrogen and oxygen. Let me think a moment. Yeah, water contains 11.188 percent hydrogen and 88.812 percent oxygen, by weight. The transmutation of heavy hydrogen into helium and heavier elements has been duplicated by modern science for brief moments in the explosion of the hydrogen bomb. But we're still a long way off from fusing hydrogen nuclei under controlled conditions in such a way that the energy released can be harnessed for constructive purposes. The difficulty is that no furnace has yet been built on earth the walls of which can withstand and contain the temperatures of millions of degrees necessary to produce nuclear fusion. The only furnace that can do this is the heart of a star.

Until now!

The Death Merchant's analytical mind reached some conclusions:

A) There were laws of nature undiscovered by man, perhaps millions of such laws. Spontaneous human combustion was the result of one of those natural laws.

B) SHC was the process of a very special kind of fusion produced by nature.

C) Some human agency, some group, some diabolical organization, had discovered this law and how it operated.

D) Not only had this group discovered the law but it had found a way, some method, for inducing artificial SHC!

The implication was like being hit between the eyes with a steel fist. Such a discovery could well become a weapon that could permit the possessor nation to rule the world. Who was to say that such a system, if perfected on a large scale, could not incinerate whole sections of nations? Hundreds, perhaps thousands, of square miles and millions of human beings?

73

* * *

The feeling of helplessness was an ice pick in Camellion's brain, causing a sensation akin to standing on a sidewalk and being helpless while a child burned to death on the third floor of a building. Even after he arrived in the United States and was at the Center, he would still be helpless. *Then the code boys will have to take over,* he mused.

Camellion finished his coffee and glanced out of the window. At 35,000 feet, there wasn't anything to see but a sea of dirty gray-white clouds. The view would still have been boring if the clouds were not there. At this height, the Atlantic Ocean would have appeared only as a gray nothingness.

He leaned back and closed his eyes, remembering quiet, rainy yesterdays. Quite a few of them had been rainy.

The quiet ones could be counted on one hand. . . .

Chapter Six

Dead end. Six weeks after Richard Camellion turned over the papers to the Central Intelligence Agency, the Company's cryptologists had not made one iota of progress toward even finding a code within the labanotation diagrams, much less deciphering them. . . .

However, there was a development in reference to the perplexing mystery of spontaneous human combustion: Stanley Michaelson Heath, the Prime Minister of Canada, and Robert Flowers, Heath's chauffeur and bodyguard, died in a garage attached to the Prime Minister's residence in Ottawa, Canada. The media called the deaths a "tragic accident." Somehow the gas tank of the car had exploded. Oh, yes . . . due to "the charred condition of the bodies, the caskets will not be opened."

The small Canadian Intelligence Service, knowing its limitations, quickly contacted the CIA and reported what had actually happened to Prime Minister Heath and his chauffeur. Both men had been found in the car—what was left of them. Heath in the rear seat, Flowers in front, behind the steering wheel. All that was left of Heath was three pounds of gray ashes. Flowers had been reduced to six pounds of ashes.

The clothes of the two men had not been consumed in the fantastic heat, only scorched from the *inside*. . . .

Even though Camellion and the two other men were inside one of the CIA's buildings just outside Langley, Virginia, the meeting was being held, nonetheless, within a

"Mother Room."[1] Bobwhite-Six, the cover name for the SHC investigation, was being conducted with utmost secrecy, albeit the Agency assumed that the KGB was working on the same problem. There was no way of knowing how many Russians had fallen victim to SHC, the news of which the Soviets had kept from the world.

"I think we're yodeling down the wrong canyon," Courtland Grojean said. "There isn't any code. But instinct tells me there has to be."

The Death Merchant's face didn't change; neither did Dr. Cottier's. Grojean had instinct the way a cobra has poison. As the CIA's Deputy Director of Operations,[2] he lived constantly with a sense of intuition and expectancy. To him, walking blindfolded on a tightrope was perfectly normal.

"Have they finished with the nihilist transposition method?" Camellion crossed his legs, leaned back in the plastic chair and folded his arms.

Grojean gave Camellion a dirty look. "Padon and his people finished with that system yesterday. They came up with nothing." His elbows were on the arms of the chair, and he began tapping his fingers together. "So far they've tried everything in the book—columnar transposition, multiple anagramming, the Gronsfeld, Porta, and Beaufort ciphers, polygram substitution, and Vigenére decryptment. Today they've started on polyalphabetical encipherment applied by groups, using each dance step as a letter. Even with the use of computers, it's a job that would give Einstein a nervous breakdown."

As usual, Grojean's face had all the expression of a flat rock—nor did he ever permit gestures and other body language to telegraph his thoughts to associates and others to whom he might be talking. Even the Death Merchant found it almost impossible to dig behind the DD/O's persona. Lucky for Camellion who wouldn't have liked some of Grojean's thoughts.

Too intelligent to be flawed by envy, Grojean at times did have fleeting moments during which he was jealous of

---

[1] A room that contains a bubble chamber in which "white-sound" generators make it impossible for any hidden transmitter —or "bug"—to pick up the conversation.

[2] The covert section—"dirty tricks" department.

Camellion. For good reasons: Camellion made a couple of hundred thousand dollars a year from the Company—all of it tax free, since IRS wasn't aware of his services for the CIA; he earned another 100 Gs or so playing the stock market; using legal loopholes and reinvestment techniques, the clever son of a bitch payed damned little taxes on that.

Such brief thoughts of envy always died a quick death, slain by Grojean's awareness of the tremendous risks the Death Merchant took, dangers that Grojean wouldn't have taken for a million in cash.

For a long moment, the DD/O studied Camellion who was wearing a gray-brown corduroy sport coat, light gray shirt, brown checked tie, gray worsted-wool slacks and brown Scotch-grain Chukkas.

"In case Padon and his group don't come through, do you have any suggestions?" Grojean asked. "What plans do you have?"

Camellion shrugged. "I haven't. I haven't any suggestions and I haven't any plans. I'm putting all my bets on Padon. I haven't learned to work miracles."

Grojean's stabbing stare swung to Dr. Russell Cottier, the biophysicist from a prestigious university in New York State. A friendly, stocky man with a short beard—he reminded Camellion of Isaac Asimov—and a friendly smile, Cottier often acted as a special adviser to the CIA on technical matters involving perplexing scientific theories.

Grojean said, "Doctor, you've heard the tape recording Mr. Camellion made, explaining his theory. I would appreciate your evaluation."

Dr. Cottier adjusted his glasses, which were very modern and curved around to cover the entire field of view.

"The problem of SHC is very perplexing," he said in a deep baritone. "There are too many unknowns, too many amorphous appurtenances involved for me to give an unequivocal answer. Due to these different integrants, I cannot form any prognosticatory evaluations."

"You do have an opinion about Camellion's theory," Grojean said. "Let's have it—and in simple language."

Camellion added, "Without ponderous prolixities and polysyllabic pomposities. I didn't bring a copy of Webster's!"

"I personally agree with your backfire aura theory, or rather your hypothesis." Dr. Cottier looked at Camellion.

77

"In part, your postulate touches on the electrodynamic theory of life. This theory was evolved by Dr. Harold Burr, Professor of Anatomy at Yale, and Dr. F.S.C. Northrop, Professor of Philosophy and Law at Yale.

In a matter-of-fact voice, Dr. Cottier explained that Burr and Northrop had become convinced that, in living organisms, a force was necessary to direct and hold together the atoms and molecules.

As far back as 1935, Dr. Burr, working with Doctors L.F. Nims and C.T. Lane, succeeded in building an ultra sensitive microvoltmeter, which was able to measure currents as small as a millionth of a volt between two points and/or with any living organism. Numerous tests revealed that all living organisms had electrical fields that varied in intensity from individual to individual.

"The results of various research programs indicated that force fields in organisms are subject to change in strength and polarity," continued Dr. Cottier. "These changes are due to internal and external events, or to biological and cosmological forces."

"This is all fact, not theory?" interposed Grojean.

"Scientific fact. I assure you," Dr. Cottier said. "These 'field profiles,' or 'biorhythms,' were first observed in trees. Similar rhythmic variations were then discovered in human subjects. I shan't bore you gentlemen with all the details. Suffice to say, extensive testing over the years proves that these force fields exist within and around every human being. This electrodynamic theory of life not only suggests a universal electric field that affects living matter but is also evidence that the human race exists in an invisible ocean of pulsating energies, with our physical bodies acting as receivers, storage transformers and electrical projectors. The human aura is simply a partial manifestation of this universal electrical field. We're not sure, but we also believe that more than electrical energy is involved."

Camellion listened attentively, his expression one of rapt interest. In contrast, Grojean's expression was flat, far from indicating the impatience he felt. He couldn't have cared less about any universal electric field. The hell with a lot of zero-base gobbledygook. His only interest was *how* spontaneous human combustion was caused and *who* was causing it.

The Death Merchant said unhurriedly, "Would you

agree that each human being is related to all life and, through the earth's magnetic field, influenced by changes in the electrical fields of the sun and moon?"

Dr. Cottier nodded vigorously. "Oh, yes. Definitely. We are indeed a part of the universal whole and are constantly being influenced by the ceaseless ebb and flow of the various energies of the infinite all."

"You'll be telling us next that we're affected by a full moon." Grojean didn't smile, and there was more than a slight trace of annoyance to his voice.

"As a matter of fact, we are." Cottier's own tone approached sharpness. "Various studies have indicated that there is a definite relationship between the full moon and emotions. During such full-moon periods, psychiatric patients are more difficult to manage. There are more crimes, especially rape, and, in general, more unrest among the general population. I might add there is proof of this in augmented voltmeter readings."

Cottier paused and looked from Grojean to Camellion. "Furthermore, other than seasonal and lunar rhythms which affect the human body, there are fluctuations in the earth's magnetic field that influence our physical and emotional behavior. Most of these changes in the magnetic field are due to various forces bombarding the planet from outer space—sunspot radiation, cosmic and gamma rays, and other electromagnetic waves that bombard our planet and our bodies."

Camellion thought for a moment, rubbing the lobe of his left ear with a forefinger. "It would seem to me that strong emotions, especially fear, would cause an increase in the bioelectric field."

The wide face of Dr. Cottier blossomed in an expression of admiration. "Excellent deductive reasoning, Mr. Camellion. You are correct. Conversely, there is a decline in voltmeter readings during narcosis, hypnosis and sleeping. In a general way, periods of high voltage are related to tension and emotion. I presume that fear and/or severe fright would send the voltage soaring. A feeling of well-being reduces the voltage."

Camellion leaned back and locked his hands behind his neck.

"Tell me, Doctor. Have there ever been any studies done in regard to this bioelectric energy and the aura. For instance, when the voltage is high, does this mean that the aura is stronger?"

"To my knowledge, only a few studies have been done," Cottier said. "The 'low' or 'high' of the bioelectric energy doesn't seem to affect the strength of the aura. By strength I refer to the intensity of color. Most of this is based on studies made in the Soviet Union, with the use of Kirlian photography. American investigators strongly suspect that there is far more to the aura than mere bioelectric energy."

Courtland Grojean stopped tapping his fingers, folded his hands and frowned severely. He had asked for an opinion and was getting a lecture.

"Doctor, I'm not interested in a scientific discussion on bioelectric forces that may or may not be connected with the aura."

Grojean got a quick, impersonal smile from the biophysicist.

"I assure you, Mr. Grojean, the human aura is a reality. I have one, you have one and so does every living thing on this planet."

"I'm not denying the existence of the aura," Grojean said, deadpan, the muscles knotting in his jaws in a manner that Camellion recognized. "We've had experience with the aura before. You've read the report about one Cleveland Winston Silvestter II and how he managed to get his hands on a device that could measure the frequency of any individual's aura. The range of the device was limited. Yet Silvester could locate any person merely by tuning in to that person's aura frequency. It was like finding a very tiny needle in a very large haystack. But Silvestter could do it."

"What happened to him?" asked Cottier.

"I killed him," Camellion answered. Then he made a thoughtful face and put his hands on his knees. "But with SHC, we're dealing with something entirely different from what Silvestter had—and a thousand times more deadly."

"Your fusion theory," said Grojean, looking from Camellion to Dr. Cottier. "Well, Doctor. You must have an opinion of Camellion's theory?"

"His hypothesis has merit," said Cottier. "I see no other answer to the mystifying problem. Of course, there is nothing mysterious about fusion, which has been going on constantly in the sun, for the last four billion five hundred million years. The sun is well into middle age. The process of fusion will continue for another five billion years, even after the sun balloons into a red giant. In a star ten times as massive as the sun, fusion would last only ten million years, mere 'minutes' on the cosmic scale of time."

"Doctor, get to the point," demanded Grojean.

"Should the answer to SHC lie in fusion of the body's atoms and molecules, combustion—and that is not the right word—would be complete within a matter of minutes, depending on the weight of the person so afflicted. Such fusion would have to be controlled by methods I can't even contemplate." He pursed his lips, and thought lines formed on his forehead. "A year or so ago, a group of scientists did accomplish this fusion in a laboratory experiment, but for only four hundred millionths of a second."

"So, science has accomplished fusion. It is possible!" Sparks of excitement flamed briefly in Grojean's eyes.

"Carrying a cup of water cannot be compared to emptying an ocean," Cottier said gently. "The fusion experiment involved only a particle, much smaller than a molecule. We can't compare this to the trillions of molecules and the hundreds of trillions of atoms in a human body." He laughed lightly as if enjoying a joke. "We might as well discuss traveling around the universe in a space vehicle powered by tachyons."

Grojean said smugly, "Camellion here thinks someone has discovered how to combust the entire body by means of fusion. If he's right, somebody, somewhere, is a hundred years ahead of your scientific theory. How about some positive answers, Doctor."

"Mr. Camellion might be correct," admitted Cottier. "He could be wrong. I don't have any concrete answers. I can give only opinions. Until you Intelligence people find out who's responsible, all we can do is stumble around in a hall that has plenty of ghosties and ghoulies and impossible monsters." His gaze turned to the Death Merchant. "After reading the scant literature available on SHC, I find it fascinating how the fire seems to first reveal itself either on the chest or the back. I wonder how this might be related to other cases of abnormal radiation of heat from the human body."

"Such as what?" Grojean sat up straight in his chair.

It was the Death Merchant who explained, saying that abnormal radiation of heat from various human beings seemed to be connected in some way to holiness, to sanctity.

"Father Herbert Thurston, in his *Physical Phenomena of Mysticism*, has written that any number of saints are said to have radiated heat of such intensity that it affected material objects and could even be a discomfort to other persons."

Grojean was skeptical. "We're not in the business of turning myth and fable and superstition into fact. You know that, Camellion."

"Not everything about religion in the Middle Ages is myth," insisted Camellion firmly. "Eventually, a lot of this 'myth' will be explained by modern science."

Grojean gave Camellion a long, questioning look.

"Almost in every case," Camellion went on, "this heat was said to be generated within the chest of the saint. To be more precise, within the region of the heart."

"Bunk!" snapped Grojean, who hated vague answers and believed only in gods he could see, feel and measure. Gods that could be terminated if the need arose.

"St. Philip Neri was one of the saints who radiated tremendous heat," Camellion said. "He also suffered from heart palpitations. After he died, an autopsy disclosed that his heart was so enlarged it had forced two of his ribs outward."

"If you can believe such religious propaganda," commented Grojean drily. "I don't, and I'm surprised that you do."

"I didn't say that I did," Camellion said. "But we must learn to sort the truth from the fiction. There's a lot of strangeness going on in what we refer to as 'civilization.' "

Dr. Cottier continued to work at a hangnail on his left thumb. "I don't find such abnormalities the least bit bizarre," he said. "There are any number of peculiar Gordian knots in the world. But some are not that strange when we probe into the causes. One can walk across the room on a thick rug and store up ten thousand volts. It takes about twenty thousand volts to produce a one-inch spark."

Grojean shot a dubious glance at the scientist. "What does that have to do with saints who had furnaces in their chests?"

Cottier quit working on the hangnail, looked at Grojean and smiled in victory. "For one thing, the National Safety

Council has in its files any number of 'human spark plugs' who store up enough voltage to be dangerous. There's the case of the oil-company driver in Arizona who burned up three trucks within several days. The poor guy was almost arrested as an arsonist before insurance investigators discovered that he was highly charged."

The Death Merchant said, "A classic case involved a baby in St. Urbain, France, back in the 1860s. The kid was charged like a Leyden jar. At times luminous rays were seen to radiate from the child, and no one could get close to him without getting a shock. When he died at only nine months of age, a luminous radiance appeared around his body, and this glow remained visible for almost five minutes. Throughout the years, there have been any number of such cases."

"None of them even give us a hint as to the cause of SHC," Grojean responded, this time not bothering to conceal his irritability.

"Indeed, it doesn't," said Cottier. "However, such cases offer proof that there is far more to the human machine than even what modern science might suspect. I recall reading about a woman in some Western state who caused a dozen fires before she was transferred to a safer job."

"But you realize, Doctor, that the heart doesn't really have anything to do with the production of this power," Camellion pointed out. "The secret must lie in the brain. I'm thinking of fire started by poltergeists. I recall a case in Texas that—"

"Gentlemen, I've had enough of this nonsense!" Grojean cut Camellion short. "*Human spark plugs* haven't anything to do with atomic physics. If your theory is right, Camellion, it's atomic fusion that's involved with SHC. I see no sense in wasting time in—"

The telephone next to him rang. Grojean picked up the phone, said "Yes?" listened intently for half a minute, then said, "We'll be right over." He replaced the phone on its cradle, lines of triumph forming around his mouth.

"They've found something in the labanotation sheets," he said to Camellion and Cottier. "Let's get over to the Cryptography Section."

The office of Raymond Padon, the supervisor of the Cryptology Section, was a large and comfortably furnished

"Mother Room." Beyond the triple-paned glass in the outer office were rows of computers, electric code machines including Aktiebolaget Cryptographs, and several hundred long desks, with two cryptologists working behind each desk. Beyond the large section of the office was the laboratory.

A short man with a bony, pale face and wiry, gray hair, Padon always wore a khaki shirt with epaulets, khaki trousers and brown Wellington boots. He had been a cryptologist for thirty-five years and was rated as one of the best in the world.

Standing between Fletcher Morrison and Jennifer Winderfer, two of his more talented assistants, Padon picked up a felt-tipped pointer and looked across the table at Courtland Grojean and Richard Camellion.

"Before I explain what we have discovered, let me point that cryptanalysis operates within two frameworks, deductive and inductive," Padon said, his voice high and nervous, for he was a high-strung individual. "Deductive solutions are those based on an analysis of frequency. As a rule, they are the general solution for any major cipher system. Probably words form the basis for inductive solutions, for example two cryptograms with the same plaintext. We can consider these special solutions."

Grojean shifted from one foot to the other, but he didn't interrupt the brilliant little code-breaking expert, who was saying, "Every method is empirical and appears in the various operations of cryptanalysis. These consist of four steps, which taken together are commonly called the *scientific method*. The steps are: *analysis,* such as counting the letters or the numerals, *hypothesis*—Z might be Y, *prediction*—if Z is Y, then some plaintext possibilities could emerge; and *verification*—they do—or negative results— they don't. Either case will then trigger a new chain of logic."

"Have you found a code or haven't you?" Grojean spoke around the pipestem in his mouth. Again, that same deadpan expression and mechanical voice.

None of which seemed to bother Raymond Padon. The DD/O was in *his* department, on *his* turf and, besides, he was one of the men who was very nearly irreplaceable and knew it.

"I have explained our methods," he said, "to give an indication of the complexities of the problems facing us in an attempt to break any cipher. None of the scientific methods worked with the diagrams."

The Death Merchant listened to his intuition. "The dance steps did not constitute the cipher. Am I not correct?"

A smile appeared on Jennifer Winderfer's pretty face. She, Morrison and Padon eyed Camellion curiously.

"Odd that you should say that," Padon said. "You're right. The labanotation figures were exactly as they appeared to be—dance steps. I hate to admit it, but it took us all these weeks to discover that simple fact."

"The labanotation sketches were a blind," Jennifer Winderfer said. "A coverup for the real code."

Thirty-two years old, Jennifer was as tall as Fletcher Morrison, who was an even six feet, but that was partly due to her piled black hair. Studying her, Camellion had the impression that she had carefully applied her cosmetics before leaving for work, but perspiration had ruined the makeup, giving her a "painted" appearance.

"Where was the real cipher?" Grojean asked. "Don't tell me it was something as old-fashioned as 'invisible ink'?" He pulled out his tobacco pouch, shoved in his pipe and began stuffing the bowl.

"No, not in the conventional sense," answered Padon, sounding vaguely disappointed, as if he were sorry that Camellion and Grojean had partially guessed what he had wanted to tell them.

With the short pointer, Padon indicated the various photographs spread out on the glass-topped table. Each photograph was an enlargement—19- by 30-inches—of each of the labanotation sheets, the various markings standing out large and distinct.

Grojean shoved his pipe into his mouth and leaned over the table. "I don't see any letters or numbers or other marks in the diagrams," he said grimly.

"*Pleeeezzzzz* be patient!" Padon said, exhibiting a great deal of irritation. "I am explaining, step by step, to save all of us time. I dislike question-and-answer sessions. They are most annoying to me."

He's the hyperthyroid type, Camellion thought. *Jennifer Windefer is also a nervous Nellie. She doesn't know what to do with her hands. . . .*

"Get on with it," Grojean ordered. "I'm pressed for time."

"After we decided that the cipher was not in any of the labanotation diagrams," started Padon, "we subjected each sheet to lab techniques. We first used black light of infrared radiation."

He reached down to the control panel on the side of the special table, switched off the bank of fluorescent lights and turned on six black-light tubes mounted in long shades over the table. There was no noticeable increase in the room's light since infrared radiation is invisible.

"We then used black light of ultraviolet radiation. That wave length was also a failure."

Padon pressed the switch that turned on the ultraviolet radiation tubes. The ultraviolet radiation also produced no visible light.

"What are you trying to prove?" Grojean protested. "Those sheets on the table are only the reproductions."

"Miss Windefer, get the original sheets and the photographs," Padon said. He glanced distastefully at a fierce-faced Grojean, who had dropped his deadpan mask, then at Camellion who had trained himself over the years to have the patience of a turtle. *Grojean,* mused Camellion, *will never realize that most people will agree with you if you'll only be quiet.*

Jennifer Windefer left the table and went over to a steel blue print cabinet. Padon, humming "Silent Night", and Fletcher Morrison began gathering up the photographs on the table, with Camellion and Dr. Cottier watching. Courtland Grojean watched, too, puffing away furiously on his pipe.

Jennifer returned to the table carrying six large pieces of cardboard under one arm and a small leather portfolio the size of an attaché case under the other. She leaned the cardboard pieces against the table, opened the portfolio, took out six sheets of paper and placed them in the center of the table, lining them up in a row.

Instantly, within the invisible light of the infrared and ultraviolet radiation, tiny letters and numerals began to glow on the six sheets of paper.

"That's more like it," muttered Grojean. He and Camellion and Dr. Cottier leaned closer to the sheets, but the shining letters and numbers, hand-printed all around the

86

Labanotation symbols, were too small to the legible. On one of the sheets were two drawings.

"We then exposed the sheets to both infrared and ultraviolet, and there before you is the result," Padon said proudly. "Using both infrared and ultraviolet at the same time was the Dutchman's idea. He's a good man. Miss Windefer, the enlargements, please, of the photographs we took under both infrared and ultraviolet radiation."

Grojean laughed bitterly. "Sunlight. All it took to bring out the code was sunlight."

"No," Cottier said. "There is more to sunlight than infrared and ultraviolet radiation. There are also protons, some X-rays and alpha particles, etcetera."

Afraid that Cottier would launch into another lecture, Grojean said quickly, "OK, OK. Never mind."

Raymond Padon gathered up the six original labanotation sheets and returned them to the leather portfolio while Jennifer Windefer spread out the six large photographs, so that the letters and numbers faced Camellion, Grojean and Cottier right-side up.

Now the enlarged letters and numbers could be seen very clearly, and so could the two drawings. The Death Merchant and Courtland Grojean picked up large magnifying glasses from the edge of the table, bent over and looked at the letters intermingled with numbers: *LGH-396. GLNH-69H-J-2099. FNJ-J2-DKYLNODHEX-2602388-GBNDQIEDHRTHJB . . .*

Camellion and Grojean studied the two drawings: ink drawings of a faceless man wearing some kind of equipment. One drawing was a full-front view; the other was a profile. The front view showed the man wearing a helmet of some kind, which resembled a large skull cap. Three metal rods protruded from the helmet. One rose vertically from the center top of the helmet; the other two were horizontal, sticking out from the sides. A knob was on the end of each rod.

There was a boxlike contraption on the man's chest, with straps leading from the box over the man's shoulder and from the bottom of the box to the belt around his waist. In the man's hands was a weird-looking device that resembled a "shotgun" microphone. A cable led from the stock of the device to another box strapped to the man's back, as shown in the profile drawing. Cables from the side of the box on his chest led to the sides of the box on his back. He wore special shoes. The soles seemed to be four or five inches thick.

The Death Merchant stared at the two drawings, instinct screaming at him: *This is it. That's the device that somehow can cause spontaneous human combustion.*

Camellion turned and looked at Grojean. The DD/O was having identical thoughts. Neither put their thoughts into words. It was no business of the other people in the office.

The Death Merchant's eyes moved to Raymond Padon. "You haven't deciphered the code."

Grojean followed up in a heavy voice, "How long will it take, Padon?"

Raymond Padon looked insulted. "The code appears to be a cipher based on the substitution method, a 'crypt within letters and numbers' we call it. First we'll try the vowel-solution method, then go to the diagram-solution method."

Grojean scowled. *Another damned lecturer!*

"I don't care what system you use. Consult a crystal ball if you want. But break that code—fast!"

He nudged Camellion, glanced at Dr. Cottier and nodded toward the door.

Explaining that he was in a hurry, Dr. Cottier declined Grojean's offer to have coffee. He took his leave and headed for C parking lot. Grojean and Camellion went to the cafeteria on the fifth floor of D building. Once they were seated at a table toward one corner of the area, Camellion asked, "Who's the Dutchman?"

The DD/O stirred his tea. "He works for Padon. His name is Rudolf Meyer. He was in the German *B-Dienst*[3] under Hitler. Later, after the war, we got him from the Gehlen Organization.[4] Like the others in Padon's depart-

---

[3] *Beobachtung-Dienst*—the Observation Service. The Nazi cryptanalytic agency that was the smallest, the least known and the most successful. The organization belonged to the OKW—High Command of the German Armed Forces, Hitler's Supreme Headquarters.

[4] Reinhard Gehlen. With the help of the CIA, he formed the *Bundesnachrichtendienst*—the BND, the Federal German Intelligence Service.)

ment, Meyer always takes a monthly polygraph and voice analysis examination. He always passes with flying colors. Why do you ask?"

"I was just curious."

Camellion unfolded a napkin and placed it over his right leg, noticing how Grojean was inspecting him, his narrowed eyes asking for an explanation.

"That coat you're wearing?" asked Grojean. "I like the color and the cut."

"I'll send you the 'Eddie Bauer' catalog," Camellion said, and took a sip of coffee.

"The drawings. You think it's the device that's used to cause SHC? If you do, tell me why you think it is?"

"For the same reason you do—intuition. At this point, that's all we have, plus the code. We'll have to proceed on the basis of any information the code might yield. Do you have a better suggestion?"

The DD/O continued to stir his tea.

As a crow would fly, Langley, Virginia, is only seven miles from the White House in Washington, D.C. The cesspool called the Potomac River separates Virginia from Maryland and the District of Columbia.

Bannockburn Heights—not quite eight miles from the White House, should a crow fly a straight-line course—in Maryland was Camellion's destination. He maintained a four-room apartment, the year around, in Bannockburn Heights, not only because he disliked hotels and motels but because Bannockburn Heights was less than 15 miles from the Center in Langley.

After leaving the visitors' parking area at CIA headquarters, he turned the sleek little Triumph TR7 onto the Dolly Madison Highway and increased speed. Unlike England and most of Europe, the eastern seaboard of the United States was in the grip of a heat wave, the temperature soaring at 38 degrees above zero.

Nice weather. Bright sunshine glinting off the snow covering the rolling Virginia countryside. Only a few scattered leftover clouds that looked deserted and out of place.

The rented Triumph convertible handled like a well-trained mechanical animal, although it didn't have automatic transmission. No matter. Camellion was used to a stick shift.

He crossed the Potomac on the Glebe Road Bridge, turned left on the George Washington Memorial Parkway and headed northwest, not at all concerned about the traffic. It was only one-thirty in the afternoon, and he'd be home before the exodus started from Washington, D.C.

The Death Merchant was always on guard, constantly expecting trouble, automatically watching any road he happened to be on, but in a manner far different from the cautiousness of the average motorist. Camellion watched cars for another reason: One of them might contain assassins who had marked him as the target.

He had first noticed the Subaru Brat when, just after he had left the bridge, his attention was drawn to the two men standing in the open bed, holding onto the curved section of the roll bar mounted behind the cab. Both men wore full-face bikers' helmets and padded parkas as protection against the wind.

The open-bed recreational vehicle had kept behind Camellion, remaining at a steady distance of several hundred feet. The Brat couldn't turn off. There weren't any side roads. Just the same, there was something about the car that disturbed Camellion. He couldn't put his finger on the reason, but it was there. He couldn't ignore it. He didn't dare. False assumptions could lead to funerals.

Camellion shifted, fed more gas to the overhead-cam engine, zipped around two cars ahead of him and maintained a steady speed, keeping a distance of three hundred feet between himself and the last car he had passed. He looked in the rear-view mirror. There was the Subaru Brat, pulling around the last car, a Chevy Townsman SW. The driver of the Brat pulled in front of the Chevy, speeded up very slightly, then kept a steady pace.

The Death Merchant's mouth formed a twisted smile. *Leaping lizards! I think someone might be trying to send me to heaven. Let's find out.*

He speeded up the TR7.

The driver of the Brat increased speed.

Camellion slowed.

The driver of the Brat slowed.

The Death Merchant did some rapid thinking: A flick of the switch and the Subaru Brat would have a four-wheel drive, but he doubted if it could outdistance the Triumph.

'On the debit side, slugs would rip through the cloth top of the convertible like buckshot going through a paper bag.

Buckshot? On the floor, in front of the front seats, was a Savage pump-action repeating shotgun. In a left-side shoulder holster under Camellion's coat was a Benelli 9mm autopistol.

But suppose they have a submachine gun? Camellion thought. *Against a subgun I wouldn't have a chance.*

He increased speed slightly. So did the driver of the Subaru Brat. The Death Merchant wondered why the enemy didn't just increase speed and try to pass him?

He must feel that he can't outrun me, and he doesn't want a high-speed chase on a major highway, a chase that might attract the attention of a police car. They've already made two mistakes. Their first was in not trying to ambush me right after I left the Center. The second is now. They should try to pass and blast me from the side. They must know, or at least suspect, that I'm wise to their game. No doubt they'll wait and try to scratch me on Wilson Lane.

Right then, the driver of the enemy vehicle proved Camellion wrong. He tried to correct what the Death Merchant had presumed was the second mistake. The enemy driver started to come up fast.

Okay, Camellion chuckled. *So you want to play*! *We'll play! Let's see how you can handle high speed on a wet road!*

Camellion pressed down on the gas and the TR7 shot ahead like an arrow, its wedge-shaped body cheating the wind. Steadily the speed of both vehicles increased to more than 80 miles per hour.

An expert driver himself, the Death Merchant had to admire the way the other man handled the Brat. He had to be damned good to keep the car on the road, to keep his machine from hydroplaning and flipping over.

The friction of millions of tires had melted the ice and snow, but there were puddles of water here and there on the four-lane highway. At low speeds, tires could push a layer of water aside and make proper contact with the wet road. As the speed of the automobile increased there simply wasn't enough time for the water to flow out from underneath the tires. The tires would "ride" up on the water—and the car would take off into space.

The Death Merchant did the only things he could do under the very dangerous circumstances. He drove in the tire wipes of the cars ahead of him. He avoided puddles by using the stab-and-steer method—cutting speed sharply and steering around the puddles. A method that seemed easy, but wasn't. Not only did the technique take practice and more practice but also expert judgment and perfect timing. It was a method used only by experts who, in order to slow down while retaining control of the steering, pump the brakes. The secret was not to pump in the manner of inexperienced drivers. At high speeds the brakes must be stabbed and hard, *but only for a split second,* the way the Death Merchant was stabbing them now.

The Triumph and the Subaru raced and half skidded down the highway, causing other drivers they passed to think that two maniacs were on the loose. Within a short while, the Death Merchant was a good mile ahead of the unknown enemy, proving that while the driver of the Subaru was good, he wasn't the equal of the Death Merchant.

Camellion felt that he could lose the Brat if he wanted to. *But that would be like running away, wouldn't it? And I want those bastards.*

The only worry he didn't have was the possibility of tire ripple—a rapid buildup of heat that can cause the tread to separate from the rest of the tire and also separate the plys. The result was a big bang or a blowout. That wasn't very likely, though, with the Triumph, which had steel-belted radials that were used in sportcar racing, tires that could resist tire ripple.

A few miles ahead, Camellion saw the long curve and the overhead sign indicating the underpass that opened to Wilson Lane, the two-laner to Bannockburn Heights. He would have to slow considerably to negotiate the curve. He looked in the mirror. The Subaru was nowhere in sight, but he estimated that it could not be more than a mile and a half behind. The driver of the Brat would almost catch up to him while he slowed to go around the curve, but the driver would also have to cut speed when he came to it. By then, Camellion would be through the underpass and on the straight stretch of Wilson Lane. He'd be able to open the throttle and easily lose the enemy. But he wouldn't. He had other things in mind for the men in the Subaru Brat.

He came to the curve, slowed, then actually began passing other cars, doing so by using cadence braking, hitting the brake very suddenly and hard to lock his wheels for only an instant, the result of which was a brief skid. This system differed from pumping or stabbing. Instead of his hitting the brake pedal in a random series of fast stabs, he hit it "in time" with the car's own natural rhythm or cadence.

Camellion concentrated on the turn, first judging the half-dry road before he made his move. Each time he stabbed the brakes, the car would rock ahead on its springs in a kind of nosedive. The vehicle would then recover and rock back. Instantly, Camellion would gradually turn the wheel . . . wait, measure, judge and "stab" again.[5]

Around the curve he went, the TR7 moving in what amounted to one long skid. He came to the turnoff, braked and, with the screaming of tires, turned onto the short incline that led to the underpass. Reaching the underpass, he gunned the engine, zipped around another car and very quickly was on Wilson Lane.

Every now and then he glanced in the rear-view mirror and cut speed slightly. Half a mile into Wilson Lane, he spotted the Subaru Brat coming out from the underpass. As soon as the driver turned onto the straight stretch, his foot slammed down on the gas and the Brat streaked forward and started to close the gap.

Thinking that there were a lot of idiots in the world, the Death Merchant fed gas to his own engine. The TR7 shot down the highway, keeping ahead of the pursuing Subaru. No matter how hard the enemy driver tried to close in and catch up with Camellion, he couldn't. He was also hampered by being on a two-lane highway with traffic coming at him from the opposite direction. The same limitations applied also to the Death Merchant, who was waiting until he could find an open stretch in which oncoming cars, as well as vehicles on his side of the road, were at least 500 feet ahead of him.

The two cars shot down the road at 105 mph. One false

[5] *Warning!* Don't attempt any of these methods until you have been trained by an expert. Such methods require a tremendous amount of practice.

move, one wrong turn of either steering wheel, and death would end the chase, quickly and violently.

Finally, the Death Merchant got what he wanted: For almost 500 feet ahead there weren't any cars on either side. Furthermore, there were no fences on either side of the road, only empty fields covered with snow.

Camellion cut speed and began very slight cadence braking. With the needle of the speedometer at 75 mph, he realized he would have to time his braking and turning to the split second, or roll over.

Now! Almost simultaneously, he jammed on the brakes and turned the steering wheel very slightly to the left. Centrifugal force did the rest. With tires screaming, the front of the car started to come to a stop as the rear end began swerving to the right. Several moments later, the entire car had spun around, reversing itself. The rear end was now in front, and the Death Merchant found himself looking down the stretch of highway that, moments earlier, had been behind him—and staring at the Subaru coming straight at him. The bootleggers' spin had been perfect.

Smiling, Camellion stepped on the gas, shifted and gunned the car forward, now heading west. All the while he continued to increase speed and drive straight at the Subaru.

Astonished at Camellion's sudden turnaround, Earl Grove, the driver of the Subaru, started to apply the brakes. He yelled at Arlie Larsen, the hood who was sweating in fear next to him, "He's nuts! You rake his side when I swing around him."

"My God! Look!" gasped Larsen, who was also a hood from Baltimore. "He ain't playing with no full deck."

The Triumph was no longer coming straight at the Subaru Brat. Camellion had swung off the highway and was plowing through the snow-covered field to the right of the Brat, headed east.

Camellion knew he wouldn't be able to get very far in the deep snow. He didn't have four-wheel drive, and the TR7 was built low to the ground. In contrast, the Subaru, built higher and with four-wheel drive, would have a much better chance of going through the snow.

The Death Merchant's TR7 slugged its way across the

field, the steel-belted radials digging into the foot-and-a-half-deep snow, the sports car acting like a wild animal that was losing its strength. The Triumph hadn't struggled more than a hundred feet into the field before the rear wheels started to spin. The Death Merchant didn't try to rock free. He didn't want to. He had planned on the Triumph's losing traction and becoming mired down, just as he had counted on the Subaru Brat charging into the field after him.

He glanced into the mirror, at the same time reaching down for the pump shotgun on the floor. *Yes, sir*, he grinned. *The dumbbells are right on schedule. The damn fools are coming to their own funerals and don't know it!*

The Subaru was turning off the highway and starting to come into the field, the two men in back bounding up and down in the bed and hanging onto the rounded top section of the roll bar. The right side window had been rolled down, and Camellion was almost certain he saw several inches of the barrel of a weapon protruding through the opening. He didn't have time to make sure; each second was too precious.

Keeping down, he got out of the sports car on the right side, his Chukkas sinking into the snow, which dropped over the tops onto his socks. Remaining low, he struggled through the snow and reached the position he wanted: the front of the car. He could tell the location of the Subaru from the sound of its laboring engine. At any moment the Subaru would be almost broadside.

Arlie Larsen, an UZI submachine gun in his hands, was so anxious to kill Camellion that he poked out the chatter-box and began firing when the front bumper of the Subaru was horizontal to the back bumper of the Triumph. The UZI chattered, 9mm slugs dissolving glass and stitching holes in the metal of the sports car.

Just as Larsen's finger squeezed the trigger, the Death Merchant reared up from the left front of the TR7 and got off the first round with the Savage repeating shotgun.

Brrrooommmm! The countryside reverberated with the crashing roar of the 12-gauge, and 85 percent of the Subaru's windshield disappeared in a shower of glass, with hundreds of the razor-sharp slivers stabbing like shrapnel into the faces of Earl Grove and Arlie Larsen, both of whom screamed in agony.

Blinded in one eye by glass and by blood in the other,

Grove jammed on the brake, sheer horror paralyzing his thinking processes. He and the three other men had been paid $15,000 each to kill one man, and that man was now killing them!

In a worse mess, Arlie Larsen had been completely blinded by flying glass, his face, like Grove's, looking as though it had been shoved into a meat grinder.

Barry Huttas and Charles Blomquest, standing in the rear, were almost thrown out of the bed as Grove shoved down on the brake pedal and the Subaru began to skid. Each man was armed with a couple of S. & W. .357 Magnums, but it was all they could do to hang onto the roll bar, let alone pull the big revolvers. It wouldn't have made much difference if they had.

The Death Merchant stepped back, almost falling in the snow, pumped the shotgun and fired again as the right side of the Subaru slammed into the TR7. Another big *brrrooommm*, and Barry Huttas got the perfect gift for the man who has nothing. His head exploded, and skin, bone, blood and scrambled gray brain matter went flying in every direction of the compass.

Camellion pumped the Savage so fast it was a miracle the 12-gauge didn't jam. *Brrooommmmm.* "Chuckie" Blomquest's head vanished like a pumpkin hit by a grenade.

In spite of being half-blind, Earl Grove opened one eye, pulled a .38 Chiefs Special from a shoulder holster, and for only a fraction of a second saw a world of red through the blood in his left eye—and the muzzle of a shotgun eight feet in front of him.

Brroommmmmm! Grove became headless. His stump of a neck spurting blood, he slumped against Larsen, who was making sounds similar to an animal being skinned alive.

The shotgun boomed again, and Larsen stopped making animal sounds. He slumped in the seat, most of his head and the top part of his chest gone, and bloody, jagged bones sticking out of the enormous wound.

Moving awkwardly through the snow, the Death Merchant inspected his handiwork. The Triumph and the Subaru would need a lot of garage work before they would be respectable on the highway. The TR7 didn't look too bad. All the windows, except the windshield, had been shot out. There were a dozen bullet holes, as well as an enormous dent, in the left side of the TR7. Blood dripped from underneath both doors of the Subaru. Huttas and Blomquest lay slumped on the bed, which was thick with blood congealing in the cold wind.

The Death Merchant looked toward the highway—cars were going by, their drivers looking straight ahead—thinking, *Worse than New York! The goofs in this part of the nation wouldn't stop for the end of the world! We'll have to attract some attention. . . .*

He first tossed down the shotgun, then trudged through the snow to the TR7, opened the door on the right side and took his overcoat from the top of the seat next to the driver's, along with half a pack of Max cigarettes that the car's previous renter had left in the glove compartment. A book of matches was stuck in the cellophane.

He put on the overcoat, waded through the snow to the rear of the Subaru, crawled up onto the bed of the truck and, pulling the Jakal from the holster on the back of his neck, cut two three-foot strips of cloth from the pant leg of one of the corpses, making each strip about an inch wide. He got down from the bed, went around to the gas cap of the Subaru and tied the two pieces of cloth together. Wishing he were back in Texas, he unscrewed the cap and began shoving the six-foot cloth strip through the opening, stopping when all that was left of it was the part between his fingers. Slowly, he pulled out the strip until most of it was outside the gas tank and, reeking of gasoline, lay stretched out in the snow.

Wind whistling around his bare head, Camellion put on his gloves, knelt down and built a round wall of snow a foot high around the end of the cloth, making certain that the snow did not press down against the cloth where it lay in a hole in the wall.

Confident that the wind would not put out the cigarette, he pulled some twigs from a bush and stuck them down in the snow over the end of the strip, pressing them down to form an X half an inch above the cloth. He pulled the book of matches from the cellophane around the pack, took out a Max and lit it, carefully puffing in order that the cigarette would be burning fully at its end.

He was just as meticulous when he inserted the burning cigarette into the top of the book of matches, closed the flap securely and pulled on the filter end until the flame

97

was only half an inch from the closed side of the book of matches. Even more judiciously, he wedged the book of matches and the cigarette in the twigs over the end of the gasoline-soaked strip of cloth.

Camellion laughed out loud as he turned and trudged through the snow, away from the makeshift firebomb. Grojean would get Excedrin Headache #10010! The police would have to haul Camellion in for investigation. How surprised they would be to find that his fingerprints were not on record anyplace. Not only had his army record mysteriously vanished but so had his prints from the FBI's Central File. Grojean would clamp a tight lid on the whole business. Of course, the wire services would report that a "Mr. Casimer Anthony Mohilowski" had had a gun battle with . . . *With who?* the Death Merchant thought. *Who cares? Grojean will "prove" that the hoods were "working for a foreign power," and that holding me will "compromise national security."*

A hundred and fifty feet from the two automobiles, Camellion got behind an oak tree and waited. Not for long. The cigarette, burning down, touched off the book of matches, and the sudden flash of flame ignited the end of the gasoline-soaked strip. In seconds, the fire raced the six feet to the Subaru's gas tank.

A crashing roar! A huge flash of fire from the rear of the Subaru, and it was all over. Flames engulfed the Subaru and quickly spread to the Triumph, black oily smoke boiling up to the sky. Soon the stink of burning metal, cloth, rubber and plastic was thick in the air. There was another odor, a very unusual one that was never in the air around Washington, D.C.—the sweet-smelling stink of roasting flesh.

The four gunmen were dead and being cremated.

The Death Merchant had not been touched.

Fate? Nonsense! *Fate is like a flirt. She always runs after those who don't care for her.* . . .

The gas tank of the TR7 exploded as three Maryland State Police cars, their sirens winding down, screeched to a halt on Wilson Lane. The Blue Jays poured out, riot guns and revolvers in their hands.

The Death Merchant raised his arms high above his head and started legging in through the snow toward the police. . . .

Chapter Seven

"No, damn it! You don't have any idea of what I've been through the last eight days!" thundered Courtland Grojean. His face contorted with rage, the DD/O shook his pipe at Camellion, the stem jabbing the air. "The Director had to go all the way up to the White House and have the President talk with the brass of NIA.[1] As keen on history and politics as you are, you know damn good and well that every President since Truman has accepted the Wilsonian credo of peace without victory."

"Yeah, I realize that," Camellion sighed bitterly. "Military victory, like the concepts of unconditional surrender, have been recognized as obsolete since the end of World War II. More danger lies in powerful individuals in some Western governments who have Marxist leanings and who belong to organizations that would like to see a world government with Moscow pulling the strings."

Grojean, who had taken time to light his pipe, stepped back and sat on the front edge of his desk. "Damn it! I should have left you sitting in jail. The Director had to talk like an Israeli trying to set up a bagel factory in Yassir Arafat's home town. And it wasn't easy, not with a Commander in Chief who has neither the backbone nor the

[1] The National Intelligence Authority, created by President Truman in 1946. Still in existence and composed only of political hacks, it's as useless as sand in the Sahara. CIA case officers refer to NIA as the "Clown Department."

intelligence to do anything about Russian troops stationed only ninety miles from the continental United States."

"It worked, and that's all that mattered," Camellion said quietly. He slumped lower in the leather chair and stretched out his long legs. "Don't forget, I wasn't exactly in paradise while I was in jail for a week. And I couldn't return to my apartment in Bannockburn Heights since Casimer Anthony Mohilowski 'committed suicide' while in jail."

"The Maryland police had to tell the press something," Grojean said. "There wasn't any other way to conclude the investigation. Your 'suicide' resolved the problem. By the way, we picked up your clothes and other stuff from your apartment."

"When I first came in, you said that Padon and his staff had broken the code. Let's have the bad news."

Grojean put down his pipe in a brass ashtray and picked up a soapstone Kyoto horse from his desk. "It's worse than we had thought," he said, studying the reproduction of the Samurai steed. "I'll give it to you in brief. Later you can read the translation, word for word."

Speaking rapidly, he explained that the contents of the code involved a plan to murder key members of the British Commonwealth.

"We could have saved Prime Minister Heath and his chauffeur if we had broken the code weeks ago. Three others were on the list, two in Rhodesia and the Governor of Hong Kong. We've already warned them to be extremely careful and to surround themselves with bodyguards."

The DD/O gave Camellion the rest of the terrible information: Included in the plan was a scheme, still in the planning stage, to murder Yasser Arafat and blame his death on the Mossad, Israel's worldwide intelligence service.

Grojean put down the soapstone carving and looked worriedly at the Death Merchant. "The plan was signed 'Director of the Brotherhood.' I think we're dealing with a neo-Nazi organization, one that is organized worldwide, has a lot of contacts, and money to burn."

"Add to that, very clever. Twice now they've sent professional gunmen after me with professional weapons. This is a clear indication that it must take a specialist to operate

100

the machine or whatever causes the SHC. There are several questions that need answering."

"Your assumption about the drawings was correct," Grojean said. "The drawings in the code are a smaller version of the mechanism that causes SHC. The device is called a Transmutationizer."

"Is that what it was called in the code—you're sure?"

"Affirmative. The code was a report to all the branch centers of the Brotherhood. Kemper Marmis was either one of the top members or some kind of special contact. Either way, we have proof that it's the Brotherhood that is responsible for SHC."

"There's no telling how much we might have learned from Marmis if one of your officers at the Embassy station in London hadn't pulled that boner with the pills." The tone of Camellion's voice was definitely resentful.

Grojean made an uncertain gesture with his left hand. "We've fired the son of a bitch and warned him that if he even hints that he ever worked for the Agency, he'll have a fatal accident." He spread his hands in a gesture of helplessness. "He blew the deal for you. What more can I say?"

He went over to the leather chair across from Camellion and sat down. "We do have one slim clue. The report mentioned that 'Professor P' was working on a new model of the Transmutationizer and that it would be ready in several months. The drawings were of the new model." He moved his hands slowly over the silvery gray hair of his temples and frowned at Camellion, who was strangely silent. "I'm not in the habit of talking to myself," he snapped. "I want your opinion."

"I was thinking of all the *luck* the Brotherhood has been having," Camellion said with thinly disguised humor. "How did they know that 'Mr. Mohilowski' would be at the Center on that particular day and taking the Dolly Madison Highway at such and such a time. Your department's been penetrated, Grojean. You've got a mole in Operations—and don't change the subject like you did when I first came in." The Death Merchant's voice became harsh and demanding. "I want an explanation."

Grojean knew that the Death Merchant was not a man who could be put off twice. "You're right," Grojean admitted, lowering his eyes. "We do have a mole, but I'm not free to discuss it with you." He looked up from the rug. "I will tell you this much: He's a home-grown traitor. We're letting him operate because it's to our advantage. When he's no longer of value to us, he'll have an accident. A public trial would be much too revealing."

"It's not to my advantage to get ambushed!" Camellion said scornfully. "I don't like playing those kind of games, and I don't intend to."

"The traitor is selling information to the KGB," Grojean replied patiently. "For that reason we haven't moved against him. There's a bit more disinformation we're going to let him get his hands on, then arrange for him to have an accident. He must be terminated in a way that will fool the KGB in Washington and New York."

"He's free-lance, then?"

"Correct. But he's not tied in with the Brotherhood—as far as I know. Nor does the KGB at the Soviet Embassy know that he tipped off the Brotherhood about you. Not that the Soviets would give a damn."

The Death Merchant's eyes glowed strangely. "Don't you dare tell me you set me up?"

"Don't be ridiculous!" Grojean said angrily. "Until you were ambushed, I didn't even suspect that the mole had even heard of the Brotherhood. I can only assume he tipped them off because there doesn't seem to be any other explanation. I don't consider him any kind of clue. I doubt if he knows for whom he's working. He probably had only half a dozen phone numbers and a contact."

"We must assume he's tipped off the Brotherhood that we've broken the code," Camellion said significantly. He got to his feet and began pacing back and forth in front of the desk. Suddenly he swung around and looked down at Grojean, who was adjusting his silk tie. The DD/O was a fastidious dresser.

The Death Merchant went on savagely, "You're gasping your last breath if you think 'Professor P' is a clue. The Brotherhood wouldn't be stupid enough to use a genuine title or initial, even in a code. Even if they had been that dumb, by now the scientist working on the device is underground somewhere in West Germany."

"Why West Germany?" Grojean's eyes narrowed.

"Come off of it! You know why!" Camellion let Grojean have a dirty look and sat back down in the chair. "Hitler's scientists were working on a lot of weird projects. Why, the Nazis almost beat us to the A-bomb."

"That's true," admitted Grojean. "There's a list of those projects buried somewhere in the Pentagon. But by the time we found them, we'd be old men. Do I have to tell you the answer?"

Camellion turned and looked coolly at Grojean. "Naturally the mole in your department knows that you've contacted West German Intelligence?"

"Of course," Grojean responded promptly. "He'd be instantly suspicious if we tried to keep it from him that the BND was checking Nazi records for us. And don't try to figure out who the traitor is! You don't know all the people on my staff."

Camellion felt like shaking Grojean's hand. He was up to his usual tricks, and Camellion appreciated a man whose mind operated constantly within a framework of total deviousness.

"How have you planned it?" asked Camellion. "And this had better be good. I can't operate in West Germany with a mole back here shooting information to the Brotherhood."

Grojean paused long enough to cross his legs and carefully adjust the creases in his tweed trousers.

"It might be that the mole was hired for only one job, to set you up for termination," he said. "He may not have the kind of contact that would permit him to keep the Brotherhood informed on a day-to-day basis."

"I've always been extremely cautious of half-truths," Camellion said. "Only fools risk getting hold of the wrong half. If the mole did set me up, we can assume that he's reporting all developments to his American contact. The Brotherhood would be foolish to pass up such a valuable source of inside information."

"My thoughts exactly," Grojean said in a pleased voice. He lowered his voice, although he didn't have to: His office was one giant Mother Room. "Which is why you won't have to worry about his knowing your every move."

"Give it to me straight. I don't intend to go over to krautland with an invisible knife across my throat."

"Without anyone on my staff knowing it, I sent a second message to Karl Otto Schneider, the Director of BND. I've requested that he wait two weeks, then have his research office send a reply that it hasn't been able to find anything in their files about a Nazi project dealing with spontaneous human combustion. However, the last part of the message will suggest that we check on some of the Nazis in Paraguay, to see if they might be able to provide a clue. Dr. Mengele has fled Paraguay, but ex-SS General Klaus Weber and other Nazis are still hiding out in the back country. Understand the direction in which I'm going?"

Pausing, Grojean looked curiously at the Death Merchant, expecting him to say that he wasn't about to go to South America, or at least to ask how the genuine report from the BND would reach the Center.

The Death Merchant only said, "Go on. Finish it."

"I'll arrange to have you fly on an Air Force transport to Guantánamo," Grojean said, his voice slightly above a whisper. "Supposedly, you'll be on your way to Paraguay. Instead, you'll fly to London and then on to Bonn. You'll work through the Company station in Bonn, but the chief of station at the American Embassy in Bonn will send only routine reports, nothing about SHC. However, the Center will receive reports from the chief of station at the Embassy in Asuncion in regard to your activities. Get the drift?"

"Yes, and I don't like it," Camellion lashed out. "Every member of your staff is an expert. The odds are that the mole will become suspicious, sooner or later. There's the level-of-incompetence factor. That, too, is working against us."

Grojean's face became more interested. "Explain."

"The principle is very simple. In any organization, every employee tends to rise to his level of incompetence. That is, if people do well in one job, they are promoted to another higher up the ladder, and so on until they reach a job they can't do well. As soon as people reach jobs they can't do, they tend to make mistakes because they've reached their level of incompetence. Understand?"

"Certainly: The cream rises until it sours."

"Applied to us, this means that someone, somewhere, is going to foul up and make the mole suspicious."

Grojean sighed heavily. "Well, we'll have to take the risk. The simpler solution—and I think that's what we have—may not be the right one, but it's the one to consider first. In this case, I feel it's the logical approach. I think you agree. Or don't you?"

"We'll do it your way. I'll want Neil Reeder, one of your London boys, with me in West Germany," Camellion said. "He's a good backup."

"I'll have him transferred immediately to the station in Bonn," agreed Grojean. "There's nothing unusual in such a transfer. No one should be suspicious."

"Not good enough," challenged the Death Merchant. "Transfer him to Bonn on special assignment, as liaison between the Bonn station and the BND, in case the krauts find something in their file pertaining to SHC. Of course, the BND won't find anything of value. Now give me that bottom line."

"The bottom line?"

"How is the BND going to transmit its real findings to the Center without the mole finding out?"

"That's the beauty of the plan," crowed Grojean. "The true report will go the Company's Bonn station and will remain with the chief of station there. His name is Milt Blome. He'll fill you in after you arrive in Bonn. All I have left to do is contact Blome and tell him the name you'll be using."

In response to the DD/O's questioning stare, Camellion said, "Get me two passports. One made out to 'Cecil Benton' and one for 'August Hillmeyer.' I'll use the 'Hillmeyer' passport for West Germany, the other one for my fictitious trip to South America. Can you get them without our friendly neighborhood spy finding out?"

"Let me worry about that," Grojean said heartily. "You just find out how the Nazi network functions and"—his smile disappeared—"get the secret of that SHC transmutationizer. My God! The device amounts to a portable nuclear reactor that can explode the atoms of the human body—if your theory is right. Stop and think of the 'impossibility' of the device! It's right out of science fiction, from the year 3,000!"

"Correction. *Implodes,* not explodes. And I have thought about it, a lot. But not impossible and not SF either. In 1930, some of the world's most respected scientists had concluded that the A-bomb was 'impossible.' Hell, every scientific achievement was once impossible."

"That may be true, but the process for SHC is the same principle that makes the H-bomb go boom, isn't it? On the assumption that your theory is correct."

The Death Merchant took several long thoughts on how to explain it to Grojean. Suppose his theory of how SHC was caused was wrong? Even worse, suppose the BND came up with a zero? *We'll be right back where we started! No, maybe not. We'll still have the mole.*

"The atom bomb is a fission," he explained. "It explodes when unstable atoms of uranium and plutonium are caused to break up, when the atoms split. The hydrogen bomb is different. It's a fusion bomb. It derives its power when two atomic nuclei of hydrogen fuse together to form a single nucleus of helium. It's the same process that causes the sun to 'burn.' What makes the Brotherhood's Transmutationizer so hideously horrifying is that one man can apparently carry the entire apparatus that can do not only what an A-bomb does but can also control the same kind of fusion that takes place in an H-bomb. Or at least causes the fusion."

"What are you saying?" Grojean was perplexed. "An H-bomb is far more powerful than an A-bomb."

"What I mean is that in an H-bomb, tremendously high pressure is required to force the hydrogen nuclei to fuse into helium. It's the A-bomb, or fission bomb of the sort that was dropped on Hiroshima and Nagasaki, that is used to ignite the hydrogen bomb. In the case of the Transmutationizer, all the necessary components and hardware are contained in two boxes that can be worn on a man's back and chest. It's fantastic!"

"It's the ultimate weapon," Grojean said miserably, "not to mention how the process could revolutionize civilization."

"Another amazing factor is that the Transmutationizer creates a kind of hydrogen bomb by using the hydrogen atoms in a victim's body. If I'm right, the process is not one that's identical with thermonuclear weapons, but depends on a force field for its source of power, a power tap completely unsuspected by modern science."

Grojean's expression suddenly became a sledgehammer looking for an anvil. "Camellion, We must find the secret of that source of power," he insisted, breathing in deeply and noisily. "I don't give a damn if you have to destroy half of Europe. Just get that Transmutationizer."

"If it's there to be gotten, I'll get it," Camellion said. "But in the long scheme of things, you and I are going to

It was exactly 3:00 PM when a *V-Mann* ushered them into a large room on the second floor and introduced Camellion and Reeder to Klaus Heinrich Hahn, a direct representative of General Karl Utt, the director of the BND, and to Otto Wesslin, a counterintelligence specialist.

The V-man left the room and Hahn, with an obligatory smile, waved a hand toward massive upholstered chairs ringed in a semicircle around a table of Gothic design on which rested a bottle of brandy and several bottles of Mosel.

As Camellion and Reeder sat down next to Wesslin and Chasteen walked over to one of the windows and looked out, Hahn went over to a black metal filing cabinet, pulled open the top drawer, took out a folder and opened it. He removed two large glossy photographs, and for many long moments compared the faces in the photographs with the faces of Richard Camellion and Neil Reeder.

"They've already given me the code pass," Chasteen called from the window. He then turned, walked across the room and sat down on the other side of Wesslin.

Hahn didn't reply to Chasteen. He returned the photographs to the folder, put the folder in its place in the filing cabinet and rejoined the group, sitting down next to Reeder. Appearing robust and athletic, Hahn gave the impression of a man who had never lost a moment of sleep in his life and who could wear a uniform without a wrinkle. Camellion estimated his age at between thirty-five and forty.

Turning slightly, one hand on his knee, the other arm on the arm of the chair, Camellion said in idiomatic High German, "Herr Hahn, do you prefer English or German?"

"I read, speak and write German, English, Russian and French," Hahn replied affably. "I suggest you use the language with which you are the most comfortable."

"I understand English," said the hard-faced Otto Wesslin, whose long face, sharp features and blond hair reminded the Death Merchant of Reinhard Heydrich—the chief of the Nazi *Reichs-Sicherheits-Hauptamt*, the Head Department for the Security of the Reich—"although I have never been able to understand why the plural of *mouse* should be *mice* instead of *mece*."

After the polite laughter subsided, the Death Merchant went directly to business, saying to Hahn, "On the way here, Chasteen told us that the BND had uncovered something in its files that might help in our investigation."

"Your investigation and ours," Hahn said very quickly, as if to remind Camellion that the investigation was a joint effort. "Only last week, one of the men who might have helped us was killed by what you Americans call 'spontaneous human combustion.'"

"We refer to the phenomena as *Der Tod Hölle*—the hell death," interjected Wesslin, pouring brandy into a glass.

Hahn looked at Camellion and Reeder and motioned to the bottles and glasses on the low table. "By the way, feel free to help yourselves to refreshments, gentlemen."

"Start at the beginning," urged Camellion. "What did you find of importance in the files?" He leaned forward, picked up a crystal wine goblet and reached for one of the bottles of Mosel.

Hahn lit a cigarette before speaking. "We gathered what files we had on the Nazi administration and searched them. We assumed that 'Professor P' was a cover cipher, but we couldn't take the chance. We looked for the name of every scientist, who worked for Hitler, whose first or last name began with *P*. The difficulty was that we had to do it all by hand. There wasn't any way we could computerize the research. We found sixty-one scientists."

"Damned good evidence that 'Professor P' was a cover," inserted Neil Reeder, after which he took a sip of brandy.

"Yes, that is true," agreed Hahn. "For that very reason, we then had to eliminate those scientists from the suspect list, one by one."

"By the association method?" asked the Death Merchant.

Hahn nodded. "All the sixty-one were involved with either research in rockets or in nuclear fission. We immediately checked the nuclear research people because of your theory of atomic fusion, Mr. Hillmeyer, which your people in Washington, D.C., related to Bonn. Incidentally, our own research people agree with you."

"What about Klaus Eickner?" inquired Reeder. "What did your research on him reveal?"

Alan Chasteen sneered and blew out cigar smoke. "He was only a petty criminal hired to do a job."

"Much more than a low thief," Wesslin said. "The local police of Kassel suspect him of several bank robberies and one kidnaping. It is unfortunate that they didn't have any evidence. *Ya,* he was a wily one, that fellow."

Klaus Hahn continued, "Our research of the nuclear scientists did not prove rewarding. Those still alive are working in the United States. Six for the American government. Two in private industry. Four are dead."

Camellion frowned. He had hoped that one of the nuclear research scientists would provide a clue.

"Next, we proceeded to research any project that might even vaguely involve fission or fusion, or one that dealt with force fields. We found only one such project: a secret weapon that was supposed to disintegrate tanks, planes, troop ships—anything. In these modern times, men of science would call such a weapon a true death ray."

Hahn paused to lean over the table and flip ash from his cigarette into a mammoth green ashtray. He then continued, glancing from Camellion to Reeder every now and then.

"This scientist's name was Helmut Koerber. He had a degree in physics and engineering from the University of München—Munich. There's no point in wasting time with irrelevant details. What concerns us is the work that Koerber did under the Nazis. He first worked on atomic research, on the heavy water project in Norway. But his theories were too radical and he insisted on doing things his way. Dr. Walter Frischauer, the boss of atomic research, had him kicked out. What happened next, as best as we can put together, is that somehow Koerber caught the attention of Himmler, who was not only a racial crackpot but a *schwachsinniger*—an idiot—about weird weapons. According to the SS files we researched, Koerber convinced the *Reichführer* that he could invent a weapon that could destroy men or objects. The exact words, in the notes we found of one meeting between Himmler, Koerber and Walter Schellenberg, were 'disintegrate by burning.' Koerber explained to Himmler that this could be accomplished by what he referred to as an 'application of reverse force fields.' "

Hahn crushed out his cigarette and turned to Camellion. "As you Americans say, 'It's all Greek to me.' But all of it sounds suspiciously like a project that could result in the hell death, or SHC."

Reeder spoke up, sounding disconsolate, "None of it

111

sounds very promising to me. It's the same as saying that the ship's cat survived the *Titanic* and calling it good news!"

"Why didn't you give me this information about Koerber?" Alan Chasteen asked darkly, his heavily lidded eyes on Hahn. "Or did your orders exclude your telling me before this meeting?"

"I had my orders," Hahn said. He looked at Reeder. "Please let me finish. You'll see that we're going in the right direction."

Hahn's gaze moved to Camellion, who was trying to decide whether the Mosel was from the Forst or Deidesheim regions of West Germany.

"The rest of our research into the Koerber matter indicated that he began the project, but never completed it. The war ended. Everything during those days was a mess. I was only four years old and don't remember any of it, but we all know from history what happened."

"I take it that's not the end of the story," Camellion said. "If it is, I'm going to start agreeing with Reeder." The Death Merchant made a sullen face as he undid the belt and unbuttoned his dark suede safari jacket. It wasn't that the room was all that warm, only that the coat did not release body heat.

"There's quite a bit more," Otto Wesslin said, taking over the oral report. "We found out where Koerber was living from the War Veteran's Pension Office and immediately sent agents to the address in West Berlin. Koerber had disappeared."

Camellion's, Reeder's and Chasteen's heads snapped up in surprise.

"That's one fine bucket of worms!" exclaimed Chasteen in utter disgust.

Wesslin leaned forward in the big chair and looked knowingly at Reeder and Camellion, his eyes gleaming eagerly. "From what our agents could find out, it appeared that Koerber suddenly vanished. No one had seen him for about six weeks. We can't be sure. It's been five or six weeks."

"How long ago was it that the BND found out he had disappeared?" Camellion asked.

"A bit over three weeks ago," answered Wesslin.

The Death Merchant's face did not register any expression. It was beginning to add up. Professor Koerber had vanished immediately after the papers had been taken from Kemper Marmis's basement safe. The Brotherhood, assuming that the CIA would break the code in the Labanotation diagrams, had tipped off Koerber and he was in hiding. There could, however, be another explanation. The question popped into Camellion's mind: Did the BND associate the disaster and Kemper Marmis's shop with the disappearance of Koerber? *If they haven't,* Camellion thought, *why should I bother to tell them?*

Nonetheless, he was concerned about West German intelligence in still another way: If Professor Koerber had continued his research after the war and if he had perfected the Transmutationizer, the BND would be just as anxious to acquire the weapon as the CIA. The question demanded an answer. *How far can I trust these krauts?* Camellion wondered. *And if there's a mole working for the KGB in the German intelligence service, then it's more than likely that the Russians are in the act. Damn! What an unholy mess!*

Neil Reeder telegraphed his concern by squirming slightly in his chair. "Then you haven't located Professor Koerber? And isn't he up in years by now?"

Wesslin finished filling his glass with wine. "We're almost positive that Koerber is still in West Berlin," he said, recorking the bottle. "He's there because he can't get out. We're watching all the crossings into East Berlin and the roads leading into East Germany. He can't fly out. We have men stationed around the clock at Tempelhof."

Alan Chasteen grimaced, deep lines appearing in his square face.

"Well," he shrugged a shoulder, "we can't discount completely the possibility that he might have been smuggled into East Berlin or East Germany. Hell, getting into the commie zones is easy. It's the getting out that takes a Houdini."

"Technically, we can't," Hahn spoke up. "As a practical measure, we can. Koerber is a fanatical anticommunist. He's been a Nazi lover and a hater of communism all his life, and seventy-year-old men don't change their political views. Psychologically, Koerber wouldn't go into commie territory anymore than I'd take up residence in the middle of Outer Mongolia."

113

"Do you have any leads?" the Death Merchant said hotly, his eyes on Hahn. "Berlin and its suburbs are big, but you have your informers and special private sources of information, I'm sure."

Surprised at the sudden energy in Camellion's voice, Hahn raised a restraining hand. "Please, Herr Hillmeyer, let me finish telling of our investigation. Professor Koerber had five assistants, technicians who helped him with the project he worked on under Himmler. Two died in the 1950s and 1960s. The other three scattered over West Germany. Gustav Hiber lives in Munich. Gunther Heusinger in Frankfurt. Erich Hammerle lived in Hamburg."

"Lived?" Camellion cocked an eye at Hahn and noticed that Reeder and Chasteen had also caught the past tense in reference to Erich Hammerle.

"Hammerle's dead," announced Hahn. He took his cigarettes from his shirt pocket. "All we found of him in his basement was several pounds of ashes, half his skull and part of a shinbone."

Neil Reeder's mouth fell open and he half rose from the chair in surprise. Chasteen almost spilled his drink. "I'll be damned!" he muttered. "Three assistants whose last names begin with *H*, and one of them dead from the ultimate burn!"

Hahn's announcement didn't faze the Death Merchant, who, being a total pessimist, had long ago resigned himself to any catastrophe.

"Hammerle is the man you mentioned earlier, the one who was killed last week," Camellion said, an undercurrent to his low voice.

"You don't seem surprised," said Hahn. He studied Camellion for a moment, then lit his cigarette.

Camellion let the remark slide by. "If you tell me next that Hiber and Heusinger aren't under constant guard, I'll tell you that the Federal Intelligence Service needs reorganizing."

Otto Wesslin smiled cynically and hooked a thumb in his belt. "The *Bundesnachrichtendienst* needs reorganizing, but not because we don't have Hiber and Heusinger under guard," Hahn said with a slight chuckle. He quickly became serious. "Gustav Hiber is in a war veterans' hospital in Munich. We were going to question all three, but didn't get around to any of them. Then Hammerle was murdered.

We have Hiber in a doctor's home on the hospital grounds. We have special agents inspecting every vehicle that enters the grounds, especially trucks."

"And Heusinger?" queried the Death Merchant.

"Agents are guarding him and his wife in his home." Hahn exhaled smoke noisily. "We haven't questioned either Hiber or Heusinger. Both men were too agitated. When we mentioned Professor Koerber's name to Herr Heusinger, Frau Heusinger became hysterical."

Wesslin joined in. "The Heusingers know something," he said reasonably. "We can question them first. Frankfurt is only seventy-five kilometers southeast of Bonn."

"We have a helicopter with pilot and copilot waiting at the airfield in Bad Godesberg," Klaus Hahn said politely, the invitation in his tone unmistakable. "We can leave at your convenience." He looked from Camellion to Neil Reeder.

Camellion drained his glass and placed it gently on the table.

"Our luggage is in Chasteen's car," he said. "I see no reason why we cant start right now."

"*Das ist gut,*" Hahn said, forgetting himself in his enthusiasm for their decision, and speaking in German. He finished in English. "By the time we get to Frankfurt, it will be time for dinner. We'll have dinner, then go out and have a talk with the Heusingers."

The helicopter, a British Westland Commando, was marked with German Maltese crosses and was a West German *Marineflieger*. By the time Camellion and the others reached the Bad Godesberg airbase, darkness had settled over the wintry German countryside and the air station was ablaze with light.

They went directly to the Commandant's office—this month it was an American, Colonel Vernon Pawaukee—and had one German noncom call the pilot and the copilot of the chopper while two more airmen placed their bags aboard the Westland Commando. Included in the luggage were two large metal suitcases.

Fifteen minutes later, at 18.30 hours, the chopper lifted off, its two Rolls-Royce turboshafts roaring and its five-bladed main rotor spinning faster and faster.

The Death Merchant looked out the fixed aft window on

the port side. There wasn't a cloud in the sky and no moon, and the stars were as big and bright and blue as diamonds the size of apples. The night was already cold and would become colder. Twenty below zero or a hundred and ten in the shade: the weather didn't count. Finding the secret of *Der Tod Hölle* and who was instigating the world-wide assassinations was all that mattered.

Camellion made an effort and shrugged off his resentment toward Germans in general. It was not only unfair but illogical to blame the Germans of Hahn and Wesslin's generation for the monstrous atrocities committed by the Hitler gang. Wesslin and Hahn and millions of other Germans had only been small children thirty years ago. To mark them with "original sin" would be the height of injustice. Children should not be forced to pay for the sins of their fathers.

The Death Merchant had been all over West Germany, and several times had made secret forays in East Germany—the "German Democratic Republic." His instincts told him that the age-old impulse to find out what made the Germans tick was a voyage of discovery that would take one's ship of search through the most fascinating realm of all: the human personality.

To those who had never visited Germany, the Germans were familiar only through the ridiculous exaggeration of caricature. Within this context the men were bull-necked, brush-cut martinets, the women either buxom, blonde, athletic Brünnhildes or mercurial, statuesque Loreleis. All spent their time eating sausage and drinking beer to the accompaniment of brass bands.

Another concept pictured the German as methodical, and fanatically devoted to authority, ready to give his life, if necessary, to the letter of the law. It was true that this trait, so savagely exploited by the Nazis, had always been characteristic of a nation where inflexible paternal authority had been so deeply etched into the soul that the nation itself became a gigantic father symbol: *Das Vaterland*.

For better or for worse, World War II had undermined this concept on all levels. There was no longer a centralization of complete authority, and the *Beamter*, or petty official, whose career was the dream of every average German, now definitely took a back seat to the worker and the businessman.

116

A German "race"? Germany was a vast conglomeration of racial types—Bavarian highlanders, Berlin sophisticates, Rühr proletarians and Baltic farmers. One can still find German *hausfrauen* for whom *Kirche, Kinder* and *Küche* (church, children, and kitchen) were the proper and moral things of life. But the majority of Germans had emancipated themselves from this old-fashioned view. Collectively, there was one thing the Germans did not want: *another war.*

19.40 hours. The helicopter put down at the American military section of Frankfurt on the Main's airport, and since the pilot had radioed ahead, several cars were waiting, silent BND drivers behind the steering wheels. Surprisingly, the night was not any colder than when they had left Bonn, and there was little snow in evidence.

"We'll go to one of our security houses and check in," Hahn said to Camellion after they had settled in the back of a Mercedes. "We'll have dinner at the Kupferpfanne, then have a long questioning session with Herr Heusinger and his frau."

"It will be at least ten by the time we get to the Hausingers," the Death Merchant said, his eyes darting through the rolled-up windows. He felt better now that he was properly dressed. While in the chopper, he had opened one of the metal cases and he now carried two 9mm Browning autoloaders in shoulder holsters.

"The Heusingers don't have anything to say about when we question them," Hahn said in clipped tones and turned down the fur collar of his black-leather trench coat. "In matters of national security, the BND has complete authority."

The driver left the airport and turned the car onto the highway that led to the Bockenheimer Landstrasse, one of the main thoroughfares of Frankfurt.

Hahn explained that Frankfurt was famous as the birthplace and home of Wolfgang von Goethe, and that there were many ironies connected with the ancient city, so old that Charlemagne had lived there in 794.

"The American bombings during the war completely destroyed the medieval part of the Altstadt, the Old Town. But the bombs missed the two most obvious targets: the huge offices of I.G. Farben and the industrial suburb of

Höchst. The I.G. Farben *Hochhaus* is now the US military headquarters in Frankfurt. Hitler would turn over twice in hell if he knew it."

They continued the ride in silence, the Death Merchant watching the passing cars and the bright lights of the highway. The BND driver of the Mercedes in which Camellion rode didn't waste any time. The car was soon on the Bockenheimer Landstrasse, the second car right behind it. Another ten minutes and the two vehicles were slowly crossing the Römerberg, a medieval square. The cars swung to the left and headed west on the Untermain Kai, which was not a *kai*, or wharf, at all, but a two-lane highway. Close by to the south was the Main River, a black, winding ribbon of darkness except for the myriad lights from boats.

A few more minutes and the two cars passed the Römer—to the left and to the south—the ancient town hall that had three Gothic gables, and for centuries had been both town hall and a memorial landmark.

"Our *Sicherheit Haus* is on the Hanauer Landstrasse," Hahn said. "The Heusingers live on the Hedderich Strasse across the river."

The BND Security House was a three-story monstrosity of stone set far back behind a tall, iron fence adorned with scrolls and other ornamental work. Camellion thought of the World-War-II movies he had seen, and of how victims had been taken to grim buildings that housed the *Gestapo*, always Gothic structures like the one behind the fence.

"Leave your coats on," Hahn said. "We won't be inside that long."

Checking in consisted of Hahn's writing a brief message that would be sent to Bonn by radio, and of taking the luggage of Camellion and the two CIA men upstairs to three different rooms.

They left the *Sicherheit Haus* and again got into the two big automobiles. This time the drivers headed west, once more driving as if they were trying to keep seconds ahead of the end of the world. Gradually, however, the drivers slowed as they neared the heavy traffic of the Altstadt.

At length they were on the Neue Mainzer Strasse and approaching the Kupferpfanne, one of the top eating places in Frankfurt. Actually the "Copper Pancake" was a part of the café on Opernplatz, with the main entrance to the pancake section on Neue Mainzer Strasse. The place was expensive; but its prices were still half of what one would pay in a second-rate restaurant in Chicago or some other large US city.

Even after he was seated, Camellion felt edgy and anxious for action. He forced himself to be patient. He had dealt previously with the West German *Bundesnachrichtendienst* and knew from experience that Germans, because of their methodical nature, were not a people who could be pressured into hurrying.

Otto Wesslin, seated next to Camellion, leaned toward him and said, "The *helles* is the light beer, the *dunkles* the dark. The dark is the best."

Camellion was further irked by where they were seated, and the soft lights, music and babble of voices and laughter from the several hundred diners didn't do anything to lessen his feeling of being exposed. He, Chasteen, Wesslin and one of the drivers—a burly man whose eyes kept moving over the crowd—were seated at one table. At the next table were Hahn, Reeder and the second driver, the last of whom sat with his back toward the driver at Camellion's table, an arrangement that permitted the two BND agents to watch all avenues of approach. But still not good enough for the Death Merchant, who didn't believe in halfway security measures.

Who could say that the Brotherhood didn't have informers within the BND? Who could say that the Brotherhood wouldn't try to turn them into a pile of ashes? An H-bomb could compress about 200 pounds of fuel into a teaspoonful of space. The Transmutationizer could reduce a 200-pound man into a pile of ashes and, just maybe, on a large scale, whole nations. The thought was mind-boggling. . . .

Camellion did enjoy the meal—*Hase im Topf*, a sublime rabbit *paté*, dumplings, cabbage, Brunswick asparagus and, for dessert, *Schwärzwalder Kirschtorte*, a Black Forest cherry cake, all washed down with *dunkles* beer and several cups of black coffee.

Nonetheless, a feeling of security did not return to Camellion until he and the others had left the Copper Pancake and were driving toward the Main River.

A talkative man, who knew how to make his points, Hahn began telling Camellion and Chasteen how Germany had changed since the war. The old war spirit was a thing of the past and the people had a "feeling for democracy." *Until the next madman starts beating a drum!* thought Camellion.

"I'll tell you another thing," Hahn said. "The younger Germans didn't cause the war and they don't feel any guilt over Hitler. No one in his right mind can condone the killing of millions of people, but the Israelis are running that 'holocaust' thing into the ground. In my opinion, the Israelis and the United States are making an enormous mistake in not dealing with the Palestinians. Why, you Americans are paying four hundred percent more for oil just so the Jews can have their Wailing Wall. Such stupidity is going to lead to another war."

"What can you expect from an administration that claims rabbits can swim and hiss?" laughed Chasteen. "The next thing you know, we'll be told that snakes can hop and that elephants *do* fly!"

Camellion only said, "How much farther to the Heusingers?"

"Not far," replied Hahn. "We're coming to the bridge now."

The Mercedes rolled over the *Unter-Main Brücke* (although "Under" the "Main Bridge" went over the river, not under it) and entered the mouth of the Schweizer Strasse.

"Everything is changing, all over the world," Chasteen said, breaking the short silence. "Everything is going to pot, even religion."

"Oh?" Hahn responded politely.

"Sure, even nuns can date nowadays," said Chasteen with a chuckle. "Of course, they have to wear a cross-your-heart bra and no-nonsense pantyhose. . . ."

Chapter Nine

The afternoon of the next day.
14.10 hours.

There had been an invisible passenger aboard the helicopter during the flight from Frankfurt to Munich—dejection, generated by the questioning session with Herr Heusinger—which could not be dispelled.

Gunther Heusinger had answered all of the questions put to him by Hahn and Camellion, but he had not known anything of value pertaining to Professor Helmut Koerber.

He had admitted he had been one of Koerber's assistants and worked in his laboratory in Dusseldorf. And the nature of the experiments? Heusinger didn't really know. Koerber had been a very suspicious, secretive man, and with SS men all over the place, no one was going to ask any questions.

"Each technician worked on a specific part," Heusinger had said, "but none of us knew the entire plan of the project. All we knew was that the experiment needed a large source of electrical power. Our power source came directly from the generating station on the Rhine. All we knew was that the project had something to do with electromagnetism. We had to work with giant magnetohydrodynamic generators and various kinds of magnetoresistors."

At this point, Gunther Heusinger had begun to sob and tremble, and so had Hilda Heusinger, his wife.

"We even experimented with people," Heusinger had confessed in shame. "Men, women and even children that the SS brought from concentration camps."

121

What kind of experiments?

Heusinger confessed that sometimes individuals were used, other times groups. The pathetic victims were made to stand some fifty feet in front of a strange-looking machine. "When the machine was turned on," Heusinger said, "they caught fire! They suddenly burst into flames! Clothes, flesh, everything burned!" Heusinger's voice had risen in horror. "They burned so fast they didn't even have time to scream."

"Until nothing was left of the body but ashes?" Camellion had asked.

Heusinger had been surprised by the question. *"Nein, asche nicht."* ("No, not ashes.") In a low voice burdened with age, the 67-year-old Heusinger had explained that the bodies were charred to the extent that they could be recognized only as corpses belonging to the human species.

How large was the machine that caused the burning? What did it look like?

"Part of it was a metal tube suspended from the ceiling," Heusinger had said. "It was easily twenty feet long, and tilted so that its needle point was directed at the people to be burned. But the tube was only part of the device, the 'barrel' you might say. The power came from magnetohydrodynamic generators. I think there were seventeen of them."

The experiment had come to a sudden end when Allied bombers destroyed the Dusseldorf power station and Helmut Koerber's laboratory—both in the same air raid, six months before the end of the war. By then, Hitler had appointed Himmler head of the German Army that was trying to halt the Russian steamroller advancing across Eastern Europe, a job for which the *Reichsführer-SS* was ill-equipped. Even if he had been a military genius, he wouldn't have had time for any of his pet projects. The technicians who had assisted Professor Koerber, including Gunther Heusinger, were drafted into the *Volkssturm*, the Home Guard. For all practical purposes, the project was ended.

"It was madness!" Heusinger had cried. "Some of the Home Guard were as old as seventy. Others were just children, as young as twelve, from the Hitler Youth. Sheer madness. . . ."

Klaus Hahn had not been verbally gentle with either Herr or Frau Heusinger. "Why didn't you tell us all this the first time we mentioned Koerber, when we placed you under protective custody?"

The Heusingers had confessed that fear had sealed their tongues. That first time, hearing the mention of Helmut Koerber's name, they suspected that Koerber had perfected his diabolical device within the past thirty years. Gunther Heusinger was also afraid that if he had told the full truth, he would have been indicted for murder because he had assisted in an experiment that had murdered almost 500 human beings. Now, they had decided to tell the truth and reveal the terrible secret.

"We could no longer live with what we knew," Frau Heusinger had said.

"You won't be indicted for anything," Otto Wesslin had reassured Herr Heusinger without telling him why, without mentioning that the secret of the device had to be kept from the world.

Camellion, Hahn and the others had spent the night at the BND's *Sicherheit Haus* and the next morning had flown in the helicopter to Munich. Again they had been met at the air terminal by agents of the BND. This time there were five security men and three cars: a Mercedes, a Volksie station wagon and a small Audi.

Deciding to have lunch at the hospital, the group of ten began the long drive to Pullach, a pretty little village eight miles south of Munich.

The hospital, just north of Pullach, was another paradox that would have caused the Nazi hierarchy in hell to grit their teeth in frustration. The hospital buildings had once been one of the SS model estates built in many parts of the Third Reich before the war. The Pullach estate had been built in 1938 and named in honor of the Führer's deputy, Wohngemeinschaft Rudolf Hess. In this and other "racial havens" the black-uniformed SS elite had lived in "pure-blooded" segregation. At one time, the estate had housed Rudolf Hess's staff. After Hess flew to England, Martin Bormann took over the place. High officers of Dachau concentration camp—Dachau, on the Amper River, was a short distance northwest of Munich—had also found the estate pleasant.

Immediately after the war, displaced persons of every nationality took over the estate. These squatters were chased out by the US Quartermaster Corps and Ordnance units; however, it was the land-grabbing US G-2 intelligence which finally acquired the estate. The G-2 turned the complex over to Reinhard Gehlen, who had been one of Hitler's chief intelligence officers. It was at Pullach that the "Gehlen Organization" began working for the newly formed United States Central Intelligence Agency. In 1956, the Gehlen network became the *Bundesnachrichtendienst*, the Federal Intelligence Service, and the estate was turned into a veterans' hospital.

The three cars crossed Stiglmaier Platz and moved onto the Dachauer Strasse. The small party would have to cross all of Munich to get to the highway that would take them to Pullach.

Sitting next to Camellion, Neil Reeder looked toward Otto Wesslin, who was on the other side of the Death Merchant. "I'm kind of curious," Reeder said. "Gustav Hiber wasn't a soldier; yet he's in a veterans' hospital. Or was it because he was in the Home Guard toward the end of the war?"

"Yes, that's it. Because he was in the *Volkssturm*," said Wesslin.

"How long has he been ill and what's his trouble?" Camellion asked.

"His liver. He won't leave the booze alone. Every now and then he has to go into the hospital and get dried out. This time it's serious—cirrhosis. He'll be dead within a year."

"He'll die sooner if the Brotherhood gets to him," Reeder said scornfully.

The driver speeded up; they were now on the open highway, with open spaces becoming more and more numerous, the fir, spruce and pine trees looking like pictures on post cards. Some farm buildings and other structures, on each side of the highway, were medieval in style, the simple late Gothic of village houses. Other structures were boxlike ultramodern—slabs of concrete and a lot of glass.

After a short pause, Camellion said to Wesslin, "I trust Hiber is conscious? If he's in a hepatic coma, we're wasting our time."

"He doesn't have cirrhosis to that extent, not yet," Wesslin said. "We read his medical report. The disease is mild in Hiber. But he's not the type to give up the bottle. He'll be conscious, but I doubt if he tells us anything revealing. How can he? He was only a working-in-the-dark technician like Hammerle and Heusinger and the other assistants. I doubt if he's seen Professor Koerber within the last thirty years."

"We can't totally ignore some of the old Nazi organizations," offered the Death Merchant. "The only flaw in that thesis is that none of them are in existence, with the exception of ODESSA."

Wesslin's voice was quick and final. "They're all kaput—*Die Spinne, Stille Hilfe, Europadienst*—finished. As far as we know, ODESSA is still in operation; yet its purpose is to keep Nazi war criminals in hiding. I'm afraid we have got to do better than that, my American friend."

The Death Merchant did not reply. Wesslin was right—and very often the bad guys won.

A high, white stone wall surrounded the veterans' hospital. At the main entrance there was a large gatehouse the size of a small cottage, both remnants of those days when the complex had housed the Gehlen Organization. Ordinarily there were only two *Wehrmacht* guards on duty at the main gate, but because Gustave Hiber was being guarded inside, three BND agents were also guarding the main entrance, carefully checking each vehicle and its occupants.

As soon as the BND agents—recognizing Hahn and Wesslin—waved the three cars inside, Camellion at once detected the atmosphere of expectancy, reminiscent of the Gehlen days when the function of Wohngemeinschaft Rudolf Hess had been the gathering of intelligence data about Soviet activities in West Germany and in other parts of Europe.

The estate did have the appearance of quiet efficiency. Along the winding roads were brick office buildings and apartment houses, the latter now filled with patients. Toward the rear of the 230,000 square yards of park land, was the long four-story building that was the hospital. Bright afternoon sunshine glittered off patches of snow, but the roads were clear and dry as a bone.

"Are you disappointed, Mr. Hillmeyer?" said Wesslin with a sly smile. "Or is it what you expected?"

125

Feeling that he had detected a condescending note in Wesslin's polite tone, Camellion turned his head slightly and looked at the man. "This is not the first former SS estate I've visited," he said. "I've visited the one in the Grünewald Forest in West Berlin. It's much larger than this estate."

Otto Wesslin's eyes showed just a hint of surprise and his jaw tightened. He recovered his composure instantly and, with a wave of his hand, indicated a group of buildings constructed of glass bricks.

"That first building, the one with the dome. It's the community center. It has a theater and a cinema. The building next to it is the gymnasium. The third building used to be a school for Hitler Youth. It's now used for hydrotherapy treatments."

The German turned and pointed to the left of the car, at a number of detached villas. "Our destination is one of those houses. Herr Hiber is being held in Dr. Wolfgang Pahl's home. Dr. Pahl is chief of radiology.

Neil Reeder's full, round face went sour. "Shouldn't Hiber be in the hospital? You said he'd be dead within a year."

"He's in no immediate danger," Wesslin said stiffly.

Camellion said, "In the early stages of cirrhosis, the only treatment is a high-protein diet, vitamin supplements and total abstinence from booze. I think Herr Wesslin meant that Hiber might be dead within a year if he continued to hit the bottle."

Wesslin brightened. "*Ya*, that is how the doctors explained the prognosis to us."

As the cars drew closer to the wide clapboard houses, they could see that each residence had a large yard with plenty of trees for shade in summer. Hedges were well-trimmed. There were concrete sidewalks in front of each house and three-foot parkways. Now and then, as the vehicle rounded a long curve, Camellion caught glimpses of tarpaulin-covered swimming pools in backyards. The SS had lived well and had enjoyed all the creature comforts.

Wesslin said, "The white house with the blue shutters and the glassed-in front porch. That is Dr. Pahl's house."

Despite the large black-and-yellow sign—*BLEIBEN SIE DRAUSSEN* (KEEP OUT)—the driver of Camellion's car turned into the wide road, drove ahead a hundred feet, then made a left turn. Another hundred feet and the driver pulled over and parked several car lengths ahead of the blue-shuttered house. The other two cars pulled in behind and the men got out onto the sidewalk, a walkie-talkie in Klaus Hahn's hand. He spoke briefly to the BND men inside the house while Camellion and the other men—two of them carrying Heckler & Koch submachine guns—waited.

Hands shoved into the pockets of his overcoat, Camellion looked around. The air had that clean country smell and, besides the fragrance of pine needles, there was the aroma of freshly baked bread. Some hausfrau apparently didn't like commercial bread.

Several cars passed, moving north, the same direction in which the three vehicles were parked by the curb. Down the road, moving south, was a three-axle truck with a two-axle full trailer, the front of the trailer reaching over the cab.

Hahn switched off the walkie-talkie and put it in one of his pockets, and the group started up the sidewalk through the hedges, Camellion on the outside to the left.

The truck came to a sudden stop in the middle of the road.

Camellion and the rest of the men were halfway between the hedge and the closed-in porch. Hearing the screech of brakes, some of the men turned and glanced behind them. So did the Death Merchant—but not out of idle curiosity. The instant he heard the driver slam on the brakes, instinct and intuition exploded in his mind.

"Watch it!" he yelled the warning in German. "It's a trap!" He spun all the way around, his right hand diving underneath his overcoat and suede safari jacket.

"*Donnerwetter!*" snarled Hahn. As he and three other men jumped from the sidewalk and dove to the ground, the man driving the truck thrust the barrel of a submachine gun through the open window of the truck, an eighteen-inch-long noise suppressor attached to the barrel.

Simultaneously, men wearing black insulated coveralls and wool Balaclava face masks, with only the eyes showing, jumped from the rear of the truck, weapons in their hands. Joseph Webber and Paul von Blosser, the two BND agents with H & K machine guns, tried to rake the driver of the truck and the black-clad men to the rear. Neither German agent had a chance. Walther Niedieck, the driver,

127

had the edge and those few vital seconds were on his side.

A long *zzzziittttttttt* sounded from the silenced MPK machine pistol and a stream of 9mm solid-based bullets ripped into Blosser and Webber, the savage blast ripping off small pieces of leather from their coats. Killed as fast as if struck by a bolt of lightning, the two corpses pitched to the ground, their blood quickly coloring the snow.

By this time the Brotherhood gunmen from the rear of the truck were racing to the sidewalk in front of the hedge, some of them carrying Czech Skorpion machine pistols, others Walther P-38s and P-08 Lugers. Hahn, Chasteen and Wesslin, who had thrown themselves to the ground, to the right of the middle sidewalk, had managed to draw their autopistols and were preparing to fire. Otto Wesslin was to the right of the three, down behind a snow drift that resembled a diminutive mountain with a miniature ski slope. The last two BND security agents were prone on each side of the walk.

The Death Merchant, his clothes full of snow, rolled behind a big oak tree, stood up and reached for the Browning Hi-Power autoloader in his right shoulder holster. He had reached the tree just in time. One of the Brotherhood gunmen chanced to spot him and opened fire with a Skorpion machine pistol. The storm of 7.65mm projectiles thudded into the other side of the tree and chipped off a cloud of bark, the *thud-thud-thud* of the slugs cutting into the hard wood simultaneous with the breaking of glass from the left and right sides of the porch as BND agents inside the house opened fire with machine guns. Their streams of flat-nosed projectiles were a river of death that dissolved the driver and scattered the upper half of him all over the cab. But the BND agents inside the house had been too late to save Charles Giebelhausen. A split second before Niedieck died, he managed to cut down on Giebelhausen, stitching him across the middle.

Hahn, Reeder, and Chasteen fired in unison, the roaring of their pistols mingling with the *duddle-duddle-duddle-duddle-duddle* of HK-53 SMGs being fired by the two BND agents from the porch. Four of the black-coveralled attackers, who had almost reached the hedge, jerked from the smashing impact of slugs and went down, one man's Skorpion MP lashing out a long whip of slugs that cut through the hedge and sent up a dozen tiny spurts of snow.

Otto Wesslin, trying to reach the northwest corner of the house, yelled in pain. One of the 7.65mm bullets had ripped across the inside of his left calf, leaving behind a bloody rip half an inch deep. Blood dripping from his leg, Wesslin reached the corner, got down, looked out and jerked back in time to avoid a chain of slugs that struck the corner and sent splinters flying.

Flattened behind the big oak, the Death Merchant calmly bided his time. Taking a calculated risk was part of the game; being foolhardy was only a stupid method for decreasing one's longevity. After all, an ignorant person is one who doesn't know something the next guy learned yesterday. It was the morons who didn't know that bravery was never enough. It was experience, knowhow and timing that counted. Mix well, laugh at the Lord of Light and season with a dash of Fate.

A third submachine gun opened fire from the front porch, which by now had lost all of its glass and been reduced to empty frames. The three HK-53 SMGs sent streams of slugs that chopped into the hedge and punched holes in the metal side of the trailer, but from the loud *zings* of ricochets it was evident that the inside wall of the trailer was covered with armor plate.

Bang! One of the left rear tires exploded and went flat as 9mm Parabellums tore into the rubber. None of the slugs, however, reached any gunmen of the Brotherhood, three of whom were snuggled sideways against the high curb; four more were behind the large wheels of the truck. One of the four then lost his nerve. He left the protection of the right front tire, ran to the rear of the truck and tried to crawl back inside. All he succeeded in doing was getting himself killed. More than a dozen projectiles chopped into his left side, ripped him apart and pitched him to the middle of the road.

Alan Chasteen, a 9mm ASP[1] pistol in each hand, yelled in German to Wilhelm Knoph and Bernhardt Loehrke, the two BND agents on each side of the sidewalk that led to

[1] *Armament Systems and Procedures, Inc.* Definitely not a weapon for combat. It's too big and cannot be used with any kind of rapidity. The Lexan grips are transparent, which gives the shooter an indication of the remaining cartridges in the magazine.

the house. Totally exposed as they were, without any hedges to hide them from gunmen who might be in the cab of the truck, the two agents were wisely lying flat and playing dead.

"Now's your chance," yelled Chasteen. "Get the hell out of there while the men inside the house have the bastards pinned down."

Meanwhile, the Death Merchant saw his opportunity. Realizing that the three streams of machine-gun fire from the house would also cover him, he got down behind the big oak and crawled on his elbows and knees, GI-style, to the thick, three-foot-high hedges. He snuggled down in the snow and waited.

He didn't expect what happened next, nor did the other men. A section toward the left center of the trailer opened, a portion four feet long and one foot high. Through the slot came two feet of long tube, a metal tube four inches in diameter. From the end of the cylinder, set in the center, was a foot-long rod. What looked like a funnel, the mouth turned toward the outside, was at the end of the rod.

There wasn't any sound. There wasn't any beam. But suddenly, Wilhelm Knoph, running in a low crouch toward the northwest corner of the house, became one huge stem of fire, the flame of a dark cobalt blue. From head to foot, he was a pillar of shining blue fire that was obviously not of the ordinary kind. The fire did not flicker or eat upward. Knoph's hat and overcoat, his trousers and shoes, crumbled and turned brown, then black. It was as if Knoph had been cloaked in an intense blue radiance.

"*Der lieber Gott!*" exclaimed Klaus Hahn in horror. With Reeder, Chasteen and Wesslin, he was safe for the moment by the northwest corner of the house. Far different with Bernhardt Loehrke, who was wading through the snow in an effort to get to the corner of the house.

He failed. The invisible beam of the transmutationizer caught him and started the process of fission. Already Knoph had "dissolved" and vanished from inside his clothing, which lay in a pile on the snow.

The *Bundesnachrichtendienst* agents on the shot-apart porch were so startled at the sight of Knoph and Loehrke turned into ghastly preternatural fire that they stopped firing, their spines tingling. This lag time in firing was all the six members of the Brotherhood needed. The three men lying by the curb reared up, saw the column of fire that was Loehrke, looked toward the house and fired bursts at the porch—a total waste of ammo, because during those four or five seconds, the operator of the transmutationizer inside the truck raked the porch with the magnetic beam, moving the weapon from left to right. Almost simultaneously, the three German intelligence agents burned blue, a hideous sight not witnessed by the Death Merchant's group.

"Where's Hillmeyer?" muttered Neil Reeder in a voice that was one-half awe and one-half fear.

"On the other side of the walk," answered Hahn disdainfully. "As far as I know, he hasn't fired a single shot. I think—"

He triggered off two quick shots with his Browning Double Action .45 as one of the gunsels at the curb swung the barrel of his Skorpion Vz61 sub-gun toward the corner of the house. The big .45 slugs chopped into the ski-masked gunman; the impact, with all the power of two sledge hammers, was more than sufficient to pitch him backward to the road.

"Get to the back of the house!" yelled Chasteen, who was stooping to help Wesslin huddled against the side of the house. "We can't fight that burn gadget here in the open."

"Reeder and I will cover you," responded Hahn. "Get going."

"My God!" choked out Reeder, who had risked sticking his head around the corner. "Look at Hillmeyer!"

The time had come. The Death Merchant, knowing that the attention of the enemy was split between the front of the house and the group at the northwest corner, calculated that the odds for living were definitely on his side.

Having taken off his bulky overcoat, wool plaid hat and deerskin gloves, he thumbed off the safety catches of the two Hi-Power Brownings, stood up, jumped over the hedge and charged the truck at an angle, an action totally unexpected by the six members of the Brotherhood.

Albert Buchdrucker was the first to spot the Death Merchant. By the right front wheel of the truck, he tried to swing to his right and bring the stubby barrel of the Skorpion on the tall man in the taupe suede safari jacket. He might as well have tried to prevent the earth from spinning on its axis.

The Browning in Camellion's left hand cracked. Buchdrucker felt only an instant's crucifixion from the 9mm hollowpoint bullet that went through his lower lip, broke off three of his lower teeth, plowed underneath his tongue and tore a bloody hole through his throat and the back of his neck. The Skorpion fell from his hands and he dropped to the ground, blood pumping out of his mouth.

Confusion on the part of the enemy became Camellion's ally. There were two men on the right side of the truck, one by the front corner of the trailer, the second man crouched behind the rear wheels. The two men, hearing the sharp report of Camellion's Browning, jerked their heads to the front of the truck.

The three men by the curb had also been caught with their guard down. While George Steinhauser had the presence of mind to drop flat, Herman Fischer and Ebert Gropius broke under the strain and started to run to the back of the truck, from where Max Weill, who had started to jump from the truck a few moments before the Death Merchant had blown away Albert Buchdrucker, was emerging.

A black metal box was strapped to Weill's back. An identical box was strapped to his chest. Cables, on each side, connected the two boxes; a single coiled cable connected the box in back to the weapon in Weill's hands—the same kind of tube, only smaller, that protruded from the slot on the left side of the trailer. A metal conelike helmet was on Weill's head, rods sticking out from the sides and top.

Weill, too, knew that something was wrong, but he wasn't exactly sure what it was. He hesitated for a moment, hearing Herman Fischer yelling frantically at him, "Behind you! Behind you!"

It requires only a single second to squeeze a trigger and put a bullet into a man or woman. Provided you don't miss. The Death Merchant never did. He didn't now. He was racing by the right side of the cab when he fired both Brownings, pulling each trigger twice. Mingled with the four loud cracks of the Brownings was the sound of autoloaders being fired from the northwest corner of the house.

Ebert Gropius cried out in pain, did a half-turn and fell

to the concrete of the road. He had made the mistake of straightening up and Hahn and Reeder put several slugs into his left rib cage.

By now George Steinhauser was nearly in a panic. Staring at the rear of the truck, he raised the HK-53 SMG and yelled "Get out of the way!" at Herman Fischer and Max Weill. Weill had opened one of the rear doors of the trailer, and he and Fischer were climbing back into the large compartment.

The Death Merchant didn't hesitate after putting to sleep forever the other two men by the right side of the truck. He raced up the right side, charged around the corner of the trailer and saw Weill and Fischer, who were in the process of hoisting themselves onto the bed of the truck. Surprise and unyielding determination flashed over Camellion's face at the sight of the metal boxes strapped to Weill's back and chest; and there was the familiar helmet on the man's head. Far better than he had hoped for.

Only eight feet away was a portable Transmutationizer!

At the same instant that Camellion saw Weill and Fischer, he spotted Steinhauser and the vicious little Skorpion. At that point, even some of the best professionals would not have been able to handle such a tricky kill situation, in which the prime factor was always survival.

Camellion jumped to the left, mentally aimed at Steinhauser and triggered off two shots with the left Browning. With the right Browning, he fired at Weill and at Fischer.

Although terrified by the sudden turn of events, Steinhauser was a good shot. Nonetheless, he had pulled the trigger a fraction of a second after Camellion started to move sideways. The Skorpion shook and chattered, and a dozen 7.65mms streamed past the Death Merchant, several of the slugs cutting slightly through the suede of his right arm. An eye blink later, Steinhauser was well on his way toward being turned into a dead man from Camellion's two bullets. One had bored into his upper chest, severed the left innominate vein and lodged against his backbone. The second hunk of lead had struck him in the lower part of the chest; it had torn through his lung and punched its way out through his back.

The Death Merchant had not missed the targets with his right Browning. A bullet had slammed into Max Weill's right hip, shattered the ilium, then plowed its way through the descending colon and the jejunum, stopping only when it hit the inner side of the left hipbone. With a loud cry of pain and despair, Weill lost his grip and started to fall backward, along with Fisher who had taken a Browning hollow-point in the right buttock. The high velocity projectile had passed through the large gluteus maximus and lodged in the ischium. Feeling his fingers slipping from the wooden floor of the trailer and a trip hammer pounding at his consciousness, Fischer wanted to scream but couldn't find his voice.

It had all happened in eight seconds!

The Death Merchant's luck changed during the ninth second!

As far as Camellion was concerned, there was only one more obstacle to overcome: the operator of the larger Transmutationizer inside the trailer and whoever else might be with him. What he had not counted on was Steinhauser's hatred and amazing physical constitution. The fanatical lover of anything Nazi—he had been in the Hitler Youth—he knew that he was dying; yet he was determined to take the man in the suede coat with him.

Growing weaker by the moment, blood pouring out of his mouth and the world spinning faster and faster around him, Steinhauser found his last bit of strength. With it he triggered off a final burst as he felt himself falling sideways and the velvet darkness dropping over his brain.

Fortunately for Camellion, he detected the movement on the German's part and threw himself back and to his right, almost as far as the rear wheels. None of Steinhauser's projectiles even came close, but four chopped into the dying Herman Fischer, who was falling from the rear of the trailer to the road. Six cut into Weill, who was lying unconscious and dying. Two ripped into his left hip. One hit him in the back of the head. Two more chopped into the box on his back. The final bullet bored through one side of the mechanism strapped to Weill's chest.

"*Schweinerei!*" snarled Camellion. He slammed two more slugs into Steinhauser, and this time he was positive that the man was on *der Weg zur Ewigkeit*—the road to eternity. One of the 9mm bullets had struck the German in the right temple.

Luck had turned its back on the Death Merchant. A

loud humming was coming from the boxes strapped to Weill's chest and back, and thin streaks of crooked lightning were arcing from the boxes on Weill's chest and back to the ends of the rods on the helmet, which had fallen from the German's head. Camellion now saw that the metal helmet was connected to the mechanisms contained in the boxes by means of two small cables.

More and more lightning jumped back and forth, so that the corpse resembled a high-voltage Van de Graaff generator or one of those electrostatic generators teachers used in high school to demonstrate static electricity.

A line from one of Shakespeare's plays raced through the Death Merchant's mind: "Heat not a furnace so hot that it doth consume thyself!"

Still, Camellion had a job to do. *And I don't intend to leave the operator of the other Transmutationizer. There's no way of knowing what he might be able to do with that weapon.*

Glancing at the dead Weill, over whom more and more spiderwebs of blue electricity were jumping, Camellion spun and faced the open door of the trailer.

As he rasied the two Hi-Power Brownings, Felix Schnabel, inside the trailer, reached out to grab the handle of the door in an effort to close it. Behind him stood Emil Heinsheimer, the operator of the larger Transmutationizer, a Walther P-38 in one hand, a Hechler & Koch HK4 pistol in the other.

The Death Merchant, startled to see the beefy Schnabel and the beanpole Heinsheimer, was much faster than the two Germans. At point-blank range, he put two slugs into Schnabel's wide chest, then ducked to let Heinsheimer's two 9mm bullets pass over his head and began pulling the triggers, the explosions of cartridges ringing in his ears. He caught a glimpse of the Transmutationizer, wooden pallets piled in the rear of the trailer and the wide-eyed Emil Heinsheimer trying to get off more shots. Three of the Death Merchant's slugs struck Heinsheimer in the chest; a fourth bored into his stomach. Eyes wide and mouth open, the kraut staggered back, almost falling onto the power pack of the Transmutationizer.

The power pack had been hit by one of Camellion's bullets. One of the high-powered slugs, missing bones in Heinsheimer's chest, had gone all the way through his body and struck the side of the power pack. But, having lost most of its velocity, the bullet only flattened out against the metal.

It was Heinsheimer who caused the damage. The dying German, ashes of defeat bitter in his mouth, fell back against the device, his arms reaching out for support. His right arm slammed against the firing tube and the force of the swing spun the rear end of the tube around. The tube hit the trailer wall, the force of contact moving the firing lever on the side of the tube upward.

The power was turned on.

The Transmutationizer began to hum.

Camellion took the only logical course open to him. He jumped back, turned to his right, dashed across the road and ran a hundred feet into the park land. Feeling that he was in the middle of a science-fiction movie, he threw himself behind a stone bench and looked at the truck. Lightning was jumping from one end of the truck to the other, back and forth from the trailer to the corpse carrying the portable disintegrater. Blue and white lightning formed a crazy pattern, a patchwork of lines of blue and white fire.

There wasn't any explosion.

The truck and corpse of Max Weill began to flicker back and forth, the images getting hazy, then returning to solidity.

"Like 'Star Trek,'" Camellion muttered to himself. "When they're trying to beam someone aboard the *Enterprise* and the subject can't quite make it!"

Several more times the truck and the corpse flickered. *Then both vanished!*

One moment they were there, solid and real. The next instant they were gone.

A slight wind began stirring several hundred pounds of metallic gray ash across the road. . . .

Klaus Hahn was still in a rage over how the guards at the main gate had permitted the truck to enter the hospital grounds. Standing with Camellion on the porch, he watched hospital workers pick up the bodies of dead men from the yard and the road, carrying them to an open-bed truck.

"Those guards—*dummkopf Schreibtischoffziers!*"[2] Hahn said angrily. "And because of their stupidity eight of our men are dead—five nothing more than handfuls of ashes!"

"It was a reasonable mistake," Camellion said briskly, "one that you or I might have made."

A check with the two *Wehrmacht* sentries and the three BND agents revealed that the driver of the truck had carried identification "proving" that he worked for the Kaufmeyer Manufacturing Company in Hannover and had a load of X-ray equipment for the hospital. He had even carried a bill of lading.

The three BND agents had checked the inside of the trailer. They had found nothing but large wooden crates, supposedly filled with the equipment to be delivered. It was not difficult to deduce what had taken place: The crates had been filled not with X-ray equipment but with gunmen of the Brotherhood. Once the truck was on the grounds, the gunmen had stepped out of the specially constructed crates, folded them and set up the Transmutationizers.

The Death Merchant was not concerned how the truck had entered the grounds of the hospital. He chalked it up to experience. To him experience was simply that which enabled him to recognize a mistake when he made it again!

There were more important matters at hand. Camellion put into words what the other men, including Hahn, were thinking. "It's not a coincidence that the Brotherhood attacked us," he said in a businesslike fashion, "and knew when and where to hit us." He stared hard at Hahn, waiting for a reply.

"The truck had to be waiting on the road," Hahn said uneasily. "They had to know that we were coming to the hospital today. They had to know that Hiber is here at Doctor Pahl's home."

"We both know what that means?"

"The leak has to be at headquarters in Bonn," Hahn said.

"What about the pilot and copilot of the helicopter?"

Hahn turned and his gaze locked with Camellion's. "*Nein.* Not Bauer and Witzblenten. They hate the Nazis.

---

[2] Blockhead desk officers.

Bauer's father was executed by the Nazis as a political dissident. Witzblenten is half-Jewish. His family went up the chimney. He was only ten years old when the war ended. He survived because some Catholic nuns hid him in the basement of the school they operated." He stepped closer to the Death Merchant and said in a more confidential tone. "The agents for this investigation are all hand-picked *Haupt-V-Männer* top V-men whose parents or other relatives suffered under Hitler's National Socialist administration. The informer is at general headquarters in Bonn. Or, for that matter, what about Herr Reeder and Herr Chasteen? The CIA isn't exactly composed of saints."

"It's possible," Camellion admitted. "But I don't think so. They were with us all the time. One of them could have passed word to someone, say when they went to the washroom. I think the Brotherhood gunmen lived in Munich. How else could the attack have been arranged so quickly! You radioed Bonn last night, and somebody at Bonn sent a message to the Brotherhood last night."

"That's logical," agreed Hahn. "What to do about the informer is the problem. We can't be letting the Brotherhood know our moves in advance."

"Well, I'm not young enough to know everything," Camellion said. "But singing '*Ich hatt einen Kameraden*' or wringing our hands won't get the job done. Let's get back inside and question Hiber, then pick up the answer from there."

"Very well," Hahn said stiffly. "But I doubt if he knows anything of value."

Turning, they walked through the broken glass, then Camellion opened the front door and went into the living room. Hahn followed, thinking of Camellion's fantastic performance on the road. There was only one man in the world who killed with such incredible ability, a free-lance adventurer who—so it was rumored—sometimes worked for the American Central Intelligence Agency. That man was *Der Tod Kaufmann*—the Death Merchant!

Hahn decided not to say anything to anyone about what he suspected was Herr Hillmeyer's true identity. Why bother? What good would it do?

The enemy bullets that demolished the glass of the porch had also shot out the two windows of the living room.

Maintenance workers from the hospital had covered the openings with fiberboard.

An ambulance had taken Otto Wesslin to the hospital. A Turkish carpet covered the floor. The furniture was upholstered in brocaded materials. Books lined one wall of the room. Yet there was still some glass on the floor.

Neil Reeder sat on a sofa, drinking a cup of coffee and smoking a cigarette.

"Where's Chasteen?" Camellion asked, unbuttoning his suede coat.

"He's in the kitchen, getting a cup of coffee," Reeder said. He stood up and looked at Hahn. "One of your men came out of the bedroom and said that Hiber could be questioned anytime."

Hahn glanced over at Chasteen, who had just entered the living room from the rear, a cup of coffee in his hand.

"Let's go question Hiber," Hahn said.

The questioning of the gaunt, bony-faced Gustav Hiber lasted almost an hour. Propped up with pillows and speaking in a weak voice, the old man, who couldn't have weighed more than 110 pounds, only confirmed the story that Gunther Heusinger had told: Professor Helmut Koerber was a brilliant but remote man. He had never been friendly with his assistants and never discussed his personal life.

"What can you tell us about his friends?" asked the Death Merchant, who sat backward on a chair, his chin on top of the chair's back. "Could you give us their names?"

"He didn't have any friends," replied Hiber, speaking in German. "At least none that ever came to the laboratory in Dusseldorf. Wait!" Hiber became excited. "I do remember one man. I remember him because of the SS colonel's uniform he always wore."

Camellion sat up straight and exchanged a quick glance with Hahn.

"His name?" demanded Hahn. "Give us his name."

Hiber rubbed a clawlike hand across his bony chin and thought for a long moment. "Let me think. I believe he was of the nobility, a Baron someone said. I can't remember his name. I can tell you what he looked like. He was a tall man in his thirties, with one of those stupid dueling scars on his right cheek. Today, he'd be about sixty-nine or seventy, if he's still alive."

"That's not much help," Chasteen said in disgust.

"Think, man!" said Camellion. "Try to think of his name."

"I can't remember it," Hiber said plaintively. "All I know is that he was a wealthy big shot and owned a mansion in Berlin. After the lab was bombed and the experiments halted, I heard that the OKW set up headquarters at the same house. This was much later, toward the end of the war. I recall that I remembered the house because I associated the place with Professor Koerber's friend—the Baron. I'm not sure he was a Baron, but it seems that someone told me he was. I wish I could remember his name, but I can't."

The Death Merchant and the other men smiled. Finding out the name of the house would be a simple matter. Preventing the Brotherhood from learning what they were doing was something else again.

Without giving any explanations to Reeder and Chasteen, Camellion and Hahn held a conference in the Volksie station wagon. Both men sat huddled in the back seat.

"The *Oberkommando der Wehrmacht*[3] was headquartered in the Spandau district of Berlin," Camellion said. "It was called Maybach One. Fortunately, it's in the Allied zone, in the British sector of Berlin. It's a gamble. We can't be sure that Koerber is holed up at the house or Maybach One."

"Hitler's bunker was south of the Tiergarten, between Voss Strasse and the Unter Den Linden," Hahn said, and looked thoughtfully at the end of his cigarette. "So what? It's not a question of finding the house, but how to go about it without Bonn finding out."

The Death Merchant's voice was low and sly. "How many BND agents in West Berlin would you personally trust?"

"Maybe a dozen." Hahn's voice was tinged with curiosity. "Why? What do you have in mind?"

"A scheme that will outwit the informer in Bonn for a

[3] The OKW. The High Command of the German Armed Forces.

140

few days, but only if you're sure you can trust the BND boys in West Berlin." Camellion watched Hahn's eyes for signals. "But I must warn you, should we fail you might be dismissed from the Federal Intelligence Service."

"I don't think so," opined Hahn, "not after I explain to my superiors about the informer. They have never accepted difficulty as an excuse for failure."

"Nor do mine."

Camellion waited. Hahn crushed out his cigarette in an ashtray on the side of the door.

"It takes less time to do a thing right than to explain why you did it wrong," he said with a touch of grimness. "Tell me your plan, Herr Hillmeyer."

Chapter Ten

After the Westland Commando helicopter landed at Tempelhof Airport in Berlin, there was a delay. The unauthorized landing demanded an explanation. US Air Force security men marched Camellion and his companions to the Commandant's office.

Out of sheer necessity, Camellion and Hahn had confided the plan to Neil Reeder and Otto Wesslin—to Wesslin because he had insisted on flying to West Berlin with the others, since the wound in his leg was not serious.

In the Commandant's office, Reeder and Chasteen explained to Major Edward Brown that they were CIA officers and that the landing had been necessary.

"That's all we can tell you, Major," Chasteen said. "For verification, radio the Embassy in Bonn. I can tell you right now that the Air Force attaché there will order you to let us proceed."

"We'll furnish the code you're to use," Reeder said, "and give you the code word that will identify us to the Embassy."

"The utmost speed is necessary," Camellion said.

Major Brown, the Commandant of Tempelhof, looked each man up and down, his expression one of resentment. He might as well have said: "Damned Spooks! Coming here with their cloak-and-dagger bullshit." On the other hand, if he didn't cooperate, he might end up a captain stationed in Alaska.

"Very well, gentlemen," he finally said. "We'll contact the American Embassy in Bonn." To let them know he had

142

the authority, he added, "You had better be telling the truth."

An hour and twenty minutes later, the Death Merchant and his four companions were in a Chevy Caprice wagon—borrowed from Major Brown—on the Gneisenau Strasse, with Hahn behind the steering wheel. Their destination was the Kurfurstendamm, the "Fifth Avenue" of Berlin. Specifically, they were headed for an apartment house on one of the small streets off the Kurfurstendamm. The *Bundesnachrichtendienst* owned the apartment house and used the entire top floor, the seventh, as a radio watchstation that monitored the air waves from East Berlin, and Eastern Europe.

"A few days at the most is all we have," Wesslin said as the car sped northwest. "By then the head office in Bonn is sure to become suspicious and start asking questions we won't be able to answer."

"A few days is all we need," Camellion said.

Hahn sounded cheerful. "I'll send a radio message tonight that we've arrived in Nuremberg on schedule, but picked up information that necessitates our flying on to Kassel. Hopefully the informer will pass the information on to the Brotherhood, who'll think we're running around in circles. All—"

Hahn stopped abruptly, noticing that Reeder, sitting in the front seat on the outside, had given a start.

"What's the matter?" asked Hahn.

"The front of that wrecked building we just passed," exclaimed Reeder, as if aghast. "It looks like it's been that way since World War Two."

"It has," Hahn said with a slight laugh. "That amputated fragment of facade we just passed used to be Weiner's Department Store. Not all of Berlin has been cleaned up. Visitors really get a surprise when they discover that some of the 'war memorials' are still around."

Speaking English, Wesslin said, "Goethe once made the remark that Berliners were *ein verwegener Menschenschlag*—'a dauntless breed.' I think he would have applied that phrase to the women of Berlin if he could have seen them work after the war. My own mother was one of them. She and thousands of others worked virtually without tools, clearing away the rubble. During those days, the population of Berlin was seventy-percent female. I barely remember it, but *Gott!* It was terrible."

"*Ya*, those Berlin women had a gift for survival in adversity," agreed Hahn. "A lot of them have survived to this day, a society of *alte Tanten*, old aunts, who can remember having once been Amazons."

From the back seat, Camellion said to Reeder, "Neil, many of the ruins we'll see have been left there on purpose, left standing as a *Mahnmal*, a warning, to posterity."

Otto Wesslin laughed. "*Ya*, the moral is: 'Don't start a war you can't win. You'll be bombed.' "

The ride continued in silence, each man with his own thoughts, the Death Merchant remembering with nostalgia the time he had escaped from East Berlin into West Berlin, using a Russian tank to shoot his way through to Checkpoint Charlie on the Friedrichstrasse.

Checkpoint Charlie was still there. And so was the Wall, the concrete barrier, averaging 12 feet in height, that separated Communist East Berlin from Democratic West Berlin, dividing Communist prisoners from free Berliners. But there was more than the Wall. On the eastern side of the modern Wall was a strip of open ground filled with tank barriers, and beyond that several electrified-wire fences. Beyond the fences, a strip of land mines. At intervals, concrete watchtowers sprang from the ground like dirty gray tulips. Three or four men in each tower, dressed in gray uniforms reminiscent of the old *Feldgrau* of the *Wehrmacht*, were constantly busy surveying the terrain through field glasses, like conscientious lifeguards at a very dangerous beach.

But Berliners, whether on the east or the west side of the Wall, had had more than thirty years to learn how to live with this schizoid barrier. They went about their daily lives indifferent to the Wall, oblivious of the guns and the guards. Only tourists came by the busload to stare at the Wall. "Like dumb cows staring at a new barn door," a Berliner had once told Camellion.

First-time visitors were also surprised to find that, instead of being that cramped, embattled outpost they expected to find, West Berlin was as comfortable as an old sock. Beyond the crowded neighborhoods at the center of the city, West Berlin is actually a community of suburbs, or a collection of towns and villages, each very different from the next and held together by the steel network of its superbly functioning trains and buses. The outer city is astonishingly green and generously endowed with parks, lakes and forests that go on and on, seemingly without end.

A thin smile crept across the Death Merchant's face. *The hell with nostalgia. Yeah, that's what nostalgia is: Longing for a place you wouldn't move back to.*

Forty-five minutes later, Camellion and the others were on the seventh floor of Number 2146 Arndt Strasse, and Hahn was introducing him and Reeder and Chasteen to Major Karl Schwitters, the *Haupt-V-Mann* of the BND station. Close to 65 years of age, Schwitters was of medium height, with his torso longer than his legs. He had a full face, but a receding chin and squinty eyes. His mouth was thin and nervous, his skin pale, sagging and somewhat spongy. His voice was husky as he acknowledged Camellion and the two other men.

The introductions over, Hahn said, "Karl, we must talk to you. It is vitally important."

"Major Schwitters, is this room safe to talk in?" Camellion asked.

Schwitters smiled and motioned for Camellion and the other men to sit down.

"Mr. Hillmeyer, you Americans won the war, but we Germans can still teach you a thing or two about security," he said in a not unfriendly tone. "We were old hands at intelligence when your Colonists were fighting the American Indians. *Ya*, we can talk here; there are no bugs." Finished with Camellion, he looked at Hahn.

While Hahn explained the overall situation to Major Schwitters, the Death Merchant thought of how Schwitters spoke in *Berlinerisch*. There was an amazing ruthlessness with which local Berliners murdered conventional High German.

High German was bad enough. The language was an abstraction. German had words for philosophy and romantic poetry, but not for music, in spite of Bach, Brahms and Beethoven. The cultural words were all derived from Latin words. And the grammar. *When you start a sentence in German,* mused Camellion, *you have to know at the beginning what the end will be. In English, you live the sentence through to its end. Emotion and thought go together; in German, they're divorced. Everything is abstract.*

Camellion did not interrupt as Hahn and Schwitters talked; to do so would have been impolite. Wise in the ways of world cultures, Camellion also reflected on another German trait: the passion for *Ordnung,* order.

Without being obvious, the Death Merchant looked around the office, which reflected this passion for order and indicated that Major Karl Schwitters was of the *ahlt Kultur,* the old culture, in which everything had its place.

The room was large but spartan. There were easy chairs on the oak floor. Everything was just so on Schwitters's desk, including the six telephones that rested side by side. A large detailed map of East and West Berlin was on one yellow-beige wall. On the opposite wall hung a long photograph of a group of World War II *Wehrmacht* officers, all members of the staff of Colonel General Gotthard Heinrici, the German Army General who had defended Berlin against the Red Army. Karl Schwitters had been a captain on Heinrici's staff.

Schwitters sat quietly and listened to Hahn explain the final part of the plan: "Once we've identified the man who owned the estate where the OKW were headquartered during the final days of the war, we'll inspect the house and the underground fortifications, if they still exist. It's the only lead we have."

"By 'inspect' you mean, of course, a surreptitious attack," Schwitters intoned, tilting back his head, "without the authority of the *Haupt-Amt* in Bonn."

"We can't inform the head office," Hahn said bluntly. "I have told you why, Karl. There's an informer in the top section. There isn't anything more I can say. Either you and your *V-Männer* at this station will help or you will not."

Neil Reeder looked as if he might speak. Camellion silenced him with a very slight shake of his head.

Schwitters frowned from Hahn to Wesslin, his expression severe.

"I could report this to Bonn right now. You are asking me and the men of this station to violate direct orders."

Hahn didn't tiptoe around excuses. "*Ya,* that is exactly what I am asking you to do."

Schwitters, his elbows raised on the arms of the chair, tapped his fingers together for several moments. He then got up, walked over to his desk and pressed one of the buttons on the panel.

No one spoke. Camellion got up and moved the heavy chair a foot to the right, watching Schwitters from the corner of his eye. He noticed how the German had viewed him with distaste over his violation of social mores by moving the chair. To Germans of the old school, it was impolite to change the position of one's chair, which explained why most German furniture is so heavy. To a German, light furniture is considered worthless, not only because it is flimsy but because people can move it easily. To move it destroys order and intrudes on the "private sphere."

The perceptive Hahn looked slyly at Camellion and smiled very faintly, signaling that he realized Camellion was testing Schwitters.

Little sparks of worry flickered in Camellion's mind. Hahn and Wesslin were extremely intelligent. The other BND officers were not fools. *Should we get lucky and find one of the Transmutationizers, what's to prevent the BND from taking over? They could neutralize me, Reeder and Chasteen, and no one would be the wiser. Suppose the leak in Bonn is a KGB mole?*

There were no answers. All Camellion could do was play it by ear. . . .

A tall, husky young man, wearing a white turtleneck sweater and salt-and-pepper trousers, opened the door, walked into the office and looked at Major Schwitters. "Yes sir, Herr Major."

"This is Albert Kaufmann," Schwitters explained. "He's our expert in research."

Kaufmann nodded politely. "I do my best."

"Albert, I went you to go through the files and bring me anything available on Hitler's OKW headquarters that was in Spandau," Schwitters said. "It could be listed under *M*, since it was coded Maybach One."

"Do you want anything specific?"

"The headquarters was located on the estate of a wealthy nobleman," Schwitters said. "He was in the SS, so he must have belonged to the Party. I want the name of the man. I want to know if he is still alive. I want to know all about him and the underground complex that was OKW head-quarters."

"It is possible that the Berlin police might have that in-formation. If the subject is engaged in any illegal activity, the regular police might have heard rumors," Kaufmann said seriously. "They have any number of informers in the pubs and taverns."

"Nein! You are not to make inquiries of the outside au-thorities," Schwitters ordered in a sharp tone. "This entire matter is top secret. I don't want you to even mention this to the other men of the station. I'll attend to that myself."

"I understand," Kaufmann said, only his eyes registering expression. "But it might take the rest of the afternoon to get the information, perhaps longer."

"Don't concern yourself about the time; just get that in-formation." Schwitters paused and thought for a moment. "How many other men are in the station?"

"Kurst, Hirschfeld and Hein, sir. Shall I send them in?"

"Yes. You may go."

It was 19.00 hours, and the Death Merchant and the rest of the men were having dinner that Schwitters had ordered from the restaurant on the ground floor of the building. The bratwurst and dumplings were washed down with *Berliner Weisse mit Schuss* (Berlin white beer with a dash of raspberry syrup). It was toward the end of the meal when Albert Kaufmann came into the office, a thick green folder under each arm.

Major Schwitters wiped his fingers on a napkin and looked pleased as Kaufmann placed the folders on one side of the desk. "Very good work, Albert. I thought it would take longer."

"I found what we needed under the Active Nazi file," Kaufmann explained. "I assumed that the subject might still be actively engaged in political activity of a doubtful nature." He tapped the top folder. "The man you want is Baron Fredrich von Hammerstein-Equord. He is sixty-nine years old and living on his estate close to the Tegeler For-est. Until the early 1970s, he published *Kampfverlag*, a weekly newspaper that praised the glories of Hitler's Na-tional Socialism."

"Ya, I remember that damned paper," growled Schwit-

ters. "It went out of business, finally, for lack of subscribers."

Speaking rapid German, the Death Merchant asked Kaufmann, "How about Maybach One? Is it still intact? What's happened to it?"

"The files show that the underground rooms are still there, half a mile north of the main house," Kaufmann replied. "At one time, Herr Gehlen was contemplating using the complex as a Berlin station, but nothing ever came of the plan. All sorts of diagrams and blueprints are in the folder."

Major Schwitters dismissed Kaufmann, and the men finished eating, after which they gathered around a conference table in another room where Schwitters spread out a detailed map of the Spandau section of Berlin and the various diagrams of Maybach I. There were also a dozen different photographs of Baron Fredrich von Hammerstein-Equord's ancestral home, a large imposing mansion, a massive, ornate affair with rows of oversized columns along its front.

Maybach I, the headquarters of OKW during the last days of the war, was a heterogeneous mixture of underground bunkers. There was a large radio room, a map room, areas for generators and air purification machinery, a telephone exchange, underground barracks for regular soldiers, officers' quarters, rooms for secretaries, kitchens, mess halls, toilets and a large water tank. One large square was marked ZEUGHAUS: Arsenal.

The entire complex was thirty feet underground, or, rather, the top of the ten-foot-thick ceiling was thirty feet underground. The outer walls also had ten feet of reinforced concrete.

"Only two entrances," said Neil Reeder worriedly, leaning over the table. "The main entrance at the north side and an emergency exit at the south end. It would take an H-bomb to shake up that place."

Chasteen put in, "And twenty air vents, the top openings disguised in various ways." He glanced across the table at the Death Merchant. "There's all kinds of gas we could drop down those air vents."

"It's almost a certainty they'll have alarms all over the place," Otto Wesslin reminded everyone, "and if they have any of those 'disintegrators' down there, who knows what could happen?"

149

Major Schwitters, smoking a thin cigar, was solemn, almost pious.

"Each entrance is armored. It would be impossible to get in either entrance without someone below being aware of it. It can't be done. We'll have to use explosives and crash in. They could destroy any of the 'burn' devices before we could get to them—or turn us into a handful of ashes." He drew himself up straight and stared at Hahn and Camellion. "Needless to say, I still find your story incredible."

"Truth is often far stranger than fiction, Major," the Death Merchant said. "The miracle of today becomes commonplace tomorrow."

Hahn remained silent, his face alive with disappointment and worry. Earlier, before dinner, he had sent a coded radio message to the *Haupt-Amt* of the *Bundesnachrichtendienst* in Bonn. The head office had demanded more information and had asked for a detailed report why he and the others were going to fly to Kassel. Hahn had stalled, replying that he would send the report the next afternoon.

"Bonn has already demanded an explanation," Hahn said at length. "The informer—and he has to be connected with the main office—might be suspicious. He could have sent a warning to Koerber and the Baron. They could be waiting for us, or on the run. At least Koerber. I think the Baron would sit tight."

"That's not the greatest danger at the moment," Wesslin said. "If Bonn shoots off a message to the station in Nuremberg, it will be a direct tipoff to the informer that we're up to something. When the station in Nuremberg replies that we're not there . . ." He let his voice trail off into oblivion.

"As I see it, we don't have the manpower for any kind of strike," Neil Reeder said. He placed his hand on one of the diagrams. "Look at the size of that underground deal. Hell, it's half a block square. That's only half the problem. We'd have to invade the house at the same time we hit the underground rooms. Why, damn it! We don't have any hard evidence that Professor Koerber is at the mansion. That drunk Hiber might have have a memory foulup for all we know."

"But we do know he's in Berlin," Hahn said quickly. "He can't fly out and he's not going over to the Reds. What better place than Baron Hammerstein-Equord's home?"

The Death Merchant licked his upper lip, stood up straight and said to all of them, "We can't make any moves until we discuss the situation with the British. Spandau is in their sector and they have top-notch security."

"Yeah, the limeys have Tegel Airport[1] to worry about," said Chasteen. "And they're fanatics about some nutty Nazi group trying to break Hess out of Spandau Prison."

The Death Merchant fixed his eyes on Major Schwitters. "Major, I suggest you phone the Commandant of the British Sector and tell him it's imperative that we confer with him. Tell him that it's a matter of vital security to his own nation."

Annoyed, Schwitters exhaled loudly and stared a long moment at the Death Merchant. Then he said, "I suppose you think the British will help us go charging in like your American cowboys?"

"That's right, pardner!" Camellion looked straight into the German's eyes. "SIS will see to it—at dawn tomorrow morning."

Major Schwitters walked across the room and picked up a phone.

[1] Tempelhof is kept open for military flights and emergencies. Tegel Airport opened in 1975 and, designed to handle five million passengers a year, is West Berlin's only civil airport.

Chapter Eleven

A cold, stiff wind blew powdery snow from the trees in the Tegeler Forest, the red-orange sun of dawn poking through the lower branches and glinting brightly on the flying snow.

From the positions of Camellion, Hahn, Reeder and the other men, it was apparent that Baron von Hammerstein-Equord's estate—that is, the north part—bordered on the south end of the Tegeler Forest. All around them were fir, linden and oak trees, but the area was totally devoid of human habitation. It was difficult to believe that all this woodland was actually a part of West Berlin. Even the air smelled fresh and untouched by man-made pollution.

In the rear of the enclosed British personnel carrier, the Death Merchant again analyzed the plan that he, Major Schwitters and Colonel Donald Winston, the Commander of the British Sector of West Berlin, had formulated.

Major Schwitters, six BND agents, ten British soldiers and Gordon Sims, a British SIS agent, would invade the mansion. At the same zero hour, the Death Merchant, Hahn, Reeder, Wesslin, Chasteen and twenty British soldiers would attack the underground complex. Two SIS agents would accompany the force which, technically, was being led by Captain Harold Cresson.

Like the other men, Camellion wore insulated coveralls, laced British combat boots and a black riot helmet with a full-face protector. There the similarity between Camellion and the British ended. Under the coveralls he wore a Second Chance bulletproof vest that protected his chest and

152

back. Alan Chasteen and Neil Reeder wore similar vests.

The American's weapons were different from the weapons carried by the British and by the Germans. The Death Merchant carried two Custom Model 200/International AutoMags with .41 Magnum barrel extensions, as well as one of the three submachine guns he had packed in one of the metal cases. An ugly little weapon, the revolutionary-type chatterbox was called the Sidewinder. It was light, well-balanced and didn't climb the target when fired.

Bascially what the Germans would call a *Volkssturm* weapon, a people's gun, the Sidewinder was 17 inches long with its telescoping stock retracted and 21 inches with the stock extended. The barrel was 9 inches and sat completely within the receiver, with the exception of the muzzle. The sidewinder was a perfect one-hand weapon for close-in attack work. The SS-1 model contained a magazine that carried 32 rounds of 9mm parabellum cartridges.

Neil Reeder and Alan Chasteen also carried Sidewinders and two 9mm Hi-Power Brownings. Neither man seemed the least bit nervous about the attack only half an hour away.

The British were armed with Webley MK-IV revolvers and Patchett/Sterling MK-V machine guns.

The Germans carried Heckler & Koch MP-5 machine guns and BDA semiautomatic pistols, preferring the Browning Double Action weapon to the Walther P-38, the standard sidearm of the West German Army. A large, burly, military-type autopistol, the BDA was one of the most advanced autoloaders in the world. Watching Klaus Hahn shove full magazines into the two BDAs he carried, the Death Merchant was not the least bit surpised that the Germans preferred the BDAs over the less reliable P-38s. After all, the BDA was almost a German weapon, since it employed the Sig-Sauer System and was manufactured in West Germany.

Camellion looked at his wristwatch, a Heuer chronograph: 06.30 hours. He turned to the other men in the personnel carrier. Included in the small group was Edward Tolson, a British SIS agent, a short-bearded man in his forties who looked uncomfortable and unhappy.

"It's six-thirty," Camellion said. "Let's get out of here."

Sidewinder in his right hand, he moved to the oval-shaped hatch.

Once outside, Camellion and the others saw that Captain Cresson and the twenty British regulars were getting out of the other two personnel carriers.

Camellion walked through the snow on the road and was soon talking to Captain Harold Cresson, who was a portly middle-aged officer. He had been in his late teens when he enlisted in the British Army during World War II, and Camellion compared him to a Model-T trying to compete in the time trials of the Indianapolis 500.

Cresson tried to sound calm and professional. "Hillmeyer, is your group all set to go?" he asked in a crisp voice, the cold air turning his breath to steam.

"Anytime, Captain." Camellion looked at the British soldiers, all young. Only a few had ever been under fire, in North Ireland. *About as useless as a meeting of the United Nations!* Camellion thought. "Choose the men you want, and keep in mind we're up against fanatics."

"I think I know my job, Mr. Hillmeyer," Cresson said stiffly, then began calling out names. As each soldier's name was called out, the man stepped forward, stamped the ground with his right foot, gave the back-handed British salute and practically yelled, "Sir!"

I think you're going to get your butt shot off! But Camellion had no intention of arguing with Captain Cresson. A closed mind is immune to any and all suggestions. With a dash of luck, Cresson and his ten men might survive. Their job was fairly simple: All they had to do was station themselves close to the emergency exit at the south end of the underground base. Should the enemy come out—shoot to kill!

"You men will come with me," Cresson said to the men who had stepped out. "The remaining ten will accompany Mr. Hillmeyer and follow his orders to the letter."

The Death Merchant patted the walkie-talkie in its case on his wide holster belt. "I'll contact you after we have planted the explosives by the door of the main entrance and are ready to blow it."

"Fine," said Cresson. "I'll let you know when we're in position."

The two groups parted, Captain Cresson and his ten men moving south, the Death Merchant and his group of fifteen heading north, each group only a quarter of a mile from its destination.

Camellion led the way, Klaus Hahn on his left, Alan Chasteen to his right. Wesslin, Reeder and Edward Tolson followed behind. To the rear were the ten British soldiers.

As the snow crunched beneath Hahn's booted feet, he became reflective, mentioning how Spandau had been bombed during the war.

"My mother told me that Spandau lost only ten percent of its buildings," he mused. "Such a minor loss was almost negligible compared to how central Berlin was bombed. This led Berliners to make the caustic remark, *'Die Spandauer Zwerge kommen zuletzt in die Sarge.'* 'The little Spandauites are last to reach their coffins.'" The German intelligence agent chuckled slightly. "The Berliners had another saying. They changed *'The Führer commands, we follow'* to *'The Führer commands, we bear what follows.'*"

"From the way things look now, you wouldn't even know there had been a war," said Alan Chasteen, breathing heavily. Although he was in excellent physical condition, the going was rough. The terrain was uneven, the snow deep in places and movement difficult.

Camellion finally raised a hand, signaling a halt. He pulled a map from his left breast pocket, consulted it for a minute or two, then returned the map to his pocket. He looked up at the sky that harbored only a few scattered clouds and the sun that, by now, was fully across the horizon.

"We're getting close to the main entrance," Camellion said to Hahn and Chasteen. "Pass the word. Tell the soldiers to spread out and be on guard, but to keep their Patchett-Sterlings on safe. I don't want any of them to get nervous and become trigger-happy."

Captain Cresson and his men made better time. The Death Merchant and his group were a thousand feet from the main entrance of the underground installation when Cresson called the Death Merchant on the walkie-talkie and informed him that he and his men were in position.

"There's a lot of broken concrete around here," Cresson said, "and we're down behind chunks of the stuff. The door to the emergency exit is a hundred feet in front of us. We tried to open it. It's caked with rust but solid. We couldn't budge it."

"All right," Camellion said, putting an emergency brake

on his temper. "You'll know when we're going in after you hear the explosion. Out."

He switched off the walkie-talkie, shoved it into its case and turned in disgust to Hahn and Chasteen, both of whom had heard Cresson's report and were shaking their heads in disbelief.

"That idiot tried to open the door!" grunted the Death Merchant. "How's that for first-class stupidity?"

Close by, Otto Wesslin spoke up, "What's the difference? If this is the headquarters of the Brotherhood, we know that they must have all kinds of alarms spread out. There's no way of knowing how many pressure alarms might be buried under the snow."

Chasteen formed his words slowly. "I hope you're wrong, Otto. If you're right, they'll be waiting for us."

"Hold on," interjected Neil Reeder. "It's also possible that we're trying to hit the jackpot on an empty slot machine. We're going to have egg all over our faces if we get down there and find nothing but dust and cobwebs and weather-worn photographs of *Der Führer!*"

"Well let's go blow that door to hell and find out," Camellion said. "We'll never know till we get below."

He hated to admit it, but he was annoyed that a blubber-gut like Cresson had gotten into position ahead of him. At a faster pace, Camellion led the group forward, around trees and bushes. In another ten minutes Camellion & Company came to the group of buildings that marked the entrance of Maybach 1. Four concrete structures that had once been painted gray, none larger than a small cottage, all as useless as Hitler's dream of world conquest. Only the main building had had windows. Now the windows were like the gaping mouths of shriveled corpses in some ancient catacomb . . . the glass gone, shattered more than thirty years ago by concussion from the terrific Russian bombardment. Icicles hung dismally from the edges of roofs. In front of the largest building was a tall rusted flagpole leaning crookedly to the west. On the front of the building, centered over the half-open steel door, was an iron German eagle clutching a large swastika in its claws, both rusty and green-black with age, the head, beak and top of the eagle's wings, as well as the top of the crooked cross, covered with snow. Massive and solid, the small buildings were a far cry from most new buildings in East Berlin—shoe-box austerities constructed of prefabricated sections, their gray, impersonal dullness relieved only by poorly executed murals.

"That's it," Camellion said, indicating the building with the eagle and swastika. "That's the building built around the main stairs."

He turned and motioned for the British soldiers to spread out and search the three other buildings, while he and the others looked inside the largest structure. He switched off the safety of the Sidewinder, approached the entrance and shoved his left foot against the half-open steel door. The large rusty hinges creaked in protest as the door swung slowly inward.

The inside was as dismal as the outside. Bits of paper and other rubble lay scattered on the floor. The opening to the entrance below was in the center of the room, a rectangular clearing in the four-foot-thick concrete floor, the back and two sides surrounded by a rusted iron railing.

The Death Merchant and the others looked down the seven-foot-wide iron stairway that slanted into the darkness below. The opening and the stairs could have been the mouth of hell.

"They could be waiting down there at the bottom," Neil Reeder said, fear and uncertainty in his low voice. Nervously he lighted a cigarette.

"We know from the diagrams that the top of the ceiling is thirty feet below ground," Camellion said lazily. "I think we can say that the stairs lead forty feet down—forty feet to the floor."

One of the British soldiers, a Corporal named Hubert Schrimshire, came into the room and addressed the Death Merchant. "Sir, the other buildings are empty."

"Thank you, Corporal," Camellion said. "You and the others keep a sharp lookout. We'll let you know when we need you."

"Yes sir." Schrimshire left the large bunker, and Camellion reached into a Gussett-type shoulder bag, pulled out a pair of strange-looking goggles and, taking off his helmet, slipped them on. Known as a holographic one-tube goggle, the device was the latest in US Army night-vision devices, amplifying visual light and near infrared radiation, then superimposing the enhanced image over the wearer's view.

"I'll go with you to furnish cover fire—just in case," offered Hahn.

"*Danke*," Camellion said. "But there's no sense in two of us risking our lives."

Hahn hunched a shoulder. "It's your show, *mein freund*.

"While I'm down there setting the charge, one of you contact Captain Cresson and let him know we're here," Camellion said. He handed Reeder the Sidewinder submachine gun, pulled one of the stainless-steel AutoMags from a hip holster, adjusted his night-vision goggles and started down the steps.

He moved quickly, all the while watching what had been the darkness below, but now, because of the night-sight goggles, was twilight. He could see that the steps slanted down to a small level landing, and that beyond the landing was a metal door twice the size of the average door.

The previous day there had been some discussion of using the service entrance, a large freight elevator situated in the middle of the base. Research by the studious Kaufmann had proved that such a plan would be impossible to execute. A lucky bomb hit had destroyed the elevator and the shaft was filled with tons of concrete.

Coming to the bottom of the stairs, Camellion walked the ten feet across the flat surface and paused before the large metal door. Even the rivet heads were rusted and partially covered with green mold. He didn't even bother to push against the large handle of the door. He could see from how the long hinges were arranged that the door was meant to swing inward. He reached into his shoulder bag, took out a half-pound block of tetryl and placed the explosive against the top hinge, the magnetic base practically reaching out and grabbing the steel. The second block he placed against the enormous bottom hinge. Still holding the AMP in his right hand, he pulled off the red tab from the bottom of each block and flipped the remote control switches, after which he backed off, turned around and hurried up the steps.

"How does it look down there?" asked Edward Tolson, the SIS agent. His voice was very steady.

"Like a steel and concrete grave without any corpses," Camellion said. He motioned everyone back from the opening, unbuttoned the flap over the right breast pocket of his coveralls and took out the remote-control detonator. He opened the metal lid of the device and grinned for a moment. "After all this effort, the Brotherhood had better be down there. Here we go."

He pushed the button.

Wwwweeerrrroooommmmmmmm! The big blast below shook the concrete bunker and rattled the brains of Camellion and his men.

Major Karl August Schwitters and Johann Kurst, both wearing leather greatcoats and sheepskin trooper-style hats, waited behind a clump of linden trees several hundred feet to the southwest of Baron von Hammerstein-Equord's mansion. Other *Bundesnachrichtendienst* officers and British soldiers ringed the house from various other positions. All they were waiting for was the signal.

"The house needs a coat of paint," whispered Kurst. "I suppose the Baron lacks the money or doesn't care. He lost all his glue factories in the war and most of his properties are in East Germany."

"I doubt if we find anyone in that house, except the Baron and his servants," said Major Schwitters. "His wife is dead and his daughter and three sons are living in other parts of West Germany."

"Didn't one of his sons, Ludwig, help him operate *Kampfverlag?*"

"*Ya,* but the last information we had on him, he was in Stuttgart."

"His other two sons and daughter?"

The Major did not answer and Kurst did not repeat the question.

To Major Schwitters this entire area was familiar territory. It had been thirty-five years ago that he had been a staff officer on General Henrici's staff, which had been quartered at Maybach II, 4.7 kilometers south of the Baron's house, only in those days, the Baron had been only a name to him.

Maybach II had been above ground, and Schwitters could still see it clearly in his mind's eye—low concrete buildings spotted among the trees in irregular rows, so spaced that they got maximum protection from the trees. Just to be sure, the buildings had been painted in drab camouflage colors of green, black and brown. Vehicles parked by the sides of barrackslike buildings beneath camouflaged netting. Sentries were everywhere at strategic points around the camp. And uniforms! Those had been the days of uniforms. Uniforms all over the Reich: the gray-green of the *Wehrmacht*; SS men in black; the *Reichsarbeitsdienst*, the labor corps, in a sort of ochre; the National Socialist *Kraftfahrerkorps* in black; the Hitler Youth in shorts, brown shirts and Sam Browne belts; girls of the League of German Girls in black skirts and white blouses; even the six-year-old *Pimpfe*, the Cub Scouts of the Nazi movement, were not left out. They dressed in black like mini-SS men. *Mein Gott!* What insanity! Hitler! That idiot! From conquering all of Europe, *Der Dummkopf Führer* had been reduced to hiding in a hole in the ground and finally putting a Walther bullet through the roof of his mouth.

Ach, the *Amerikaners* had even less sense! All that marvelous technology, and now they were letting themselves be destroyed from within by millions of ever-increasing aliens and by the very people with whom they had fought a war they had not wanted to win. *Ya*, a nation of blockheads whose society was falling apart because of childish and unrealistic leadership, a leadership of fools who didn't even know the meaning of the unceasing political warfare being conducted by Communist nations.

Herr Hillmeyer! *Ya*, a very clever and dangerous man. But even if he was *Der Tod Kaufmann*, the BND had a surprise in store for him.

The rumbling explosion to the north pulled Major Schwitters from his reverie and snapped him back to the present.

"There's the signal," he said. He took a whistle from his pocket and blew it loudly. "Now we move in," he said to Kurst.

The smoke and dust was still settling at the bottom of the long flight of steps when Camellion said, "I'll go down first. If it's a trap and we're caught bunched up on the stairs, we won't have room in which to maneuver." He glanced over at Alan Chasteen, who was coming into the bunker followed by the first of the British Tommies. "I'll call out when I'm sure it's safe."

"You mean if you don't end up a pile of ashes on the floor!" grunted Chasteen. "You don't know what the hell is behind that door."

"I'll soon find out." The Sidewinder in his hands, the Death Merchant went to the opening and started down the stairs. The other men clamped lights to their helmets and plugged in the end of the cords to 12-volt battery packs on their belts.

Through the dust and smoke, Camellion found that the tetryl had blown the steel door off its hinges and tossed the heavy slab of metal, as well as the hinges and chunks of concrete, ten feet into the next room. Everywhere was dust, desolation and the promise of death.

He hurried to the blasted opening, and looked around the foot-thick right frame of the opening, his eyes raking the next room through the night-sight goggles. There were rusted metal chairs and what had once been a massive table. The table had been struck by the door and was now a mass of giant splinters. More rusted chairs on the other side of the room and at the east end—*an anteroom of some sort!*

The only door was across the room and painted black. Camellion moved through the trash and inspected the door, which was the same size as the one he had blown off its hinges. He found that the paint was not peeled, nor was there a speck of rust anywhere. *The door was not thirty-five years old!*

He backed out of the room and, once he was in the foyer, called up the stairs in a loud voice, "Come on down. There's no one here."

Immediately, he saw bright white shafts of light flashing downward and crisscrossing each other, and heard feet pounding on the metal stairs.

Hahn and Reeder were the first to reach Camellion. Quickly, Chasteen and the others gathered around, with most of the British soldiers still on the steps.

"Are you telling us that we did all this for nothing?" Reeder ground out, disbelief flowing all over his sweaty face.

"Simmer down," Camellion reassured him in an easy manner. "There's a door in the next room. It's painted jet-black and the paint can't be more than a year old."

Reeder brightened up and Chasteen exclaimed, "By God! We've found them. We've found the headquarters of the Brotherhood!"

The Death Merchant sighed. "We can't be sure that we've found anything, not until we get beyond the next door. We can't as yet say this is the main base of the Brotherhood. We haven't the slightest idea who their leaders are."

Klaus Hahn took a deep breath and pushed back the helmet on his head. "We might as well get on with it," he said slowly in English. "What is your American expression? It is a hard row to hoe?"

The Death Merchant wasn't sure because of the contrasting light, but had he seen a look of understanding pass between Hahn and Wesslin?

"It will be an even harder row if the enemy has any of their devices that affect combustion pointed at us," Wesslin reminded all of them. "There's no beam and they're noiseless."

"Mr. Hillmeyer, I would like to know exactly what it is we're up against!" spoke up Corporal Hubert Schrimshire. His accent distinctly Welsh, Schrimshire was acting as spokesman for the British Tommies. "I think we have a right to know," he finished.

The Death Merchant told him, concluding with, "But it's not a conventional fire. It's actually a magnetic 'fire' that turns human flesh to ash—within minutes. Tell your men that if they see any of the enemy wearing a box on his chest, a metal helmet with rods, and holding a metal tube, they had better shoot damned fast."

Schrimshire only stared at Camellion, in a kind of dumb astonishment, as if he expected to hear a clap of thunder and see lightning flashes.

"Another thing," Camellion said, "when we go inside the room, you and your men take positions along the side of the far wall, to the right of the door. You got that?"

"Yes, sir!" Schrimshire looked as if he might be holding his breath.

"Don't call me *sir*. Now get the word to the men and tell them what's expected of them."

Schrimshire nodded, turned and began whispering to the other British soldiers.

The Death Merchant became all business. "Let's get this show on the road."

He turned and headed for the other room, smiling to himself when he heard Neil Reeder mutter to no one in

162

particular, "I should have become a mortician. You don't get rich, but you get to drive a big car."

Camellion thought of Hahn and Wesslin. *There are three kinds of people in the world. The Yesterday People are always living in the "Good Old Days." The Tomorrow People are dreamers. They're the "This will happen tomorrow" jokers. Hahn and Wesslin are realists; they're interested only in the Right Now. They're Today people. That's what makes them dangerous. They want the Transmutationizer for the Federal Republic of Germany.*

It didn't take too long to do what had to be done. "We'll use TH-Three on the door, then toss in a dozen sand grenades and follow up with three blinders," Camellion said. He reached out and took the heavy shoulder bag that Reeder handed him and placed it on the concrete floor. "Neil, you can help," he said.

Workng in the light furnished by Hahn's and Edward Tolson's helmets, Camellion removed a coil of silvery rope-like material from the bag and a dozen magnetic U-shaped clamps. He placed one end of the half-inch-thick rope at the top right hand corner of the door and secured it with a magnetic U-clamp, while Reeder held the length of the thermate charge and the other men watched with a macabre fascination.

Camellion continued to clamp the rope charge to the door until the top, bottom and side edges were completely covered. Once the charge was secure against the door, he took an electric detonating timer that Reeder handed him, got down on his knees and pushed the two prongs into one end of the charge, the bag of spare Sidewinder magazines clanking around on his left hip. He paused and looked around. The British soldiers were in place, but they carried neither sand grenades nor blinder bombs. *And it might be a good idea to split up Hahn and Wesslin!* the Death Merchant thought.

"Chasteen, you and Hahn get to the right of the door with the soldiers," Camellion ordered. "After the door's gone, you won't be able to cross over, and we don't have enough room on one side for four of us to throw the stuff."

Klaus Hahn and Neil Reeder moved to the right.

"Tolson, shine your light on the timer," the Death Merchant said.

As soon as the beam had fallen on the timer, Camellion turned the tiny black knob to 1-M, got to his feet and moved ten feet to the left of the steel door. Reeder, Hahn and some of the British soldiers moved back to the right.

In sixty seconds the thermate exploded with a loud *whooshing* sound, and the four edges of the steel door blossomed with intense white fire, which sizzled as the thermate, a mixture of thermite, barium nitrate and sulfur in an oil binder, burned at a temperature of almost 6,000 degrees Fahrenheit. The edges of the door began to melt, the red-hot molten steel dribbling to the floor.

The process took only four minutes and sixteen seconds; then the door fell inward into the next room and hit the floor with a loud, ringing crash.

For a few moments there was a terrible stillness, the silence deafening; yet there wasn't a single sound from the other room. Not a single shot; and if a magnetic beam from a portable Transmutationizer was pointed at the doorway, no one knew it, and no one was about to expose himself by standing in the opening. Going up in blue flames was not the answer.

The opening did prove that the complex was far from deserted. Yellow-white light streamed through the smoking rectangle. Now, with the realization that the installation was not deserted, Camellion, and Chasteen, Reeder and Hahn moved as close as they could to the hot doorway and went to work with a vengeance. As quickly as each man could, he pulled a sand grenade from a shoulder bag, pulled the pin and tossed it around the hot edge of the doorway into the room beyond, spacing out each grenade so that as much of the area as possible could be covered.

The sand grenades were officially M14L special-purpose offensive weapons. They didn't resemble the old pineapple-type from WW II, nor were they serrated to facilitate fragmentation. Although the body was sheet steel and the filler was nine ounces of TNT, the shrapnel consisted of thousands of tiny steel balls, each one no larger than a grain of sand. In effect, each M14L was a miniature sand blaster—a very deadly weapon since it had an effective casualty radius in open areas of 2.6 meters.

Roar after roar crashed against the ears of the Death Merchant and his force of fifteen, each exploding grenade throwing out thousands of steel balls with the force of a cannon. There were a few brief screams from some of the doomed members of the Brotherhood inside.

All together, Camellion and the three other men pitched twelve sand grenades into the room beyond. Then each man took a different kind of grenade from one of his shoulder bags: a blue canister with two green stripes running horizontally around the middle. Designated K42C in the British Army ordnance manual, the body of the grenade was aluminum, the fuse of the impact-detonating type, the filler 15.2 ounces of concentrated photoflash powder (barium nitrate, aluminum powder and potassium perchlorate).

Hahn and Reeder threw their blinder grenades first. Far inside the other room, the canisters exploded not with a roar but with a loud hissing and a blinding flash that, for only an instant, was brighter than the sun. Brotherhood gunmen, thinking that the sand-blast bombardment was over, were rearing up from behind crates of equipment and leaning out from behind square concrete support columns when the sunburst of light hit them. Men yelled in terror. Some screamed like women, believing they had been blinded; and for the moment they were, including Hellmut Weidling, the man who had been pointing a portable Transmutationizer at the door.

Before any of the neo-Nazis could recover their senses, the Death Merchant and Alan Chasteen lobbed in their photoflash canisters. There were two more blinding flashes of dazzling light that momentarily blinded some of the men the first two bursts hadn't caught. Some Brotherhood members had closed their eyes in time. But others were so unfortunate as to have been reblinded. Having been caught in the first two bursts, they had been blinking furiously in an effort to dispel the blackness when Camellion and Chasteen's flare-ups caught them.

The Brotherhood didn't have time to reorganize their defense. After throwing the blinder bombs, Camellion and the other men had turned their heads toward the opposite door, the one that opened to the stairs. Yet each flash from the other room shone brightly through the red-hot doorway, making the area as bright as daylight at high noon.

The instant the last two flashes flamed out, the Death Merchant stormed in low through the burned-out doorway, firing short three-round bursts with the Sidewinder, the slugs ripping into half-blinded Brotherhood members thirty feet ahead of him. Some of them were still dropping to the floor as he darted behind the first concrete column to the right and looked around its right side. The north wall was ten feet away. Up ahead, all along the right side of the columns, the area was clear.

Right behind Camellion charged Hahn, Reeder, Wesslin and the rest of the small force. Hahn and Reeder jumped behind the first concrete-support pillar to the left, Wesslin running to the column behind which Camellion was crouched. The remainder of the men, who had charged through the doorway, went either left or right, then threw themselves to the floor, since it was far too dangerous to try to reach the next columns in line. Besides, only two men could safely stand behind each column.

The snarling roar of submachine guns was terrific. By now, the gunmen of the Brotherhood had partially recovered, and although ten of the Nazis were still half-blinded, they had dropped down behind boxes and crates filled with concrete rubble, and were returning the fire. So were the six Germans whose eyesight had not been affected. They had been down behind the crates when the four sunbursts of photoflash powder had blossomed.

The Death Merchant shoved a full magazine into the Sidewinder and thought of what he had seen during the fleeting moments he was racing to the pillar. He judged the room to be forty feet long and thirty feet wide. The enemy was at the west end of the room behind crates piled in front of the entrance to the next room, a large entrance that was easily eight feet by seven feet. The Nazis of the old days had been practical in that steel bulkhead doors had not been placed between the inner rooms of Maybach 1. It would have been a waste of good steel. If the Red Army had reached the underground citadel during WW II, the Russians could have blown it sky-high from above ground.

A British Tommy, rearing up to get off a burst of P-Sterling slugs, cried out loudly from the shock of enemy projectiles cutting into his upper chest and fell flat on his face, blood pouring out of his mouth and nose. Other HK MP-5 bullets struck the floor so close to Alan Chasteen, Edward Tolson and the British soldiers to the right that dust and sharp chips of concrete splattered against the plastic flip-up face shields of their Ballistic Helmets. The Tommies down to the left were faced with the same danger of instant death. The only reason all of them had not been slaughtered was that the two lines of columns were between them and the gunmen of the Brotherhood. The neo-Nazis couldn't spread out, because if they did, they would have to totally expose themselves.

Clutching his HK MP-5, Wesslin swung to Camellion savagely, fury and alarm in his eyes. "We can't stay here," he said in German, his tone as firm as his stance was determined. "We must charge and take our chances. I see no other way."

"I do," the Death Merchant said. "A direct charge and they'd cut down half of us before we reached the halfway mark. We'll—" He stopped talking and stared over Wesslin's shoulder. Seeing the look of sudden concern on Camellion's face, Wesslin turned and saw the reason for his alarm. Edward Tolson, the SIS operative, and four British soldiers had gotten to their feet and were attempting to reach the concrete supports that were second to the last in line from the east.

"Mein Gott! They're crazy!" gasped Wesslin.

The Death Merchant knew it was too late to yell a warning at the five men. Hahn, Reeder, Chasteen and the other soldiers tried to give cover fire to the five running fools. The difficulty was that, since they were down on the floor and had the concrete columns between them and the enemy, they didn't have a full view of the defenders. And each time Neil Reeder and Klaus Hahn tried to fire around the right side of their column, they were met with streams of 5.56mm slugs.

It happened suddenly without any warning. Tolson and the four British soldiers stopped as if they had been jerked back by invisible wires, the submachine guns falling from their hands. Instantly, each man became one large glow of intense blue shininess. The five men didn't move. They didn't scream. They just stood like statues, as if frozen between the past and the present. For almost two minutes they stood bathed in the blue radiance. Then they were gone, erased forever. Their clothes—cloth, leather, metal, plastic—and equipment collapsed in piles on the floor.

The "fire" had not exploded one cartridge or one grenade—only flesh and bone and blood.

What had been five human beings was now five small piles of gray ash. . . .

Chapter Twelve

Big game hunters are prone to say that when an animal is hunted its survival instincts combine with its basic intelligence to produce a "nobility." But none of these sportsmen have hunted Man. When Man combines intelligence and ferocity, he becomes the most unpredictable and the most dangerous of all big game.

With this thought in mind, the Death Merchant told Wesslin what had to be done. The German agreed, all the while staring at the five piles of clothes only ten feet to his left.

Wesslin turned and faced Camellion. "Klaus and Reeder could use the same tactics," he said, removing his helmet and moving his fingers through his thick blond hair. "A two-pronged attack would force the enemy to divide its fire."

"*Nein,*" Camellion said. "There's a greater chance for success if only you and I attack from the right. These columns are five feet square. We can get close enough to lob in sand grenades before they can stop us."

Wesslin only grunted and nodded his head.

The Death Merchant looked around the right side of the column. The length of the area was clear. He couldn't see the last crate because of the intervening supports. That was all right, too.

He and Wesslin left the protection of the column and started running forward—a straight-in dash to the first pillar. They had covered three fourths of the way when the enemy to the right spotted them and machine-gun slugs started hitting the supports and the north wall. Several times Camellion and Wesslin felt projectiles tugging at their coveralls, and once Camellion thought he had bought the Big One. A bullet passed through one shoulder bag, the one containing the M14L sand grenades. Fortunately the swaged lead missed the grenades and went harmlessly out the other side of the canvas.

So fast were Camellion and Wesslin moving that they almost collided with the back of the first support column. Only fifteen feet to the front was the Brotherhood line of defense.

Listening to the scream of ricochets flying off both sides of the column, Wesslin panted, "You throw. I'll cover you."

"We'll both throw around each side," Camellion said, his voice a final order. "You stick your head out and they'll blow it off. We'll give them two each—and throw high. Then we'll move it and send those swine into hell to join Hitler."

They pulled down the face plates of their helmets and then went to work—two grenades each, which they threw around either side of the column, the roars a symphony of pure pleasure to their ears.

The first two grenades, thrown by Wesslin to the right, exploded and did little damage, except to sand-riddle one side of a Brotherhood gunman. He started screaming and continued to scream from what felt like a million needles stabbing into him. Other Nazis dropped down behind the crates and covered their faces, terrified of the tiny steel that could very easily blind a victim.

Both of Camellion's grenades landed behind the line of crates and, exploding twenty-two seconds apart, sand-riddled practically all of the remaining twenty fighters, five fatally. Those who could still fire a weapon grabbed their machine guns and tried to poke the barrels over and around the end of crates, but it was too late. A second after the first sand grenade had exploded, Hahn, Reeder and the rest of the men raced forward. Now it was pure slaughter. The moment an enemy gunman exposed himself, he was hit by either HK or Patchett/Sterling projectiles. The Death Merchant and Otto Wesslin put an end to the brief but bloody battle by hosing five men with 9mm Sidewinder and 5.56mm HK MP-5 bullets. Men cried out, jerked violently from the the impact of certain death and died, the corpses falling over each other until the area was littered with dead flesh.

One of the last to die was Helmut Weidling, the young German with the portable Transmutationizer. In agony from steel "sand" that had riddled both legs, he made a feeble attempt to aim the field-energy tube at the two men who were killing him and all his companions. Neither Camellion nor Wesslin had a choice. Both wanted the device, but being turned into a pile of ashes was not the way to get it. They raked Weidling from head to ankles, the high-velocity projectiles ripping into his body and into the mechanism in the box strapped to his chest. Instantly, both the chest box and the box on Weidling's back began to hum and blue-and-white lightning began to jump from the metal rods on the helmet to the funnel-shaped end of the firing tube. A few seconds more and the corpse of Weidling, as well as the body of the man on whom he had fallen, began to flicker, hazy one moment, solid as a brick the next. One-two-three! *Both corpses and the Transmutationizer vanished.*

The light bulbs, screwed into sockets hanging from the ceiling, suddenly went out and the huge room was plunged into tar-black darkness.

"Don't switch on your helmet lights," yelled Camellion. "Stay where you are. I'll come over to you."

Camellion took off his helmet, slipped the night-sight goggles over his eyes, replaced the helmet and reloaded the hot Sidewinder. Verbally directing Wesslin where to walk, the two men soon made contact with the other eight men. The Death Merchant outlined his scheme: He would proceed into the next area to the west and, if it was free of the enemy, contact them by walkie-talkie. They could then turn on their helmet lights and come forward with a measure of safety.

"Listen, there are only ten of us left," Alan Chasteen said. "We don't know what's up ahead. I'm for contacting Captain Cresson and having him blow the emergency door. He and his men can come in that way and take some of the heat off us."

"No dice," Camellion said flatly. "Cresson and his boys would be ripped upside-down and backwards. Those Tommies are only kids. Look at the stunt Tolson and four of them pulled!"

In the twilight produced by the holographic goggles, he could see anger and resentment jumping all over the face of Corporal Hubert Schrimshire and the four other soldiers.

"Sorry, men," Camellion apologized. "I don't mean to insult you, but a hit job like this calls for judgment based on experience."

Minutes later, Camellion crept into the next room, saw that it was empty and, with the walkie-talkie, told the men to switch on their helmet lights and move forward. For the next fifteen minutes, he and the tiny group crept through the deserted dark rooms, some filled with moldy furniture and rusted filing cabinets, all filled with ghosts from the past.

Camellion estimated that they were almost to the center of the underground installation when they came to a twenty foot by twenty-foot room the west entrance of which was blocked by a narrow steel door. No rust, no mold, no moss! The Death Merchant put his ear to the door and listened: He could hear a faint humming sound.

"We could have found the laboratory, if there is one," he whispered, "and maybe even Professor Koerber. We'll know shortly."

"How?" Neil Reeder put his skepticism into words. "I've a gut feeling that thermate and sand grenades aren't going to work this time."

"He is right, Hillmeyer," Klaus Hahn said, annoyed. "We have no way of knowing the size of the area beyond or the kind of protection the enemy might have."

"I'm going to blow the whole damn wall," drawled Camellion, "and let the concrete act like shrapnel. Ten pounds of tetryl should do the job very nicely."

It took him only ten minutes to space out ten one-pound blocks along the center length of the wall, taping each block to the concrete, including one he taped between the hinges of the steel door. He pulled off the red tabs, flipped the toggle switches in the ends of the blocks of explosive, then hurried to the rest of the men, who had taken cover in the next room to the east. They watched him screw earplugs into his ears and take out the remote-control detonator, and heard him say, "When I say 'yell'—yell! It will

171

lessen the pressure." His finger on the button, he said, "Now yell!"

Nine shouts erupted from nine throats. The Death Merchant let out a loud bellow and pushed the button.

Blllammmmmmmmmmmmmmm!

The wall in the next room dissolved in a sheet of red flame and smoke, the concussion of such pressure that the wall protecting Camellion and his men shook violently as if from an earthquake. Chunks of concrete slammed against it and shot through the wide doorway, while echoes from the thunderous explosion bounced back and forth throughout the complex of rooms filled with ghosts and dead Nazi dreams.

Camellion dropped the earplugs in a pocket, grabbed the deadly little Sidewinder, secretly muttered "*Dominus Lucis Vobiscum*—you bastard!" and shouted, "Let's move it!"

He took the point and, with the other nine men, tore through the wide entrance and ran across the floor of the room, the west wall of which had disappeared, jumping over or racing around chunks of concrete. They leaped over a foot-high section of the wall that was still standing and saw at a glance that they had indeed hit the jackpot. The area behind the demolished wall was a laboratory, or, rather, had been a laboratory but was now a wreck. At least a good part of it had been wrecked by lumps and masses of jagged concrete, some pieces no larger than marbles, other hunks as leviathan as a washtub. Yet eighty percent of the cloud of rock had slammed into either men or electrical equipment. Bodies lay everywhere, men who were either dead, dying, or unconscious from concussion. But other members of the Brotherhood were on their feet, with pistols and automatic weapons in hand.

Through the swirling smoke and settling gray dust, the Death Merchant had only a few seconds to catch sight of faces and huge machines. There were rows of huge degaussing coils and even larger generating magnetometers that were connected to strange-looking machines, some of which still throbbed with power.

The next instant, Camellion was surrounded by men whose smoke-smeared faces could not conceal the pathological hatred they felt for him and his pathetically small company.

Amid shouts, yelling and the crashing of gunfire, the Na-

172

zis charging the Death Merchant found that they were walking on the water of dreams and could only sink. In a crouch, using his right foot as a pivot, Camellion spun and moved the Sidewinder back and forth, the machine gun belching out slugs that, in 4.2 seconds, ripped into eight of the men and knocked them back screaming. In one expert moment, Camellion dropped the empty Sidewinder and his hands flashed to the butts of the two .41 AutoMags.

All around Camellion, the men of his force were firing steady bursts from their machine guns, the barrels hot from chains of slugs that cut through brown uniforms, bored into flesh and knocked over bodies to the extent that it seemed an invisible hand might be trying to stack corpses. Neither side had had time to drop down or seek cover behind machines and other equipment; and now the Nazis didn't want to. They outnumbered the Death Merchant and his men four to one. Each side had exhausted the ammo in the automatic weapons, and now men reached for pistols and knives.

Cecil Greathouse, one of the Tommies, was the first of the nine to die; he caught a 9mm bullet low in the groin. A second slug ripped through his stomach. With a long, low moan, he fell back, doubled over and sagged against Alfred Nichols, another British soldier, who didn't have a ghost of a chance against the two Nazi gunmen charging him. Nichols fired at Ewald Spiedel with his Webley .38, but the very fast Spiedel ducked about the same time that Fritz Dehnner, the second man, fired three shots from a Sauer autopistol. All three 7.65mm projectiles hit Nichols in the chest. He died instantly.

To the astonishment of the Brotherhood, they found that it was far more difficult to kill the remaining eight.

The most experienced trigger artist in the world wouldn't be able to hit the side of an extra-large barn if he couldn't first control his nervous system. During hell-fight moments like this, the Death Merchant was as tranquil as a sleeping oyster, due to years of training and discipling himself in the various schools of the Oriental martial arts, mainly karate of the *Goju-Ryu, Shito-Ryu,* and *Tae-Kwon-Do* schools, coupling these deadly arts with Eastern Indian yoga techniques in breathing.

Calmly, firing both AMPs simultaneously, Camellion

blew up four of the Brotherhood, three who were getting ready to aim down on him and one who had crept up behind Alan Chasteen and was about to tickle one of his kidneys with a bayonet blade. All four were dead before they had time to even suspect they were headed for the depths of hell to join Hitler, the huge flat-nosed .41 Magnum bullets hitting them with the force of a minigrenade.

Camellion killed a fifth kraut who was aiming down on Klaus Hahn with a Swiss-made 06/29 version of the Luger. The German was only ten feet away and the .41 projectile, hitting him in the back of the head, exploded his skull in a bloody shower of bone and brain.

Detecting movement behind him, Camellion half turned and delivered a right reverse roundhouse *Yoko-Geri-Kekomi* kick, the back of his foot crashing into the kraut's back and knocking him forward. The Death Merchant counted off the seconds in Korean, *"Hana, Dool, Set!"* He said, *"Net,"* and put a .41 bullet in the left side of the man, the tornado impact of the projectile almost lifting him off the floor as it pitched right into two other Nazis, who had been trying to close in on the rest of Camellion's group but were not having too much success. Every one of the men had exhausted his supply of ammo, and there wasn't time to reload. They did the only thing they could; they used the pistols to bash in faces and crack skulls. Reeder, Chasteen, Hahn and Wesslin were particularly deadly. All four were experts in various forms of karate and were using their elbows, feet and legs with vicious efficiency.

Hahn slammed the side of his Browning Double-Action pistol against the side of one man's skull and used a powerful side kick to a second man's forward knee. He used the muzzle of the BDA to mash a third Nazi's Adam's apple, then applied a front snap kick against a fourth kraut whose back was turned to him. The German, a knife in his hand, had almost reached David Bromfield, one of the British Tommies. He stopped and let out a long *"Aaghhhhhhhh!"* when Hahn's boot came up between his legs and the tip of the BND agent's foot connected with his testicles. The man's scrotum exploded with an agony that sent the German into a state of half-unconsciousness. Hahn's blow, however, did not save Bromfield. The gagging, moaning Nazi fell forward and the knife blade found a home between his shoulder blades. Both moaning, the Nazi and Bromfield sagged together to the floor.

Chasteen and Wesslin fought back-to-back, Wesslin holding his two empty BDA autopistols by the barrels with the butts outward, Chasteen clutching his Browning Hi-Power auto in a similar manner with his right hand, while he stabbed and jabbed with an Armament Systems "Vindicator" which he held in his left, the double-edged stainless-steel blade ripping through cloth and enemy flesh.

Yet the Cosmic Lord of Death was greedy. Dwight Hamlin went down under a bombardment of blows from two men. As he fell, a third man pumped two 7.65mm Mauser HSC pistol slugs into his body—both in the head.

Only a short distance away, Neil Reeder had preferred to defend himself by using two "Quicksilver" knives, slashing in every direction, his hands firmly gripped around the two hollow aluminum handles. The backs of his hands were wet with blood as were the two 4.25-inch stainless-steel blades.

The three Nazis who had terminated Dwight Hamlin now came face to face with Eternity. The Death Merchant spotted them while Jurgen-Erich Koster was swinging the muzzle of the Mauser HSC toward Reeder. Both Auto-Mags roared with all the crashing sound of two small cannons. A flat-nosed .41 bullet hit Koster in the chest and blew away his entire breastbone before it zipped through his torso, pulverized several vertebrae and tore a hole in his back the size of a Golden Delicious apple. Ewald Speidel caught a .41 slug in the stomach. Bent over double, he went flying at the same time that Oscar Prinzt, the third Hitler-lover, was slammed against the backs of two other Nazis who were trying to kill Bruce Childress, the last British Tommy alive. The .41 slug went sideways through Prinzt's body, wrecked his lungs, then struck one of the Germans in front of Childress, hitting him in the back. An instant later, Prinzt crashed into both men—an unexpected bit of help that gave Childress the opportunity to stab the other German in front of him with a bayonet. Weak and panting, Childress dropped beside the dying men and, with trembling hands, started to reload one of the Patchett/Sterlings the Tommies had dropped.

* * *

It wasn't by accident that the Death Merchant spotted the man he felt was Professor Helmut Koerber. The tall, stooped figure was hurrying up a short flight of steps to a metal platform six feet above the floor level, thirty feet to the west. The platform was bolted to a large machine that resembled a giant core magnet. Other strange-looking mechanisms were attached to the humming machine, some of them arcing crooked lines of electricity, causing the Death Merchant to think, *Koerber is either going to shut down the big deal, or else he has some other vital business up there!*

Straining to see through the smoke and dust partially obscuring the ceiling lights that had not been broken by concussion, Camellion saw what that other business might be—a portable Transmutationizer plugged into the machine.

The realization was still fresh in Camellion's mind when he saw another member of the Brotherhood come from the west side of the large machine. This man carried a portable Transmutationizer, the two boxes strapped to his body, the weird helmet on his head, the firing tube in his hands.

Deduction produced the answer. The Brotherhood was losing the battle, and the ruthless Professor was going to end it and gain victory by turning the attacking force and his own men into ashes. He would have to kill his own people because of their close proximity to Camellion and his force, such as it was.

The Death Merchant made his decision. He wasn't sure yet what Koerber was going to do. He didn't want to terminate him unless he had to. It was different with the other man, who was adjusting a dial toward the rear of the tube—*getting ready to fire!*

Camellion holstered the left AutoMag and, using both hands, aimed carefully at the man. Gently, he squeezed the trigger, the roar of the AutoMag a sweet song following the .41 Magnum projectile that struck Ludwig Hammerstein-Equord in the stomach, several inches below the box on his chest, and rocketed out his lower back. As good as dead, the eldest son of Baron von Hammerstein-Equord was knocked back from the terrific impact, the firing tube falling from his hands. He hit the corner of the machine, sagged to the floor and died.

There's our portable Transmutationizer, thought Camellion. *Intact!*

The Death Merchant's elation was short-lived. Detecting movement to his left, he sidestepped to the right and ducked an instant before Alfons Leckscheidt pulled the trigger of a P-38 Walther. The 9mm slug missed the left side of Camellion's neck by only a quarter of an inch. Misses never counted. A quarter of an inch might as well have been a hundred feet.

Camellion spun and fired. The AMP roared. Leckscheidt's face exploded in blood, spewing a torn-apart upper jawbone and ripped pieces of flesh. Camellion didn't have time to fire at the second man. Fritz Dehnner grabbed his right wrist and tried to smash his solar plexus with a high kneelift. Quicker than a cobra, Camellion stopped the right kneelift with a left-legged block and aimed a terrific back first *Yikwon* at Dehnner's right temple. Very quickly, Dehnner employed a *Suki-Uke* sweeping block to wreck the intended strike, twisted the AutoMag from Camellion's right hand and tried to apply a left top of the foot *Kogan-Geri* to Camellion's groin. Again Camellion blocked, much faster this time. The Death Merchant knew he was up against an expert and didn't intend to waste time. He couldn't. Another Nazi was jumping over bodies and coming to help Dehnner.

Chasteen and Wesslin had their hands full fighting four Germans, Wesslin with his two BDA "head-crackers," Chasteen with his empty Browning autopistol and deadly Vindicator. Sooner or later, someone had to make a mistake, and it was one of the Germans who made it: He didn't jump back quite fast enough. Chasteen took advantage of the mistake by ripping upward with the Vindicator, the razor-sharp blade cutting through the man's brown shirt and slicing deeply into the deltoid muscle of his left shoulder. A few moments later, the German was as good as dead.

So were the other three members of the Brotherhood!

And so were Alan Chasteen and Otto Wesslin!

Very suddenly, all six men were bathed in a blue sheen, in the death glow of the magnetic wave produced by the Transmutationizer. The six stood there, frozen between life and death, between the Here and the There.

The large blue glow, throwing an azure coating over the entire area, also caused Neil Reeder to drop his guard for a fraction of a moment against the man in front of him. It took only a second. The kraut sliced in with a long-bladed boot knife and pushed the blade into Reeder's stomach. But in his enthusiasm for the quick kill, the Nazi had forgotten about the two Quicksilver knives in Reeder's bloody hands. Pain exploded in Reeder's gut and he felt his legs turning to water. Only one thought pounded in his brain: *Kill the son of a bitch!* With his last bit of strength, he brought the left blade upward with such force that the stainless steel not only ripped lengthways through the German's throat but actually tried to slice through the chinbone; and there it buried itself. His eyes bulging, the dying man started to sag, blood jumping out of his mouth and throat, and splashing all over Reeder's face and chest. Reeder wasn't aware of it. Dying, he was falling through an endless tunnel of darkness—a few seconds ahead of the Brotherhood gunman Klaus Hahn had just killed. Hahn had kicked the man in the stomach and then had cracked his skull with the BDA, all the while watching the other man rushing in at him from the left.

It was the roaring of Bruce Childress's Patchett-Sterling submachine gun that came to the aid of Hahn and Camellion. For three to five minutes not a single shot had been fired, and there had been only the sounds of grunting, of heavy breathing and of blows being landed. The roaring snarl of the P-Sterling broke the silence and caused the last three Nazis in action, as well as Camellion and Hahn, to jerk their heads toward the savage firing.

By now the blue glow was gone and the four Germans, Wesslin and Chasteen had been reduced to ashes, leaving behind only their empty clothes. Childress had been horrified. But he had seen Professor Koerber on the raised platform. He raised the machine gun and fired it on full automatic a split second before the tall, white-haired scientist could swing the tube to Hahn or Camellion.

Almost a full magazine, 32 high-velocity slugs zipped into Professor Koerber and the box strapped to his chest. A single eye blink and Koerber was dead, his corpse being knocked back against the side railing, his white smock and clothes full of bullet holes and dripping blood. He fell forward on his face, the boxes strapped to his body shooting out lightning that arced to the firing tube and to the ends of the three rods of the helmet fastened firmly to the head of the corpse by means of a chinstrap.

The fadeout began. Koerber's corpse flickered and was gone. Then it was back again. Then gone. Once more the body reappeared. It then vanished forever, leaving only ashes within clothes riddled with bullet holes.

Mouth open, Bruce Childress stared at the empty platform.

Fritz Dehnner quickly recovered from his surprise at hearing the British machine gun; yet he was still in deep trouble and knew it. He was a third-level *Dan-Goju* stylist and had won numerous trophies in Germany, France and Great Britain. But it hadn't been until now that he realized that fighting a bout in some *dojo*, or in an exhibition or a tournament, was far different from the real thing. Here, there wasn't any protective body padding. His opponent wasn't wearing thick grabber gloves or boots padded with foam rubber. In an exhibition match, one could only lose. Here—*Mein Gott!*—if you made a vital mistake, you would die.

Deep fear crept into Dehnner's defense, and fear brought uncertainty, which interfered with his timing and reflexes. He aimed a *Nihon-Nukite* double-piercing finger strike at Camellion's solar plexus, but missed when Camellion jumped back. Too late, Dehnner discovered that he had left himself open for an attack. Camellion jumped, his right leg shot out and up, and the back of his boot caught Dehnner in the left temple with a *Bal-Twikumchi* heel blow that rattled the Nazi's teeth and sent the room reeling around him. Staggered, Dehnner was helpless for the moment, all his defenses down. A single fraction of time was all it took to finish him off. The Death Merchant's left hand shot out in a full five-finger spear-hand *Kwansu*, the tips of his fingers digging into Dehnner's throat and crushing the top of his windpipe. Choking, the German fell back, gasping and gurgling sounds coming from his throat, his fingers clawing at his chest. His face as red as a cherry, Dehnner sagged to his knees, and the Death Merchant spun to his right and executed a high *Shito-Ryu* roundhouse kick. The heel of his right boot crashed into the face of the other man charging him, the grand-slam smack breaking the man's upper jaw and his nose. The man let out a squawk with all the volume used by a frightened chicken that knows the ax is about to fall. Blood pouring out of his nose and from cavities where teeth had been, the man fell back.

Bruce Childress had recovered from emotional shock in time to see the second-to-the-last enemy still alive running toward "August Hillmeyer." He had tried to bring the man down with the Patchett-Sterling, then remembered that the SMG was out of ammo.

In a half-daze, the young British soldier looked around. Bodies littered the floor, lying in all sorts of grotesque positions. My God, it was worse than the killing floor of a slaughterhouse. The stink of burnt gunpowder and smoke stung his nostrils, and made his mouth and throat very dry.

Childress looked and saw "Hillmeyer" bring down the man who had charged him. To his left, he saw that Hahn was killing the last man of the Brotherhood. Hahn was in back of the man, had forced him to his knees and was strangling the new Nazi with a rear double-armed Commando hold.

The Death Merchant had caught only a glance of the man's face before slamming him out with a kick. *He's so damned ugly his face should be wanted all over the world for indecent exposure,* he thought.

He looked down at the beaten man who lay on his right side, groaning, the fight gone out of him.

Pulling the left AutoMag, Camellion watched Klaus Hahn, thirty-five feet to his right, shove a fresh clip into a BDA, pull back the slide and place a cartridge in the firing chamber. Forty feet ahead and slightly to the right, Bruce Childress was shoving a box magazine of ammo into the Patchett-Sterling. Everyone else was dead.

"Soldier, get over here on the double and watch this man—move it!" Camellion called out sharply to Childress. He pointed with the barrel of the AMP at the groaning man at his feet, all the while watching Hahn from the corner of his eye, feeling that Hahn was doing the same thing.

Camellion switched the AMP to his right hand, turned and started west at about the same time that Hahn did, stepping over chunks of concrete and walking around dead bodies.

Hahn carried his BDA autopistol like Camellion, hanging loosely in his hand.

Together they walked around the platform, came to the west end of the humming machine and looked down at the corpse of Ludwig Hammerstein-Equord. The corpse was just another rotting pork chop. It was the intact portable Transmutationizer that interested them.

Klaus Hahn and Richard Camellion—seven feet apart—looked at each other, both sensing what the other man was thinking. *Each man might kill the other. But what would it prove?*

"We both have a job to do, *Tod Kaufmann*," Hahn finally said. "You are the Death Merchant. But you needn't answer that."

There had not been any fear in Hahn's voice. There was no surprise in Camellion's voice, only very faint amusement.

"One of us might get lucky. At this short distance, I doubt it. If you attempt to move, I'll have to fire. If I attempt to step back, you would have to do the same."

A faint smile spread over Hahn's smoke-smudged face. "Exactly. We have come to—what is the phrase in English? A 'Mexican standoff?'"

Camellion was almost positive that he could terminate Hahn and not be touched by the other man's bullet. The British soldier? If Hahn did blow Camellion away, he could kill that Tommy before the poor kid knew what had hit him. But Camellion didn't want to kill the West German, not unless he had to. Hahn was basically a decent fellow. He hated the old Nazis and despised the Brotherhood with equal vigor. *Let him play his hand. . . .*

"What would you suggest?" Camellion said. "I know the *Bundesnachrichtendienst* wants the device. That's natural enough. The secret of the burning blue death would give any nation an edge, particularly a large version of the Transmutationizer."

"So that is what the device is actually called!"

The Death Merchant nodded, his gaze burning into Hahn's eyes.

"There are times when a man has to forget his sworn loyalties and what is best for the world," Hahn said evenly "I think you will agree to that."

"Meaning?"

"Nuclear power is already a threat to all humanity. Why add to the threat? No matter which nation gets the device, the secret would get out. The KGB would steal it and the result would be proliferation."

"We could knock each other off for nothing," Camellion mentioned. "The Transmutationizer might contain a self-destruct device that excludes its being tampered with. I don't think Koerber left any plans or blueprints. He wasn't the type. He was too egomaniacal."

"We can't be certain," said Hahn, "not until a search is made of the house and this installation."

The Death Merchant's expression became grave. "I'm open to any suggestions you may have."

"We destroy the Transmutationizer. All we have to do is put slugs in the box."

Camellion's slight laugh was tight. "Your Mr. Seifert wouldn't take kindly to our doing that."

"Neither would your Mr. Grojean. But who's to tell them? The British soldier doesn't know what's going on up here. He can verify that Koerber's dead. He's the one who killed the swine."

The Death Merchant thought for a moment. *He's too intelligent to be lying!* "All right. We move our weapons together, slowly, and each fire two shots. Agreed?"

"Agreed."

Each man watching the other, Camellion and Hahn swung their barrels toward the box strapped to the back of the corpse. They fired two shots each into the box; then knowing they no longer had to watch each other, they relaxed and moved twenty feet away. They watched the lightning play, studied the fadeout and saw the body and mechanism vanish. They holstered their autopistols and started back toward Bruce Childress, Hahn remarking, "It's strange that throughout all this one of the British soldiers should be alive."

'It's not strange at all," said Camellion. "He was safe all the time. Death didn't want him. It wasn't his time."

Hahn gave Camellion an odd look. "I'll contact Captain Cresson and Major Schwitters and let them know we're finished down here. I'm anxious to learn what Schwitters found in the mansion. It's a shame we couldn't get one of the Transmutationizers. Of course, I won't use that word in any oral or written reports."

"Good enough. I'm going to get my other AutoMag."

Hahn stopped and pulled a walkie-talkie from a case on his belt.

The Death Merchant continued on his way toward the spot where the member of the Brotherhood had twisted the AMP from his right hand. *No, Grojean wouldn't be happy,* he thought. *The hell with him. Hahn's right. The world doesn't need thousands of Transmutationizers—and why bother to tell Hahn that his solution was the same one I had chosen weeks ago?*

Nonetheless, Camellion felt a vague uneasiness. A question mark was struggling in back of his mind. Professor Koerber was dead and the secret of the burning blue death had probably died with him. Yet Camellion still felt that he had not heard the last of the Brotherhood of the Fourth Reich. . . .

DEATH MERCHANT

by Joseph Rosenberger

Over 3 million copies in print!

☐	40-483-2	Death Merchant	#1	$1.50
☐	40-417-4	Operation Overkill	#2	1.50
☐	40-458-1	Psychotron Plot	#3	1.50
☐	40-418-2	Chinese Conspiracy	#4	1.50
☐	40-419-0	Satan Strike	#5	1.50
☐	40-459-X	Albanian Connection	#6	1.50
☐	40-420-4	The Castro File	#7	1.50
☐	40-421-2	Billionaire Mission	#8	1.50
☐	220594-6	Laser War	#9	1.25
☐	220473-3	Mainline Plot	#10	1.25
☐	220561-5	Manhattan Wipeout	#11	1.25
☐	220642-3	KGB Frame	#12	1.25
☐	40-497-2	Mato Grosso Horror	#13	1.50
☐	220796-7	Vengeance: Golden Hawk	#14	1.25
☐	220823-9	Iron Swastika Plot	#15	1.25
☐	220857-7	Invasion of Clones	#16	1.25
☐	220880-5	Zemlya Expedition	#17	1.25
☐	220911-2	Nightmare in Algeria	#18	1.25
☐	40-460-3	Armageddon, USA!	#19	1.50
☐	40-256-2	Hell in Hindu Land	#20	1.50
☐	40-019-6	Pole Star Secret	#21	1.25
☐	40-043-6	Kondrashev Chase	#22	1.25
☐	40-078-5	Budapest Action	#23	1.25
☐	40-352-6	Kronos Plot	#24	1.50
☐	40-117-8	Enigma Project	#25	1.25
☐	40-118-3	Mexican Hit	#26	1.50
☐	40-119-1	Surinam Affair	#27	1.50
☐	40-254-6	Nipponese Nightmare	#28	1.50
☐	40-272-4	Fatal Formula	#29	1.50
☐	40-385-2	Shambhala Strike	#30	1.50
☐	40-392-5	Operation Thunderbolt	#31	1.50
☐	40-475-1	Deadly Manhunt	#32	1.50
☐	40-476-X	Alaska Conspiracy	#33	1.50

PINNACLE-BOOK MAILING SERVICE
P.O. Box 690, New York, NY 10019

Please send me the books I have checked above. Enclosed is my check or money order for $_____ (Please add 50¢ per order and 10¢ per book to cover postage and handling. New York State and California residents add applicable sales tax.)

Name _____

Address _____

City_____ State/Zip_____

Please allow approximately four weeks for delivery.